DADDY'S SWEET GIRL

LAYLAH ROBERTS

DADDY'S SWEET GIRL

Laylah Roberts

Laylah Roberts.

Daddy's Sweet Girl.

© 2019, Laylah Roberts

Laylah.roberts@gmail.com

laylahroberts.com

Cover Design by: Allycat's Creations

Editing: Celeste Jones

❀ Created with Vellum

LET'S KEEP IN TOUCH!

Don't miss a new release, sign up to my newsletter for sneak peeks, deleted scenes and giveaways: https://landing.mailerlite.com/web-forms/landing/p7l6go

You can also join my Facebook readers group here: https://www.facebook.com/groups/38683042506991I/

BOOKS BY LAYLAH ROBERTS

Doms of Decadence

Just for You, Sir

Forever Yours, Sir

For the Love of Sir

Sinfully Yours, Sir

Make me, Sir

A Taste of Sir

To Save Sir

Sir's Redemption

Reveal Me, Sir

Montana Daddies

Daddy Bear

Daddy's Little Darling

Daddy's Naughty Darling (in the Dirty Daddies Anthology)

Daddy's Sweet Girl

Daddy's Lost Love

A Montana Daddies Christmas

Haven, Texas Series

Lila's Loves

Laken's Surrender

Saving Savannah

Molly's Man

Saxon's Soul

Mastered by Malone

How West was Won

Men of Orion

Worlds Apart

Cavan Gang

Rectify

Redemption

Redemption Valley

Audra's Awakening

Old-Fashioned Series

An Old-Fashioned Man

Two Old-Fashioned Men

Her Old-Fashioned Husband

Her Old-Fashioned Boss

His Old-Fashioned Love

An Old-Fashioned Christmas

WildeSide

Wilde

Sinclair

Luke

The Hunters

A Mate to Cherish

A Mate to Sacrifice

1

Abby Reynold contemplated murder.

She glared at old Pete who was on his sixth cup of coffee. Who the hell sat in a diner and drank coffee at ten p.m.? She glanced longingly over at the booth seats. She could just sit, lay her head down and go to sleep.

Or she could go home and sleep if it wasn't for old Pete. She sighed. She knew she should be nicer. He was obviously lonely and looking for company. But it wasn't like he ever talked. He just sat there and drank coffee until she was ready to scream.

This really wasn't worth the meagre tip he'd leave. She heard a snore coming from the kitchen where Oscar was several shots into his not-so-secret whiskey stash.

If Gloria, the owner, would just set a closing time Abby could have shuffled old Pete on. But no, Gloria had this policy that they didn't close until the last customer left. Even if the last customer was drinking endless free cups of coffee.

Finally, old Pete left. With a sigh of relief, she swiftly switched the sign to closed and turned off the lights, heading out the back. Everything was already closed down and cleaned. She passed

Oscar who was sitting on a chair, his head against the wall behind him, snoring.

She figured Gloria only kept him on because he was her brother. His cooking was average and his personal hygiene was very, very questionable.

She pulled on her coat and grabbed her purse then left. Cool air assaulted her, making her shiver. Reaching into her handbag, she grabbed her keys. She hated leaving the diner at night. The front was well lit but out the back, Gloria hadn't bothered with security lights. Of course, Gloria always left before it grew dark and she didn't seem to be particularly worried about her staff's safety.

Abby bit at her lip, preparing to make the mad dash to her car. She'd had to park at the back as she was on the late shift and everyone else had grabbed the closest spaces. They didn't think about leaving her one near the back door. No, that would be too thoughtful.

Stop being a bitch.

She winced at even thinking that word. Nana would box her ears if she ever heard her swear. But then, Nana was gone now. She pulled out her small flashlight. Her phone was so ancient that all it could do was call people and send messages. No fancy flashlight apps for her.

"Okay, let's do this. One, two, three." She raced towards her car, not glancing around, just focused on her goal. Suddenly, her foot hit something, crushing her toes as she dove forward, her hands and knees scraping painfully along the hard gravel. Her keys and flashlight flew from her hands. She let out a cry of pain, lying there for a moment in shock, panting for air. Slowly, she rolled onto her butt.

"Shit," she muttered. Well, if ever there was a time to swear it was now. Her flashlight must have turned off when it bashed against the ground because she could barely see a thing. Where had it gone?

"Looking for this?" a low voice asked.

Abby screeched as her flashlight turned on. A huge man dressed all in black stood a few feet away. He kept his face in the shadows, but the flashlight bobbed in his hand. She managed to spot her handbag about a foot away and reached for it with a trembling hand. She didn't know who he was, but she figured someone hanging around in a dark parking lot after ten p.m. dressed all in black maybe wasn't going to be a good guy.

"Leave the bag where it is," he commanded in a low voice.

She froze. Her heart was racing so hard she was scared she might pass out.

Calm down, Abby. You need to stay conscious if you're going to fight him off.

Oh hell, who was she kidding? She was a chubby, unfit wimp who couldn't even kill a spider. What chance did she have against this guy if he decided to hurt her?

"You know, usually by this stage people ask me who I am and what I want," he drawled. His voice was dark. Cold. And she shivered. She wanted to get off the ground but she was too terrified to move. "Don't you want to know what I want from you, little rabbit?"

"I'm pretty sure I don't."

"So, she does speak. Thought I might have terrified you into paralysis."

She licked her lips. "I-I don't have any money."

"Your brother has something my boss wants."

Crap. She should have known Max would have something to do with this. Everything shit in her life had Max all over it.

"I-I'm paying off his debt," she whispered. Why was he here? She paid regularly. Three hundred dollars a week. It was as much as she could afford and even then, she barely had enough to cover her expenses. Thank God, she'd inherited the house she lived in from Nana. She'd thought about selling it to clear what Max owed, but it was the only home she'd ever known.

Besides, she was pretty certain with the way Max racked up debt that she'd soon find herself in this position again. Anger filled her. Why was it up to her to pay off her brother's debts?

Because they'll kill him if you don't.

Even worse, they'll kill you.

"Mr. Markovich said I could pay him in installments." And if she was late, she knew she'd end up with late fees tacked on. Probably in the form of a missing finger or toe. She bit her lip to stop herself from whimpering.

The man whistled. He still held her flashlight, while she remained sitting on the cold ground. She shivered continuously. "Little shit owes money to Markovich, does he?"

"You don't work for Markovich?"

"I don't work for Markovich. The man I work for is far scarier than Markovich. I'm surprised he'd let you pay off a debt. He must like you."

Not as far as she could tell.

Her stomach bubbled. What was going on? What trouble had Max gotten himself into now? Nana always said the Reynold men were born with an abundance of charm and a complete lack of morals. They could sweet talk someone into bed, then rob them blind while they slept. That was how Uncle Jack had made a living until one of his marks woke up and whacked him over the head.

"May he rest in peace," she muttered.

"What?"

Shit. She froze. She hadn't meant to speak out loud.

"Was that a threat, little rabbit?"

Okay, she'd thought his voice was cold and harsh before. Now he sounded just nasty. Pull-your-teeth-out-with-pliers-nasty.

She really, really needed to stop watching crime shows on T.V.

"A t-threat? Have you l-looked at me? What s-sort of threat could I b-be?"

There was a beat of silence.

"Yeah. True. Max said you were a pushover. Bit of a wimp. That you spend all your time watching T.V. and have no life."

Hurt stabbed her. Okay, it was one thing to know your brother was a jerk and an idiot. But it was another to hear that he was saying such hurtful things about her.

Like none of that was the truth?

Well, it didn't matter if it was, it was still hurtful. She took a deep breath, trying to push back the pain. So, what if Max was saying stuff about her? What was so great about his life? And why was it that his issues kept landing on her plate?

"Whatever money Max owes your boss has nothing to do with me," she told him in a low voice, surprising herself. She didn't usually fight back. She usually let people walk all over her.

"Is that so, little rabbit?" he whispered.

Okay, maybe now was not the time to find her backbone. Now was probably the time to say whatever this guy wanted to hear and get the hell out of here with all her fingers and toes attached.

"It i-is so."

Damn it, Abby. Just say whatever he wants to hear to get away from him safely.

The big man crouched down and shone the flashlight in her face. She placed her arm over her eyes, trying to shield them. He grabbed her arm, making her whimper in pain.

"Now, listen here," he said threateningly. "I want to know where your useless prick of a brother is."

"I d-don't know." She was so terrified she felt like throwing up.

He made a low, angry noise and his hold on her tightened. Tears welled in her eyes.

"But he calls me once a week," she lied. "I spoke to him yesterday. Next time he calls, I'll find out for you."

"You fucking better. And you best not be playing me. I don't like when people lie to me, got it?" He dragged her closer until she was nearly gagging on the smell of his breath.

"I u-understand."

"And don't try to run or bring anyone else into this or things will go much worse for you."

His threat made, he disappeared into the shadows, dropping her flashlight on the ground.

Abby sat there for a moment, trying to bring her emotions back under control. The urge to vomit warred with her desire to just sit there and cry.

Reynolds don't cry, Abigail.

You can't let them see you hurting.

Abby tried to be brave. To be stoic. To never show her fear. But damn, it was hard. Most of the time, she just wanted to build a fort and hide from life.

But right now, she had to get off the ground, gather up her stuff and go pay her weekly installment for Max's debt.

Wasn't it enough to have one bad guy in her life? Seemed not. Seemed she was just an over-achiever.

KENT JENSON SLAMMED his gloved hand into the boxing bag, trying to exhaust himself enough that he might be able to sleep tonight. The door to the gym slid open. He landed a few more upper cuts before someone grabbed the bag, holding it still for him. He glanced over and saw Zeke.

"Thanks," he muttered.

"No problem, chief," Zeke said easily.

Kent punched in silence, until sweat dripped down his face and stung his eyes and his lungs burned. When he was breathing hard, his muscles shaking with fatigue, he stepped back and started undoing his gloves.

"What you doing here this time of night?" he asked.

"I was working in the security hub, saw you were in here, thought I'd come get a workout."

Right. And Kent also believed there was a pot of gold at the end of the rainbow.

"Some of the boys are going to a club in the city this weekend," Zeke offered casually. "Maybe you should go with them."

Kent wiped his face with a towel then walked over to the fridge to grab a bottle of water. Once, he would have jumped at the chance to visit a BDSM club. But now, the thought of it just made him feel tired. Empty.

"I'll pass," he said.

Zeke raised an eyebrow. "Might help you sleep better."

"What makes you think I'm not sleeping?"

"Chief, it's obvious to anyone that looks at you. You look like shit. You're as mean as a rattle snake, you've been stomping around here snarling at anyone who moves for the last few weeks. You need a session at the club."

"Tell you what I don't need and that's someone sticking their nose into my business."

"If this was anyone else who wasn't sleeping, you'd be the first to get all up in their business."

"I'm the boss."

"That means we don't get to worry about you?" Zeke replied.

"Jesus," he muttered and took a long drink of water.

"Hey, I don't want to have this talk, but I drew the short straw."

They were choosing straws to see who had to come speak to him? Had he been that much of an asshole? He thought over the past few weeks and realized he probably had been.

Fuck.

"We just figured a few sessions at the club would help ease some tension."

Once upon a time they might have. He needed the feeling of being in charge. These nightmares were something he had no control over. A session at the club, taking command of a sub, a scene, it used to give him back that control, to help him quiet the nightmares.

Now, he wasn't so sure. He didn't feel the pull he once had. The nightmares seemed to be coming more frequently and he couldn't run off to a club each time they did.

"I'm not going to the club. But I am sorry I've been such an asshole. I'll do better."

Zeke sighed. "Chief—"

"You want to spot me for a while?" he asked.

Zeke stared at him for a while longer. Then he nodded. "Sure. I live to serve."

"Asshole."

Zeke grinned. "That's your new nickname, not mine."

Kent just shook his head. "The lack of respect around here is disturbing. Maybe I should have stayed in the military."

No, getting out was the best thing he could have done. He just had to find a way to combat the nightmares.

ABBY WALKED out of the back entrance to the bar and let out a low breath. A shudder rolled over her. She'd been coming here every Friday night for the last three months and she still left feeling dirty and nasty and like she wanted to cry.

At least she didn't have to walk through the notorious biker bar anymore. She'd done that the first night and nearly hadn't made it out alive. Someone had grabbed her and pressed her up against the bar, his hands hard and heavy on her body and...

She bit her lip. *Don't think about it.* Gray, one of Mr. Markovich's assistants, had seen her and intervened and since then, Mr. Markovich had let her come in the back way. And, unlike the diner, the bar's back parking lot actually had security lights. Although it seemed darker tonight than usual.

She grabbed her keys in one hand and her bag in the other. She had to think about investing in some pepper spray. Or maybe she should start carrying around the police baton Nana had given her when she turned eighteen. It weighed a ton, though.

But it was better than walking around completely unarmed and helpless. She walked swiftly towards her car, coming to a sudden stop as she heard someone cry out. She froze, looked around. The sound had come from her right, behind a large van. She hesitated.

The cry came again. Female. Scared.

"Get away from me, you assholes."

Shit. Was that who she thought it was? It couldn't be. What would Eden Jensen be doing here? Everyone knew the Jensens. Eden's brothers were gorgeous, rich and powerful. Clint was the oldest. Stern and slightly scary. His younger brother, Kent was much more easygoing. He always had a smile for her and he was a hell of a tipper.

Too bad she always turned into a fumbling, tongue-tied idiot around him.

She dropped her keys back into her bag and grabbed out her cell phone, fumbling with it as she heard a thumping sound then a pained cry.

She dialed 911, noting that her battery was nearly at the end of its life. She hadn't had time to charge it before driving here. She'd raced home from the diner, quickly gotten changed and came here to meet with Mr. Markovich. He didn't like to be kept waiting.

She didn't want to find out what happened if you did keep him waiting.

"911 what's your emergency?" the calm voice asked.

"My name's Abby Reynold, there's an assault on a woman happening in the parking lot of-of Suck 'n Blow bar." She hung up. She didn't want whoever was with Eden to overhear her.

Another cry sounded. Shit. Shit. Shit. She wished she wasn't a wuss. Why had she never taken up Karate or Judo or gone to a damn self-defense class?

At another pained noise, she knew she couldn't just stand here while Eden was assaulted. She ran forward, creeping her way around the van, her whole body trembling with fear. She spotted two men looming over Eden, who was sprawled on the ground. One of them pulled back his leg as though to kick her.

Oh, hell no!

"Hey! I've called the cops. They'll be here any minute!" she yelled out. "You better leave!"

"Fuck, who's that?" One of the men turned, spotting her. She guessed her ability to blend into the shadows needed work. This looked so much easier on T.V. "Well, here's another bitch."

She swallowed nervously. "I mean it, I've called them. You need to leave."

"You haven't called anyone, bitch. Grab her, Ron," the other one said, reaching down to grab Eden. She bit down on his hand and he screamed. "You fucking cunt."

Abby yelled and whacked the man coming for her across the face with her handbag. That police baton would really come in handy right now. "Fire! Fire!"

"What the fuck? Why you screaming fire, bitch?"

"Fire! Help! Fire!" she continued to scream

He grabbed her and flung her against a car, her side slammed into the mirror and stole her breath. Shoot. That was going to bruise.

In the distance sirens sounded. To her shock, both men froze.

"Fuck, this bitch really did call the cops! Let's go!" her assailant yelled.

"I'm not leaving this one, she fucking bit me." He kicked Eden in the leg, making Abby gasp. "Fucking cunt."

"You really need to work on your insults," Eden told him, sounding breathless and in pain.

He pulled back his leg again and Abby dove forward, placing herself in front of Eden. She knocked Eden's assailant back onto his ass. He climbed to his feet and reached around his back for something. "Fucking bitch, I'm gonna put a bullet in you!"

Oh God. Oh God.

This was it. She was going to die. What the hell had she done with her life except work and pay off Max's debts? Nothing.

And now she was going to die in this dark parking lot with absolutely nothing to show for her life.

"Hey! What's going on! Hey!" a deep voice yelled. "What the fuck!"

"Shit, that's Gray! Fuck!" one of the men yelled. "Let's get out of here."

Both men took off. Abby lay there. Had that really just happened? Had she nearly died?

Oh, hell.

Eden moved then whimpered.

Abby, pull yourself together.

"Eden, are you okay?" she asked, turning towards the other woman. "Where are you hurt? Do you need an ambulance? What am I saying? Of course, you do. Let me find my handbag. Shoot, I don't know where it went."

"Abby, it's okay, take a breath. You're going to hyperventilate." Eden's voice was surprisingly calm. How could she be calm?

"It's not okay, you were just beaten up. Who were they? Oh hell, here comes Gray."

"Gray?" Eden asked. "Who is Gray? Help me sit, will you? And can you see my chair anywhere?"

"What the fuck is going on?" Gray asked as he approached, his voice a low growl.

She placed an arm around Eden's back and helped her sit. The other woman hissed and winced. Where had her handbag gone? She needed some light to check whether Eden needed an ambulance.

"Abby, what the fuck is going on?" Gray demanded.

"You know this guy, Abby?" Eden asked.

"Yeah, that's just Gray," she muttered absentmindedly as she found her handbag and reaching in, grabbed her flashlight.

"Thanks for the ego boost there, babe."

She turned on the flashlight and shone it straight at him. He cursed and stepped back, shielding his eyes. "Jesus, Abby, watch where you're aiming that."

"Oh, sorry, are you okay?" She lowered the light, noted a few people from the bar were standing behind Gray. That wasn't good. She knew firsthand the type of people who hung out at Suck 'n Blow. And they made Gray look like a choir boy.

"Damn it, sometimes I think you're some secret weapon Max sent in to destroy us."

"Me? A weapon? I don't think so." She laughed nervously. The idea was absurd.

"Well, you're something, babe. Just haven't worked out if the sweet, clumsy, naïve thing you have going on is an act or not."

"It's not an act," Eden said from where she leaned against the car behind her. "Now can you two stop talking and find my damn chair? Not too fond of sitting here in the dark on the ground."

"Chair?" Gray asked. He turned to Eden, studying her for the first time. "Fuck, please don't tell me you're who I think you are."

Eden said nothing.

"Umm, I'll find your chair." Abby stood.

Gray held his hand up. "Stay where you are. Rex, find Ms.

Jensen's wheelchair. Now. Fuck. What the hell happened?"

"Well, I was trying to get to my car when two assholes assaulted me, they dragged me from my chair and told me they'd always wanted to fuck a cripple," Eden told him. Her voice didn't sound shaken or scared. But there was more than a hint of bitterness. "When I objected, they decided to beat on me instead."

Gray let out a series of curse words that had Abby blushing. Although she filed away some of the words for future reference. At the rate her life was going to crap she would need them.

"Your brothers are going to fucking lose their shit," he muttered.

"Yes, they will."

Rex, who she recognized as one of Mr. Markovich's other associates, wheeled over a chair and placed it by Eden. "Umm...you want a hand?"

Eden glared up at him. "I've done this a few times."

But not while injured and Abby really wasn't sure she should be moving around without being checked out. "We need an ambulance."

Those sirens were close now and Gray cursed under his breath.

"No way, no ambulance," Eden said. "I am not going to the hospital."

"Fuck, who called the fucking cops?" Gray asked.

"I did," Abby said.

He swung towards her. Fury came off him in waves, beating at her. She took a step back.

"You called the fucking cops?"

"Those assholes were hurting her! What did you expect me to do?" Wasn't calling the police the normal reaction in that situation?

"Come and find me," Gray roared.

"Stop yelling at her," Eden told him. "It's done."

"Shit. Fuck. Rex take 'em to the back room and stand guard at the door. No one gets in or out except me or the sheriff. Got it?"

"Umm, I really think I should just go home," Abby said hesitantly.

"Abby get your fucking self and your fucking friend into the fucking back room. Fucking now. Got it?"

He stood there, heaving for breath.

She said the only thing she could in the face of such anger. "Yeah, I got it."

Eden was struggling to pull herself up into the chair and Abby couldn't take it anymore. She stepped forward. "Can I help?" she asked quietly.

Eden froze then nodded tiredly. "Yeah, just grab me under one arm and help me get up."

She was heavier than she looked. As Abby tried to lift her, Eden groaned.

"Abby, let her go."

Gray stepped forward and gently brushed her away then lifted Eden into the chair with a care that frankly surprised Abby.

"She needs an ambulance," Abby told Gray.

"I'm fine," Eden said.

"You're not fine."

"Abby. She said she's fine," Gray stated.

"But—"

"Abby, shut the fuck up," Gray snapped.

"Hey, don't talk to her like that," Eden told him.

"Both of you are pains in my ass. You wanna know what I do with pains in my ass?"

"Take some Advil?" Abby asked. As soon as it left her mouth, she couldn't believe she'd said that. To this extremely scary guy.

Both of them just stared at her. Her flashlight bobbed as nerves threatened to get the best of her.

"Or maybe an enema," Eden added, turning Gray's attention

to her.

Oh no. That wasn't good. Gray wasn't a good guy. He was a dangerous guy. And Eden didn't know that. She needed to get his attention back on her.

"Or a colonoscopy."

Gray growled. Actually growled. "I was thinking more of a bullet."

"Now that's gonna hurt," Eden said sweetly. "And seems a bit drastic."

He sighed long and loud. "Rex get them into the back office."

"I know the way," Abby pointed out.

"Well, now, wouldn't want anything else to fucking happen to you on the way, would I? Trouble seems to follow you around."

No, it didn't. She led a boring life. Nothing exciting ever happened to her. And any trouble she did have was entirely due to her no-hoper brother.

And she could definitely do with less of it.

She saw the flashing lights of a police car as they neared the back of the bar. Abby pushed Eden's chair around to the door. The fact that the other woman didn't protest told her she was hurting more than she let on.

"Shit," Eden muttered. "This isn't good."

"It doesn't sound like Gray's planning on hurting us," Abby said. Although she wasn't entirely certain.

"Not worried about Gray. Although I wouldn't trust him as far as I could throw him, which obviously isn't that far. I'm worried about Clint."

"Clint? Your brother?"

"Only Clint I know."

She pushed Eden through the back door and into the room she always met Mr. Markovich in. Thankfully, he was gone. If Gray was a bad guy, then Mr. Markovich was a...well...shark. Handsome in a really terrifying way. And the worse things were, the more he smiled. It was the weirdest freaking thing. She'd never thought that she would be petrified of a smile.

"Clint will hurt you?" She was shocked. She didn't know him well, but he was always polite, if a bit brusque. Except when he was with his girlfriend. Charlie softened him. When he looked at her, his eyes filled with warmth. It was obvious they adored each other.

It was sweet.

She wanted that. She wanted adoration. She wanted sweet.

She didn't have a chance in hell of finding it.

Eden stared up at her. Abby winced as she saw the other woman's right eye was mostly swollen shut.

"Oh hell, Eden. Your eye."

"Yeah, that's not going to be good. I could really use a bag of frozen peas."

She strode over to the small fridge, opening the door. "He's got crème de cacao, and crème de menthe. That's weird. That's weird, right?"

Eden shrugged then winced. "So, he likes grasshoppers."

"It's Mr. Markovich." And she could not imagine him drinking grasshoppers. Not that Abby wouldn't mind a grasshopper right now.

"I'm not really sure who Mr. Markovich is," Eden told her.

Right. Because Eden didn't live in the underbelly. She lived in the light. She had two brothers who loved and protected her. Well, Abby thought she did. Now she wasn't so sure about Clint.

"He won't hurt you, will he? Clint?" She closed the fridge and slowly stood. Now that the adrenaline was draining away, she could feel every one of her aches and pains. Her knees, her hands, and now her side.

"Clint? Clint would never hurt a hair on my head. But the man can lecture. You do not want to be on the receiving end of one of those." Eden sighed tiredly.

That's what she was worried about? A lecture? At least it meant that her brother cared.

"I lost my cell, do you have yours on you?" Eden asked. "Since Gray the goon won't let us leave, I need to call Kent."

"Sure." She searched through her bag. "Um, Eden, why are you here? At this bar?"

"I was meeting someone," Eden muttered. "They didn't turn up. They chose the place, not me. Won't make that mistake again."

Someone knocked on the door and Ed stepped inside. The sheriff was a big, intimidating man with dark hair and smoky gray eyes.

His gaze took in everything, running over first Eden then Abby. "Well, shit. Have you called your brother yet?"

"Just about to," Eden said, taking Abby's phone from her hand. She stared down at it. "What the hell is this?"

"A phone." Abby blushed at Eden's disbelieving look.

"I didn't think they still made phones like this. I've never held one."

Yeah, well, Eden wasn't hurting for money. Her whole outfit probably cost more than Abby made in a month.

It doesn't make you less than her.

"Eden," the sheriff said in a low voice. She turned to stare at him. Slowly. How hurt was she? "You're being rude to Abby."

Abby gaped at the sheriff. She couldn't remember the last time someone had stuck up for her. The sheriff had always been kind, but she'd never really spoken to him for any length of time. Mind you, she'd been trained to avoid cops.

Eden glanced up at Abby. She winced at the other woman's swollen face. "Sorry, Abby. I tend to be a bit grouchy after assholes kick the shit out of me."

The sheriff's face clouded over. "Who exactly kicked the shit out of you?"

2

She heard a commotion out the door. A deep voice barked something. Demanded. Whoever that was, he was furious.

Eden sighed. "Kent's here."

That was Kent?

The sheriff had insisted on calling the paramedics. He'd taken Eden's statement while waiting for them. Now a paramedic was checking Eden over while Ed took Abby's statement.

The door to the room opened and in stepped Kent Jensen. Her whole body heated. He was wearing sweatpants and a sweatshirt. How could he still look hot in that outfit? Nobody looked hot in sweatpants.

Except for Kent.

His light-brown hair was kept short, drawing your gaze to his gorgeous features. He was sporting a five o'clock shadow, which just gave him a more rugged appearance. His deep brown gaze roamed the room. She'd noticed that about him. He always took in his surroundings no matter where he was. She guessed it came from being a former Navy SEAL. Or maybe it was because he owned Jensen Security International.

Once he'd glanced over the room, his gaze immediately locked on Eden. For some stupid reason, she felt a stab of jealousy. Idiot.

Someone moved into the room behind him. A big guy also wearing sweatpants. Although he didn't rock them the same way Kent did. This man gave the room a similar glance. She'd seen him a few times before. She knew he worked at Sanctuary although he rarely came into the diner.

His cool gaze touched her briefly before Eden became the entire center of his focus. Kent was already crouched beside his sister, talking to her quietly. The other man moved to her side.

And here sat Abby. Alone. She took in a deep breath.

"Abby, you okay?"

She jumped. The sheriff, who was sitting across from her, gave her a worried look. She forced herself to smile. She'd forgotten he was even there.

"I'm fine."

"Rye, check Abby over," the sheriff ordered the hunky paramedic.

"I'm fine."

"You're getting checked over," Ed said in a firm voice. She shivered slightly at that tone.

"Really. They didn't even touch me," she insisted. "I don't need to be checked over."

"Then how'd you get those grazes on your hands?" he asked.

"What grazes?"

She glanced up in shock as Kent asked that question. She hadn't even seen him move and now he was standing next to the sheriff, staring down at her. She froze. She didn't know what to say. His blue eyes were serious, his face cool. Was he angry with her? What had she done? Was he mad over the grazes?

She tucked her hands under her thighs, concealing a wince at the pain.

Kent raised an eyebrow. "Hiding them doesn't mean you don't have to show me, sweetheart."

Warmth filled her at the endearment, even though she told herself he probably called lots of women that.

Kent moved his gaze to Ed, and she was able to breathe once more. "Eden told me what happened. I'm telling you right now, you better find these assholes before I do."

Ed sighed. "You can't say things like that in front of an officer of the law, Kent."

"Just stating a fact. Two assholes beat on a woman who couldn't even fight back. You think that sort of thing is gonna go down well? Fact that she's my sister, belongs to Sanctuary, you can bet you're gonna have a whole lot of angry people breathing down your neck."

Ed rubbed the back of his neck as though he could feel it already. Then he stood. He looked down at Abby once more.

"Abby, let Rye check you over."

"Promise it won't hurt a bit, darlin'," Rye told her with a wink.

Abby blushed and turned her gaze away, feeling uncomfortable.

"Back off, you're crowding her," Kent told the paramedic with a scowl. He came and crouched in front of her. "Where are you hurt, sweetheart? You can tell me."

His soft voice brought tears to her eyes. She couldn't help it. She knew he was just being nice. Across the room, the other big guy was crouched in front of Eden in a similar position. Was he her boyfriend? If he was, then what was she doing in the parking lot of Suck 'n Blow? That guy didn't seem like the sort of man who would let someone he cared about come here.

Two fingers were placed under her chin and her head was turned so she was staring up at Kent once more.

"Abby, sweetheart, I know you've had a fright. But I need you to stay here with me, okay? I'm here now. I'll look after you."

She stared into his deep blue eyes and heard the sincerity in his voice. How amazing would it be to have this man protect and take care of her all the time? It was a dream that would never come true. But right now, she just wanted to sink herself into the safety he represented.

"O-okay."

"Where are you hurt? Eden said those guys shoved you against a car. Is your back sore? Did they hurt you anywhere else?"

"N-no. That...that's all that happened. Eden is the one they hurt."

"What about the scratches on your hands?"

"I fell over earlier. I'm a bit clumsy sometimes," she whispered in an ashamed voice. She wished she was tall and elegant and graceful.

Not short and clumsy with too much boob and ass.

"Hey, come back to me." His voice was still soft but there was a core of steel that had her obeying him immediately.

She met his gaze and that whoosh of arousal ran through her body. Jesus, he was potent.

He gave her a warm smile. "There she is. Good girl. You're doing well, Abby."

She was? She thought she was one step away from losing it.

But he had called her a good girl.

"Huh, like that is it?" Ed asked.

"You got a problem, Ed?" Kent asked, without glancing back at the other man.

"No problem." The sheriff stared down at her, studying her. What was it? Was there something on her face? She reached up to rub at her cheek and Kent took the opportunity to grab her hand. He gently turned it over to study the scraped palm. The blood had dried and gone all crusty but there were still bits of gravel and dirt stuck in the cut.

She winced. That was gonna be hell to clean.

"This didn't happen recently," Kent said. "And it hasn't been cleaned."

"It happened a few hours ago. Wasn't looking where I was going and tripped over something in the car park." She didn't mention the threatening man. She knew better than to talk to cops about Max's shit.

That was a definite way to lose more than your fingers and toes. A shudder rocked her body.

"It's okay, Abby. You're safe now," Kent reassured her.

If only that was true.

"I'm going to go and talk to Gray again. You got this?" Ed asked.

"Yeah, I got this." Confidence filled Kent's voice.

"I can take Abby home—"

Kent turned to Ed. "I got this, Ed."

His firm tone sent a shudder up her spine. He immediately turned back to her.

"Easy, sweet girl. Everything is okay now. You really should get these hands cleaned."

"No," she whispered.

He gave her an incredulous stare. "No?"

She peeked over at the paramedic and just shook her head. Her hand trembled in his.

"It's him or me, little one."

Little one? Okay, she'd been called a lot of names over the years that alluded to her height. Shorty, pipsqueak, shrimp, small fry, midget. The list went on. But never little one. And certainly, never said in such a warm voice.

"I can do it myself."

"Now, those weren't your choices, were they?" That core of steel was back and her heart leaped into her throat. The paramedic or him? Seriously? Those were her choices? Bad enough he was touching her now, much more and she thought she might self-combust.

"Kent, Eden needs to go to the hospital and get checked out," the other guy told him.

"I'm not going to the hospital, Zeke," Eden stated.

Zeke stood, arms folded across his chest, the look on his face intimidating as hell. If Abby was Eden, she would have already capitulated, unable to take the pressure of such a glare. But Eden was matching his scowl with her own, obviously determined not to back down.

"Eden," Kent said in a low voice. "You could have broken ribs."

"They're not broken. I know what broken ribs feel like, remember? They're just bruised and there ain't nothing that can be done for them either way. I'm not going to the hospital."

Kent stood, stared at his sister thoughtfully. Then he turned to Zeke. "Take her to Doc."

"Chief," Zeke said in a warning voice.

Kent's face morphed into that cold mask once more. "Take her home to Doc."

"Where are you going?" Eden asked.

"I'm taking Abby home. I'll take care of her."

I'm taking Abby home. I'll take care of her.

She should protest, but when was the last time someone had taken care of her?

"Zeke, take Eden home in her car. I'll take my truck. Make sure she gets checked over by Doc."

"And Clint?" Zeke asked in a stiff voice. "We telling him that his sister was at a dive bar and got accosted by two bikers?"

"In the morning," Kent said tiredly. "I'll deal with it. After Eden and I have a chat."

"Awesome," Eden said sarcastically. "I look forward to it."

Abby felt sorry for Kent. There were dark crescents under his eyes. She had the feeling he had to deal with a lot on his own. She wished she could rub away the frown lines on his forehead, massage his tight neck muscles. But it wasn't her place. He was just being nice to her. None of this meant anything.

"Abby, thanks for helping me," Eden said to her.

Abby smiled. "You're welcome. Not that I was much help."

"Umm, one question? Why did you call out fire instead of help?"

"Oh, I watched this documentary once where it said people are more likely to respond if they hear the word fire than help." She shrugged.

"Come on, Eden," Zeke said firmly. "Let's get you home and checked over. I'll call Doc on the way."

Eden groaned. "Great, he's even more grumpy when he's woken up."

"Well, just think of it as a warm-up for when Clint hears about this," Zeke replied.

"Fuck my life," Eden said tiredly.

"You should be damn thankful you're not mine," Zeke told her as he walked around the back of the chair, taking hold of the handles. "'Cause not only would you be headed to the hospital, but once you were better, you'd be over my knee."

Abby froze in her seat, Eden's reply drowned out by the roaring in her ears. Did he just threaten to spank her? She'd heard some rumors about Sanctuary ranch, but they'd always been sharply shut down. She'd never put much credence into them. But now...

"Abby, you okay?"

She peered around the room. There was only her and Kent left and he was giving her a concerned look. She blushed and tried to jump to her feet. But as she did, she knocked into him, sending him sprawling backwards.

"Oh my God, I'm so sorry."

Why did she have to be such a clumsy dork? She held out her hand to Kent who was staring at her incredulously. "Here, let me help you up."

He climbed to his feet without taking her hand. Rejection flooded her. He didn't want to touch her.

Well, you were the one to knock him over.

She dropped her gaze to the floor. Idiot.

"Abby, look at me," he said to her in a low voice. "Look at me." This time his voice was firmer. Not so easy to ignore.

She sighed. Glanced up at him.

"Honey, I weigh twice as much as you do and you've got some nasty grazes on your hand. Plus, I'm a guy. I'm a little old-fashioned about some things. And that means, in my world, a little thing like you doesn't try to help me up. When I'm around, you don't open doors or carry things or pump gas or pay for the bill. All right?"

She blinked, trying to take that in. There were men like that? She'd kind of thought they didn't exist. Not anymore. Then it hit her. He wasn't rejecting her. He was being thoughtful.

"Oh."

He smiled. The skin around his eyes crinkled as amusement filled his face. He tucked a lock of hair back that had fallen out of the bun she usually kept her hair confined in. "Come on, sweet girl. Let's get you home and into bed."

Her body went on high alert.

He doesn't mean it that way.

And sure enough, his next words proved that. "You look completely wiped and it's way past your bedtime." He took gentle hold of her wrist and guided her from the room, and yes, he actually held open the door for her.

"I don't have a bedtime."

"You should."

She frowned. What did he mean by that? He led them out the back door of the bar as though he'd used it plenty of times before.

"Have you come here often?" she asked.

"Here? God, no." His voice was very definite. "Love to know why you're here, though."

She tensed up. Crap. She was going to have to think of a good excuse.

"And before you tell me that lie you're trying to concoct, I would warn you that I don't like to be lied to. Ever. I'd rather you said nothing at all than lie to me. Understood?" There was no bend in his voice and even though she couldn't see his face, she knew that he meant every word.

Okay, note to self. Don't lie to Kent Jensen. Probably not going to be a problem, since before tonight she'd barely spoken to him and she fully expected things to return to normal tomorrow. Tonight, was just some weird aberration where he was taking care of her because he was a good guy, because he was grateful she'd helped Eden.

Yeah, that had to be it.

bby frowned as Kent guided her over to a huge ass black truck. "My car is over there." She waved her free hand towards the left.

"Is it?" He beeped open his truck.

"Umm, yes, so I guess I'll just say good night here."

He opened the passenger door and the inner light went on. Then he turned to her. "Abby, didn't you hear me say I was going to take care of you?"

"Umm, well, yes, but—"

"And that I told the sheriff I would take you home?"

"Well, I heard that, yes, but that doesn't mean—"

"That I told the paramedic I would look after those cuts on your hands—"

"Yes, but you see—"

"And I told Zeke and Eden I was taking you home in my truck."

"Urgh! Could you please just let me talk!"

There was a moment of silence. She opened her mouth to speak, finally he was going to be reasonable.

"No."

No? No? He couldn't be serious. He reached down, grasped her around the waist and lifted her up into the passenger seat. No doubt she would have had to take a running jump to get up but he'd lifted her in as though she didn't weigh a thing.

"Kent!" she squealed.

"Yes?"

"You can't just lift me like that!"

"Why not?" He grabbed the seat belt and pulled it over her, his arm brushing against her already stiff nipples. Oh Christ, he couldn't feel them through the layers of clothing, could he?

"Because I'm too heavy."

More silence. Only there was disapproval in this silence.

"You did not just say that."

"Umm…" Why was he mad?

He grasped hold of her chin and turned her to face him. He seemed to have this thing about her looking at him when he spoke. "Listen to me, Abby. Really listen and take this in. Talking bad about yourself is not allowed. Saying things like you are too heavy is a surefire way to end up in trouble with me, you got me?"

No. She didn't get him. She didn't get him at all. Trouble? Why would she get into trouble over speaking the truth? She was just trying to save his back. She didn't see how it was such a big deal anyway.

He sighed. "You don't got me."

"Not really."

"Do you know anything about how Sanctuary Ranch is run?"

"I-I've heard things."

He snorted. "Probably the wrong things. You already know I have some old-fashioned values. I believe the man should be the head of the household. It's how I grew up. What I want for myself. It's what all the men on Sanctuary believe in. Not a dictatorship, I'm always going to listen to my woman's opinion. But the ultimate decision falls on me. I make the rules. I enforce them. Now I can tell by the look on your face that you're about to tell me I'm a complete Neanderthal asshole. But you haven't heard it all. The women living at Sanctuary are cherished, protected, completely respected by me. Their happiness, safety, health come before everything else."

She didn't know what to make of any of this. She didn't know what he expected her to say or why he was even telling her all of this. It did explain a few things about the men who lived on Sanctuary Ranch. They always had this dominant vibe going on. And whenever any of their women were with them, they were extremely protective and attentive. It had always made her jealous and a bit sad.

Because it wasn't something she'd ever have.

"I would never disrespect my woman. I certainly would never allow her to disrespect herself. You get what I'm saying?"

She wanted to point out that she wasn't his woman. That none of this applied to her. But the words were frozen on her tongue.

Instead, she nodded.

He studied her for a moment then shook his head. "Just don't put yourself down again." He ran his gaze over her. "Christ, you're so short your feet don't even reach the floor."

She peered down to find her feet swinging in the air.

"You need a booster seat."

"I do not!"

"Can you see out of the window?"

"I'm not that short."

"Honey." He placed his hand on her thigh and warmth filled her. She quickly pressed her thighs together as her clit throbbed. "I like that you're short. You're cute."

Cute. Right. Cute was what you said about puppies and kittens and little kids. All of them usually short as well.

"But I'm concerned about your safety. How tall are you? What height is it safe to be out of a booster?"

He couldn't be serious. Oh my God. He was. He was actually being serious.

"I'm five foot," well, not quite, "and I'm nearly twenty-six years old, I'm way too big and old for a booster seat." She wasn't about to tell him what she weighed.

He grunted. "I'll have to look that up."

Look it up? What the hell? Before she could say anything, he'd shut her door and moved around the front of his truck, leaving her to wonder what the hell that meant.

"Wait," she said as he got in. She undid her seatbelt. "I just remembered I have the early shift tomorrow at the diner. I need my car."

"Call in sick."

"I can't call in sick." She gaped at him.

"I'll do it for you."

"You will not." What was going on? "I have never called in sick."

"How long have you worked there?"

"Five years."

"Five years and you've never once been sick?" he asked incredulously.

"I'm hardly ever sick," she allowed, remembering his warning never to lie to him.

"You go into work when you're ill? You're not concerned about spreading germs to your customers?"

"I wouldn't go in if I was contagious," she protested.

"So, if you weren't contagious, then what was wrong with you?"

How had they gotten onto this conversation? She remained silent. He shifted, turning towards her. "Not gonna answer, huh?"

"You said you'd rather I didn't say anything than lie to you," she pointed out softly. She tensed, waiting for him to get angry.

"Fair enough. I appreciate you not lying to me."

She spun, staring at him in shock. The overhead light had already turned off so she couldn't make out his features, unfortunately.

"Abby, it's nearly two a.m. You've got to be exhausted, I'm sure your boss will understand if you call in sick for a day."

She didn't think Gloria would understand at all. "I need the money."

"I'll give it to you."

He did not just offer that.

"Y-you won't." Maybe someone as broke as her shouldn't have any pride, but she did. And she was not taking money from this man.

"I will. Tell me how much you'd be short by and I'll make up the difference."

She leaned over the console between them, determined to make herself understood. She wasn't an aggressive person. She didn't like confrontation. But this was not going to happen.

"You. Will. Not."

He drummed his fingers against the steering wheel. "Gotta say, didn't think you'd have this stubborn streak."

She wasn't sure it was stubbornness so much as anger over what he obviously thought of her. That she was the type of person to take his money. She wasn't. She might have none. Things might be getting desperate enough that she was in jeopardy of losing her home, but she would not take his money.

"Fine." He started his truck. "Let's get you home so you'll get some sleep tonight."

"I really need my car, though. How will I get to it in the morning?"

"I'll get one of the boys to drive it to your place before your shift. What time do you start?"

"Six," she whispered, knowing he wouldn't like that.

"Shit. Barely even worth going to bed."

Yeah, she'd had that thought herself. The cab of the truck was filled with his anger.

"I'm sorry," she told him, unable to help herself.

"What are you sorry for?"

"I'm sorry you're upset with me for not doing what you wanted."

He snorted. "I'm not happy that you have to go to work on little sleep, that you were threatened and scared tonight. I like to be in control. And I definitely don't like the word no. However, none of that means that I'm upset or angry with you."

"Really?" she asked incredulously.

"All right. I'm upset. But not the sort of upset that you need to apologize to me for. You're doing what you think you need to do. My opinion differs. Were you mine, my opinion would win. But you're not."

"Women really agree to relationships like the one you want?" she asked, unable to help herself.

"Yes. They thrive with that sort of relationship. They need it. It makes them feel safe and cherished."

She'd love to feel safe and cherished.

"Where do you live, sweet girl?"

"What?" she asked.

"Where do you live? I need the address so I can get you home and into bed."

Want to join me there?

Lord, she wished she was brave enough to ask him that. And she was also glad she wasn't brave enough.

Jesus, could she ever make up her mind about anything?

She managed to rally herself enough to give him her address.

He didn't bother to use the fancy GPS built into the dashboard, obviously he knew where her street was. They pulled up in front of her house after a mostly silent drive. She was glad it was dark enough that he couldn't see how rundown her tiny house was. There wasn't exactly spare money for the repairs that needed doing.

"Uh, thanks for the ride," she said, reaching for her belt.

"Don't get out of the truck yourself," he ordered. He climbed out and came around to open her door. Okay, it seemed that he was going to escort her to the door of her house.

He really was a gentleman.

He grabbed her, lifting her down. When her feet touched the ground, her legs nearly collapsed under her.

He held her. "Do you need me to carry you?"

"No," she said hastily.

He stepped back slowly. "Lead on then, sweetheart."

She walked up towards the small porch that ran along the front of the tiny two-bedroom house. She and Max had shared a bedroom when they were younger. Once they'd gotten older, Max had moved into Nana's old camper. Abby had sold the camper after Nana died to help pay for some of the funeral expenses.

She grabbed her keys and unlocked the door. "Thank you for —" her voice trailed off as he reached around her and opened the door then slid by and walked inside. "What do you think you're doing?"

"I still need to take care of those grazes on your hands, sweetheart, remember? It was obvious you were trying to brush me off so I figured I'd cut through the bullshit and come inside." He unerringly managed to find the light switch as he moved into the house.

"Kent, I really just want to go to bed." This whole night had been shit. And to think she'd been complaining about old Pete having too many coffees. Turns out that had been the least of her problems. She pinched the top of her nose between her finger and thumb.

"Hey." Kent gently pulled her hand away from her face. "I know this is all overwhelming. You're exhausted, sore, and you're letting a man you don't know very well into your private space."

"I'm not sure that I let you in." She sent him a teasing smile.

He grinned. Her heart went into overtime. When he smiled, he went from gorgeous to stunning.

"I have been accused of being bossy once or twice."

"Once or twice? Now, who's lying?"

"So, there is a sense of humor under that quiet exterior."

She winced and lowered her gaze. Quiet. A word that basically meant boring. Forgettable.

"Abby? You okay?"

"I'm fine. Just a bit sore. I need a shower."

He grasped hold of her chin, raising her face so he could study it. "I get this night hasn't been easy and you'd probably like to be well rid of me so you can climb into bed and collapse, but tonight you jumped in and helped my sister when you could have walked away. Or called the cops and kept yourself safely hidden until they arrived. I wouldn't have even blamed you. Little thing like you shouldn't be wading into situations like that."

"You don't owe me anything, Kent." Because it's obvious that's where he was going with this speech.

"But I do, sweetheart. My entire family does. You saved Eden from getting a worse beating than she did. And she told me how close you came to a bullet." His face darkened and she grew tense as she saw the fury in his gaze. He looked away, took in a deep breath then turned back to her. "That sort of situation crops up again, you ring the cops and you keep safe. Understand me?"

He was using his you-better-listen-to-me-or-else voice again.

"That doesn't require a lot of thought to agree," he said in a warning voice.

Shit. She hated to disagree with him. It wasn't really her nature to argue. Well, most of the time. Sometimes she took a stand, like when he said he was going to give her money to make up whatever she would lose if she called in sick. She had pride. And principles. And there were some things she just couldn't agree to.

"I'm not sure I can agree. I'm not saying I'm brave or anything. I was scared shitless. I froze. I took too long getting there. When I did get there, I didn't know what to do. But if it ever happens again, I'm not sure I can promise to keep myself safe while someone else is getting hurt."

He raised his eyebrows. "You dove in to defend someone else even though you were scared and you think you're not brave? You've got so much courage in you it's enough to have a man shaking in his boots."

"I really don't understand you."

"I know. Not sure I understand me either. I just don't like the idea of you getting hurt."

Well, that was sweet.

"If it makes you feel better, I don't like that idea either. And I don't plan to ever get in that situation again."

"You go back to that bar, it could well happen," he warned in a low voice.

She didn't tell him that she had to go back, because that would lead to a conversation she wasn't going to have.

He grunted as though he understood what she was trying not to say.

"The thing is, little Abby, I do owe you. I'm going to make sure you're all right, which includes taking care of those scrapes and making sure you're not hurt any worse than you say you are. I wish you would let me handle things so you could get more than an hour or two of sleep, but that seems to be out of the question."

"It is," she said firmly.

"All right, so just for now will you let me take care of you?"

"Okay."

He smiled and it lit his face. She melted. "Okay. Go have a shower, baby. I'll get you something to wear."

"Umm, no. I'll get something to wear. You...ah...sit here." She moved into the living room and pointed at the sofa.

He raised one eyebrow but he seemed more amused than annoyed. She grabbed the T.V. remote and gave it to him. "Knock yourself out."

"Okay."

She just stared, completely frozen by the sight of him. Kent Jensen. In her living room. Sitting on her sofa. Watching her T.V.

It was like she'd entered the Twilight Zone. Where all her dreams had come true. Well, except for a bad guy threatening her, scraping her knees and hands, encountering a pair of women-beating jerks and bruising her. Otherwise, yeah, dream come true.

"Abby? Abby."

She blinked, stared down at Kent who was watching her with some concern mixed in with his amusement now.

"Yes?"

"Shower, baby," he said to her gently.

"Right...shower...yes."

"You want me to come help you?"

That shocked her out of her dreamy state. "No!"

"Well, you better get to it, or I'm going to think you need my help."

She saw his grin before she swiftly turned away and practically raced into the bathroom. Then she realized she didn't have her pajamas and opened the door, walking into her bedroom to grab some things.

When the bathroom door was safely closed and locked, she leaned against it to catch her breath.

Wow. Just wow.

LITTLE THING SURE WAS RATTLED.

His amusement faded as he set the remote down. He didn't intend to just sit here and watch television. He was used to Abby freezing up around him, stuttering her words. Once she'd nearly dropped a whole plate of food in his lap. Luckily, he'd seen what was about to happen and had snatched it safely out of her hands.

Yeah, he rattled her. And in some ways, he liked that. Liked that he could so easily read every expression on her face. She didn't know how to hold back. He knew she was attracted to him. Every time he touched her, her breathing sped up, her body grew tense. When she'd been staring at him before, he knew she was a million miles away. In Abby-land.

He guessed Abby-land was a better place for her to be than her reality.

He really wanted to change that. He groaned and rubbed his hand over his face tiredly. What was he thinking? What was he doing? He couldn't lead Abby on. She wasn't the type of woman he was looking for.

Because he was pretty certain she was a Little.

He'd never thought of himself as a Daddy Dom. Not like Clint or Bear. He'd never been involved with a Little. He wasn't the kind of guy who could nurture and guide her. Not like a Daddy. He didn't even know if she knew what she was. If she knew anything about BDSM or age play.

Nope, getting involved with her wouldn't work. And she definitely wasn't a one-night type of girl.

Why was he so attracted to her? Why was he even here? He could have driven her home, walked her to her door and left. He could have insisted she go with that paramedic who hadn't been able to take his eyes off her. He clenched his hands at the memory.

You've got no business being jealous.

He also had no business making demands on her. He knew some of his comments could have been misleading. Where had that stuff about the booster seat come from? He'd obviously spent too much time around Clint and Charlie.

Step back. Cool things down.

He'd already gone too far, telling her about what sort of relationship he desired. No doubt she was completely confused by his comments. But he wanted to see if he could get past the layer of defenses she had up. With time, he could get her used to his touch, his presence and she might open up. Then he'd see the true Abby. He'd gotten glimpses of her. Flashes of her sense of humor. And after the way she'd come to Eden's defense, he could now see her courage.

She was far too brave for his peace of mind.

Crap. This whole night had turned into an absolute shit-storm. Although he was damn glad that Eden had called him and not Clint. Mind you, that was a given. He knew she was expecting him to intervene between the two of them.

Clint was going to be pissed.

And he had every right to be. Eden had no business being at that bar, where the worst scum of the state hung out. And neither did Abby. He was dying to know what she had been doing there. He'd see if Eden could shed any light on that.

You need to distance yourself.

Right. But that didn't mean he couldn't intervene from afar. He got up and prowled into the kitchen, pouring himself a drink of water. The house was freezing cold and had a tired feel to it. The wallpaper came from the seventies and was curling up at the edges.

On a hunch, he opened the pantry. He sighed. Christ, why didn't she have any food? Sure, could be that she didn't like cooking and ate out all the time. But somehow, he didn't think so. There was coffee, some staples like salt and pepper along with a bag of rice and a few cans of food. He opened the fridge. Milk and half a block of cheese and half a dozen eggs.

How the hell was he meant to pull back now? Clearly, she didn't have anyone to take care of her.

Not your problem.

She helped Eden.

Shit. Shit.

He knew he could tell Clint about all of this and his brother would take care of things. They never left a debt unpaid. But he didn't want Clint taking care of her. Kent wanted to be the one to do that. Even if he had to be careful not to overstep and lead her on.

He heard the water turn off and left the empty glass in the sink. He'd just sat on the sofa and turned the T.V. on when she walked into the living room. Her chestnut hair was pinned back in that horrid bun once more. She was covered head to foot in a man's robe. Jealousy struck him and he had to fight it. The robe looked well-worn. Old-boyfriend or current? Wide, hazel eyes stared at him.

"Abby, I never asked if there was someone you wanted to call."

She frowned slightly. "Call?"

"Like a boyfriend." The words tasted sour in his mouth.

She blinked a few times. "I don't have a boyfriend, if I did I..."

"Wouldn't have accepted a ride home with me?" he guessed.

"Well, yes. Sorry."

"Nothing to be sorry about. If you were my girlfriend, I'd expect to be the first person you called when you got into trouble. Of course, if you were my girlfriend, you wouldn't have been at that bar in the first place."

Her eyes widened at that. Before she could say anything, though, he nodded at the robe. He could tell she was fading fast. She was exhausted and needed to get to bed. For two hours of sleep. He was seriously not happy about that.

"Lose the robe, baby."

Her mouth dropped open and she just stared. He stood and moved towards her, reaching slowly for the robe, not wanting to frighten her. He knew he intimidated her and he never wanted her to be afraid of him.

"Abby, I need to check that your injuries aren't worse than you're letting on. Then I need to clean those hands. Any other injuries I should know about?"

Her hands closed around his. "It's really not necessary—"

"I believe we've already had this talk, haven't we?" He made sure his voice was firm. He didn't intend to argue over anything that had to do with her health. "I don't want to go through this again. I'm going to make certain you are all right. End of story."

She frowned at him. "You're used to getting your way, aren't you?"

He grinned. "Most of the time, yep. Occasionally Clint over-rules me on things, but not very often. Now, lose the robe and tell me where your first aid kit is." He'd untied her robe by now and she hadn't tried to push him away again so he took that as a good sign.

"Umm...well..." She nibbled at her thumbnail. He'd noted before that her fingernails were bitten to the quick.

He gently pulled her thumb free from her mouth. "Baby, spit it out."

"That's not really my thing," she muttered.

He grinned. "I kind of figured that out already. But we don't have time for you to think about what to say, so just say it."

"I don't really have a first aid kit."

"You got antibiotic and some cotton swabs?"

"I think so."

"Then problem solved." And tomorrow, he'd get her a proper first aid kit.

So much for keeping your distance.

"Right. Problem solved. Easy as that." She was gazing at him as though he was a problem she wished she could solve as easily.

He tugged at the sleeve of her robe, pulling it slowly off, gentling his touch as she winced. Was she hurt worse than she'd been letting on? It itched at him to find out. To take care of her. To tuck her into bed and make certain she rested.

And the best way he could do that was to climb into bed beside her.

Okay, he couldn't think of that right now. Once the robe was off, he studied the pale blue pajamas she wore, with pictures of cows on them. They were faded and obviously well-loved. He placed her robe over the back of the sofa then took hold of her wrist and gently steered her into the bathroom. "Where is the antibiotic?"

"Umm, in the cupboard under the sink."

The bathroom was full of steam and yet still felt cold. It was spotlessly clean like the rest of the house but needed a complete gut. All the fixtures had to be at least thirty years old. He easily found the antibiotic, cotton swabs and some Band-Aids. He placed them down then reached for her and lifted her up so she was sitting on the counter.

"Kent!" she protested.

He just gave her a look. If she started to talk about how she was too heavy for him to lift then he wasn't going to be happy. She must have read that in his face because she pressed her lips together. He took gentle hold of her right hand. The shower had cleaned off a lot of the dirt, but there was still some embedded in her scrapes, so he set about carefully cleaning them off. She winced several times and he knew it had to be hurting, but her hand remained steady in his and she didn't complain.

Brave little thing.

"Good girl, sweetheart. I know it doesn't feel nice, but you are being so good for me." He didn't know where the words came from. Sure, he'd praised subs before for doing things they weren't comfortable with. For letting him push them. For giving themselves wholly to him.

But never for something like this and never in that tone of voice.

He placed a large band-aid on the worst of the scrapes and took hold of her other hand. He started cleaning it up. "I know it hurts. Not too much longer."

"There's my knees too," she whispered.

"What?"

"I scraped my knees when I landed."

"All right, we'll get to those as well." When he finished both hands, he stepped back slightly to study her pajama pants. "You got panties on?"

"What?" She gaped at him.

He swore, he'd never had to repeat himself so much in his life. But he knew she'd had a hard night. Plus, he was pretty certain she wasn't used to having a man in her house, invading her space, ordering her around.

"Do you have panties on?"

"Yes," she said in a voice that implied he was crazy for suggesting she wouldn't. His lips twitched. He'd rather expected that reaction.

"Good. Be easier to deal with your knees if you take your pajama pants off." Before she could react, he lifted her off the bathroom counter. He stood back a little, waiting. Wasn't really in his nature to wait. He was generally a man of action.

But she didn't know him well and he was in her space, ordering her around.

So, he waited.

"Umm...ahh...I can't take my pants off," she said in a rush.

"Sweetheart, I promise you, all I am interested in is taking care of you and getting you into bed. Scout's honor." He held up his fingers.

She watched him suspiciously. "Were you ever a scout?"

"No, but I was a Navy SEAL, does that count?"

Her whole face softened. "Thank you for your service."

Sweet as fucking pie.

"Take the pants off, sweet girl. Let's take care of you and get you into bed."

He figured it was a sign of just how tired she was that she just nodded and slipped off the worn pajamas. He got a glimpse of her panties. Pale pink with little rainbows on them.

Fucking adorable.

Shit. What was wrong with him? He was used to lacy, sexy lingerie. Since when did he think of underwear as adorable? He lifted her back up before he could think about his reaction to her too much. Then crouching, he stared at her knees. "Oh, sweetheart, these have to hurt." They were red and the scrapes were angry looking.

"Every time I'm still for longer than five minutes, I seize up," she admitted to him. "Funny how much more it hurts to fall as an adult than a kid. Shower helped a bit, but they're still sore."

He bet they were and she was going to feel even worse in the morning. He clenched his jaw against saying anything.

Damn near killed him.

He stood. "Okay, your knees are done. Let me see your back where you hit the car."

She just stared at him, then she opened her mouth.

"And I know you're not going to argue with me because you know how futile that will be."

"You're stubborn."

"Yep," he agreed. "More stubborn than you are."

"Not going to get an argument from me about that."

"Oh, so there's something you won't argue with me about?" he teased as he lowered her to the floor and turned her to face the bathroom counter.

"I never argue."

He snorted. "Could have fooled me."

"I don't." Her voice had a childish note to it.

"Darling, you're not exactly doing a good job of proving your point right now."

"Oh. Right. Yeah. Guess you could more truthfully say I don't argue with anyone but you."

He had her top up, and was hoping their conversation would keep her attention directed away from the fact that he could see a large expanse of her creamy skin. Jesus, the urge to lay kisses along her back, down over what he knew had to be a perfect ass was nearly irresistible.

He took a deep breath then examined at the angry red mark that started on her back and wrapped around her ribs.

Shit.

"Why is that do you suppose?" he asked in a low voice as he gently prodded at her ribs, hoping like hell she hadn't damaged them badly. What had he been doing lifting her up and moving her around when he knew she was injured?

His rational side was pointing out that if her ribs were that badly damaged, she would have been showing some sign of favoring them. And she certainly would have reacted when he first picked her up. But right now, he wasn't interested in listening to his rational side.

She winced and he paused. "Sore there?"

"A little."

Hmm. He wondered what exactly 'a little' meant. He had a feeling she was used to hiding her true feelings.

"Should have taken you to the hospital to get checked out."

She tensed. "Ahh, no you shouldn't have. It's a bruise and some scrapes. I'm fine." She tugged at her top. He let her right her pajamas as he put everything away. When he stood, she had her arms crossed over her chest, gazing at him nervously.

Time for him to back off. She'd reached the limit of her endurance.

"All right, sweetheart. I'm going to go now. One of my boys will bring your car to you in the morning, what time do you leave for work?"

"Quarter to six. Are you sure that's not too early?" she asked anxiously.

"It's fine. You wake up and you're too sore or tired I want you to call in sick, okay?"

He could tell by the stubborn look on her face that she wouldn't be doing that. His hands itched to land a few smacks on her ass. Not that he would even if he had the right, with her injured and exhausted. Of course, if she were his, then he'd make damn sure she would stay in bed until those dark circles under her eyes disappeared and there was a spring back in her step.

"All right, sweet girl." He pulled her close, laying a kiss on her forehead. "Walk me to the door."

She nodded, staring up at him in surprise. He ignored the voice whispering at him to give her a real kiss.

Not happening.

He turned and walked swiftly out of the bathroom, slowing halfway down the hallway as he realized she was struggling to keep up. He hated that. Hated that she was hurt. So, his voice might have been a bit gruffer than he'd intended when he turned back to her at the front door.

"Lock this door behind me and get yourself into bed immediately. Good night." He opened the door then shut it and waited until he heard the lock click into place. And if he heard a quiet good night come through the door then he put it down to his imagination.

4

She was dead on her feet.

She didn't even know it was possible to be this tired and still function. After Kent left in the early hours of this morning, she'd slipped into bed, grabbed Bun-bun, her stuffed rabbit toy, and fallen asleep as soon as her head hit the pillow. When her alarm went off it had felt like a bad dream, but she'd managed to force herself out of bed and into the shower. Her cuts had stung like crazy as the water hit them, her knees were starting to bruise and her side was turning a puke green color.

Awesome.

She'd shuffled through her routine, and stumbled her way outside to find an extremely hot guy leaning against her car in the driveway. He'd straightened when he saw her, watching her walk towards him. It wasn't fully light out, so she hoped he couldn't see her wince as she moved but somehow, she thought he did. She figured that being one of Kent's 'boys' he didn't miss much. She'd seen a number of them over the years she'd been working at the diner, and they all had this dangerous, watchful thing going on. No doubt he was some sort of superhero with excellent night vision, amazing abs and enough testosterone to power a jet engine.

"Hi, I'm Abby," she introduced herself as she grew closer. She stopped a few feet away, aware that he was still standing between her and the driver's door of her car.

"I know," he drawled. What sort of accent was that?

She blushed. Of course, he knew who she was. Dumb ass.

"I'm Macca. You don't need to be afraid of me," he said suddenly, surprising her.

She blinked, pushed her shoulders back. "I know."

She sensed amusement coming from him, but told herself she had to have imagined it. He didn't appear to be the type to be amused by much. He had wide shoulders, stood at least a foot taller than she did and had a neatly-trimmed beard. She wasn't much into beards, but on him it looked hot. She couldn't see much more in the semi-dark.

"Street lights here aren't very good," she muttered. *You're acting like an idiot.* "Hope I didn't keep you waiting long. You should have knocked on the door and come in where it was warm."

He tensed. "You shouldn't ever let a strange man into your house when you're alone."

She sucked in a breath. "You work for Kent, right?"

"I do."

"So..."

"Doesn't matter who I work for. You don't know me; you don't let me into your house. That's your safe place. Now, someone intent on real harm, they'd probably find a way to get inside, but you don't make it easy and invite them in, got me?"

She got that he was scaring the crap out of her.

"You think someone could break into my house?" She wished she hadn't asked as soon as she said it. He was right, it was her safe place. But of course, someone could easily get in. She'd seen enough crime shows to know that. Hell, it was one of the reasons she slept with a police baton by her bed.

He shrugged. "Sure. You got no security system to scare them off. Your door doesn't even have a deadbolt on it. No locks on your windows. Lighting outside ain't good and your neighbors don't strike me as the type to come running if they hear a ruckus."

Well, she couldn't argue with that. She'd lived here for a long time and her neighbors had changed so many times that she had given up trying to keep up.

"How do you know what sort of locks are on my door and windows?" she whispered. Now he was really scaring her.

"Chief told me," he said easily. "And now I've scared you."

"Well...umm...yeah." What was going on here? She'd thought he was just here to drop off her car, not lecture her.

And why had Kent told him that? Why had Kent even noticed? She guessed as a security specialist it was his job to notice. She wasn't certain if that made her feel better or worse.

"Good," he replied, surprising her. "A single, attractive female living alone can't be too careful. So, don't ever invite me or any bloke you don't know into your house when you're alone, understand?"

And now she was getting a lecture. What accent was that? Australian? "Oh, you don't need to worry about that."

He gave a brisk nod. "You sure you want to go to work? You look like you need to take a couple of painkillers and climb back into bed."

Okay, how could he go from terrifying her one moment to acting all concerned the next? This conversation had to be one of the most confusing in her life.

"I'm fine. Could I get to my car, please?" The sooner she was out of his presence the better. "I'm going to be late."

"Sure." He moved away from her car then opened the door and

held it for her. "But your car is making a squeaking noise that I'm certain is the fan belt. And your tires have hardly any tread."

He wasn't telling her things she didn't know. Well, she hadn't known that about the tires. Or the reason for the squeaking. She knew next to nothing about cars.

She slowly climbed into her car, aware of his gaze on her. She reached for the door handle but he crouched low, peering in at her. The interior light in the car was on, letting her see more of his face. She noted the small scar that intersected one eyebrow and the hazel-green eyes that were staring at her intensely.

"I really am going to be late."

"Chief ain't going to be happy with how stiff you're moving. You sure you're well enough to go to work?"

No.

"I'm fine," she said firmly. "Now, thank you again but I have to go."

"Seatbelt," was all he said.

She sighed and did up her seatbelt. "Do you all have to pass some bossy test before he hires you?"

He blinked for a minute and then a smile lit up his face, magically transforming it. Suddenly, he wasn't just handsome. He was breath-takingly gorgeous.

"Something like that," he replied with a chuckle. "I'm gonna drive behind you, make sure you get there okay so don't be concerned if you see my headlights."

"That's not necessary, I drive this route nearly every day." He really had done enough.

"Not after being injured and getting next to no sleep, you don't," he replied. "Just think of it as part of the service."

Right.

She wondered how many other women had received these services.

No, best not think about that, Abby.

"Well, thanks for bringing me my car. And everything else. I think," she muttered.

He gave her a nod. "Sweet. Chief said to treat you like one of our own." He shut the door before she could ask what that meant. Actually, she was pretty certain it was a good thing she didn't know what that meant. Because it might just be more than she could handle right now.

That had been about eight hours ago and her shift was nearly over. Thank the Lord. She just wanted to go home, take some pain killers and crawl into bed. She didn't care about food or anything else.

Home. Pain killers. Bed.

"Abby, I need to talk to you."

She groaned at those words. She didn't have the energy for Gloria right now. But the older woman was her boss and Lord knew, she needed this job. She walked slowly to where Gloria sat in a back booth, trying to school her face into something pleasant. Or at least so she didn't look like she'd enjoy wrapping her hands around the older woman's chicken neck and …

All right. Enough of that. She wasn't usually given to murderous urges. But she was exhausted.

Gloria didn't even glance up, didn't invite her to take a seat in the booth seat across from her even though Abby had been on her feet all day. She had her laptop open and documents spread out across the table. For Gloria, this was work. But it was mostly show, since she was usually socializing with her friends or online shopping.

Oh well, she was the boss so Abby figured it wasn't any of her business. It was a little annoying that she took up an entire booth which could be filled up with paying customers during peak times.

But again, not her business.

"Oh, there you are. Took your time."

Abby wanted to point out that she'd been standing there for at least a minute before Gloria had bothered to raise her dyed-platinum head.

But again, her boss. Not for her to argue.

"Sorry," she muttered.

"I'm going to need you to work tomorrow."

Abby froze. That wasn't happening. Normally, she'd take all the extra hours she could get her hands on, but she'd gotten through today by telling herself she could relax tomorrow.

"I can't." The words left her mouth before she even thought them.

Gloria's bright blue eyes narrowed. "Rachel needs tomorrow off and I need you to cover for her."

She wanted to ask why Rachel needed the time off, because she was pretty certain it was because Gloria wanted her to go to the club with her tonight. Republic was the place to be seen in Wishingbone. Not that Wishingbone was trendy. It wasn't a big city. However, if you wanted to be seen, you went to Republic.

She should just agree to work the shift. She didn't want to get on Gloria's bad side. She had the habit of exacting revenge against those who pissed her off. The only reason she'd never turned her bitchiness on Abby was because she barely even noticed her.

"I don't feel well," Abby told her, surprising herself. Since when did she lie? Although it wasn't entirely a lie. She was feeling flushed and light-headed, but she knew that was from exhaustion not a virus.

Gloria waved a hand away. "Are you contagious?"

"No," she admitted.

"Then you'll be fine. You do look like shit, though. You might try putting on some make-up. Our customers don't want to be put off their food."

The insult sucked the breath from her lungs. It hurt. And she wished to hell she could tell Gloria where she could stick her job.

But unless she wanted to end up homeless or find herself missing a few fingers or toes then she knew she couldn't say a word.

"I've got you down for the early shift. You can go now."

Abby just turned away. She hated being stuck. Hated feeling like a coward. But what choice did she have?

So, she turned around and shuffled out the door.

By the time she got home, she was so tired she could barely see straight. She stumbled into her house, shuffled down to the bathroom to grab some painkillers and wash her face. Then she moved into her bedroom, pulled on her pajamas, threw her uniform into the laundry pile, pulled the curtains and slid into bed.

Bliss.

KENT POUNDED on the door again.

No answer.

Where was she? Her car was in the driveway. Had she gone for a walk? In this neighborhood? Okay, so it was the middle of the afternoon and probably safe but he still didn't like the idea.

Overprotective much?

He knew he shouldn't feel this protective of someone he wasn't involved with. And he definitely had not intended to find himself here today.

But he couldn't ignore the urge to check on her. Especially after Macca had told him how slowly she'd been moving this morning. He'd also made Kent aware of the state of her car's tires and that it needed at least a tune-up. He'd be talking to her about that as well. Didn't she know how dangerous it was to drive around on bald tires?

Images of her skidding off the road, crashing, injured or dead filled his mind. Anger pounded through him at the thought and he banged his fist down on the door again.

"Abby! You okay? You in there?"

Still no answer. What if she was ill? What if she'd fallen and hurt herself? Worry mixed with the anger.

She could just be asleep. Or have gone for a walk. He knew he should walk away.

But he wasn't going to.

He eyed the door. She wouldn't appreciate him breaking it down. He grabbed the handle, turning it. As the door opened, fury once again flooded through him. What the hell? Worried now that something really had happened to her, he rushed inside.

"Abby! Abby, where are you?" He ran through the house searching for her. Not in the living room, kitchen, bathroom. His gaze jumped to the shut bedroom door. He strode towards it and knocked.

No answer.

"Abby!"

There was a murmur of noise on the other side. He opened the door and walked in. The room had twin single beds and a dresser against the wall between them. It was painted a pale green that had probably once been pretty but had faded to a murky yellow-green that made him feel nauseous. One bed had a lump under the covers and he could spot some chestnut-colored hair poking out of the top of the covers.

"Abby?" Her face was covered and he became worried about her breathing. At least that's what he told himself as he pulled the covers down. She was wearing the same pajamas as last night. Her skin was still too pale. And she was clutching something in her arms.

Something that looked like a stuffed rabbit.

"Abby!"

5

Abby thrashed around. "No! No!"

Shoot. Was she having a nightmare? He reached for her just as she opened her eyes and screamed. Her fist shot out and caught him right in the nose. He fell back on his ass with a groan as pain engulfed his face.

Shit.

"Oh God. What's happening? Kent! Did I hurt you?"

"I'm fine."

"Shit. Shit. Shit." Her voice was frantic, nearing hysterical. "Why did I do that? Oh God, I didn't know it was you. Crap."

"Stop swearing," he said firmly then he gentled his voice, "I'm fine, baby." Well his nose was throbbing and he had to take a moment to breathe through the pain but he was fine. He'd live. He'd had a lot worse.

"I broke your nose, didn't I?" she wailed. "I'm such a stupid klutz."

He frowned, not liking that.

"Abby," he said in a low warning voice. He glanced up to find her climbing from the bed, her hair a tousled mess. And the throbbing in his nose took a back seat to the rush of arousal that filled him.

"Do you need some frozen peas? I'll get some peas."

"I don't need any damned peas, Abby. Sit," he growled when she went to move. "My nose is fine. I've had far worse."

"I'm so sorry. I was having a bad dream and then I woke up and saw someone looming over me..." Her eyes widened. "You're in my bedroom." She looked like she couldn't quite believe her own words. Then she did something rather odd.

She started laughing.

What was going on with her?

"Oh, I get it now. This is a dream. Well, thank God for that." She sounded so relieved he felt a bit insulted.

She frowned at him. "I'm not usually clumsy in my dreams about you, though." She stared at herself. "And I never wear these pajamas. Or have Bun-bun with me."

"You don't?" She dreamed about him? Bun-bun?

"No, that's not exactly normal, is it? Or sexy. A twenty-six-year-old sleeping with a stuffed toy is weird."

Not as weird or unusual as she might have thought. At least not on Sanctuary. But he wasn't going into that right now.

"Baby, listen to me. You're not dreaming." He knelt, ignoring his aching nose and placed his hands on her legs just above her knees as he braced himself.

This was going to come as a shock.

"Yes, I am."

Okay, that wasn't quite the reaction he was expecting. But then he was starting to learn that the unexpected was normal when it came to Abby.

"No, you're not."

"Yes, I am. Because if I'm not sleeping then you've come into my house unannounced. Because if I'm not sleeping then you're in my bedroom. And you now know that I'm a twenty-six-year-old who sleeps with a stuffed toy!" Her voice got louder with each accusing sentence and he winced.

"All right, you're still sleeping," he agreed trying to calm her down.

"No, I'm not!" she yelled as she struggled to stand. He applied pressure to keep her seated.

"And here I always thought you were a quiet little thing."

"I am until someone creeps into my bedroom and wakes me up." Her eyes were wild as she glared down at him.

"I can assure you, I did not creep," he said, offended.

She gave him an incredulous look.

Part of him admitted that he could have handled this whole thing differently.

"I knocked. Several times. On the front door which was unlocked, and don't think we won't be having a chat about that." He'd prefer that chat happen over his knee, but he'd have to settle for giving her a very stern talking to. He also hadn't forgotten what she'd called herself just before.

Stupid klutz?

Nope. She needed to learn that wasn't acceptable either. Safety and respect were important.

"You knocked? A chat?" She seemed bewildered as though she didn't understand what he was saying.

"You always wake up so befuddled?" he asked.

"Befuddled?"

He was going to take that as a yes.

"Once I was inside the house, I called out several times. I expected to find you collapsed and unconscious on the ground since that was the only reason I could think of for the door not to be locked and you not to be answering me. Then I knocked on your bedroom door and called out again. I heard something, probably you having a nightmare, so I came in. Do you always sleep that deeply? To the point where a man can be in your house and you don't even wake up? Do you know how dangerous that is? What if I had been someone intent on doing you harm? Just what were you thinking leaving your door unlocked?"

HUH.

So she was getting that he was mad. Only she didn't entirely understand why. Because she hadn't answered the door? Because she hadn't woken up when he'd called out for her? Was it an ego thing? He didn't like to be ignored? She hadn't done it on purpose. She had honestly been so tired that she'd forgotten. Simple as that. Sure, it had been stupid.

But she didn't get why he was so mad at her about it. It wasn't his door she'd forgotten to lock.

Which question should she answer first? Which was the least likely to make him madder? She didn't really know what to say so instead of saying anything she settled for biting on her thumbnail and not saying anything at all.

His eyes narrowed. "Oh no. That is not the way this is going. You get to keep quiet on some things. But not this. Not when it comes to safety. Now, tell me. Do you normally sleep that deeply?"

Well, shoot. "Yes."

His jaw tightened and a small tic developed by his right eye.

"And the reason that the door wasn't locked?"

She squirmed around on the bed. Part of her still hoped this was a dream. *Please, please let it be a dream.*

"Abby, you would do well to answer me right now."

Shit. The look in his eyes told her he wasn't going to give up on this. And let's face it, he could easily out-stubborn her. She took a deep breath, braced herself. "I forgot."

"You forgot?" he asked in a quiet voice. That was unexpected. She'd thought he would yell.

"Umm, yes, see I was so tired when I got home that I just

wanted to take some Tylenol and get into bed and I forgot to lock the door. But it was the middle of the afternoon. Lots of people don't lock their door when they're home alone during the day."

"They should. Especially when they're a five-foot nothing female who lives alone in a less than desirable neighborhood and sleeps like the dead."

"Do you lock your doors?" she challenged, hardly believing her daring. You didn't dare a man like Kent Jensen.

"I own the top security business in the world. I lead a group of the most well-trained, most dangerous men in the world. I have the best security system—"

"Let me guess, in the world," she said dryly. It was a wonder his ego could fit into her small bedroom. And later, she knew she would completely flip out at the fact that Kent Jensen had seen her extremely childish bedroom. Seriously, what other twenty-six-year-old slept in a twin bed with a lacy, pink bedspread and a bunny?

Yep, she was going to totally lose it later. Right now, she had to concentrate on Kent. When he was in the room, there was little else she could think of.

Deep breath in, Abby. He's not for you. His world is so different from yours it's impossible.

He raised his eyebrows as though hardly daring to believe her daring.

Him and her both.

"Yes, in the world."

"So, you don't lock your doors," she guessed.

"I do," he said, surprising her. "I can hardly lecture you on something that I don't or won't do myself, can I?"

Well, he could. But it would make him a hypocrite. And a bit of a jerk. He could be stern. Demanding. Overwhelming.

But he wasn't a jerk.

"So, let me get this straight. You sleep like the dead, so deeply that you don't even hear someone enter your bedroom calling your name, and yet you forgot to lock the door. Not that the lock is that great, but it could be reasonably expected to keep most people out."

"Well, I don't think most people would just wander into someone's house even if they did find it unlocked," she pointed out, her temper starting to stir. Who did he think he was? He was the one in the wrong here. He was the one inside her house without invitation, invading her privacy. And he was going to lecture her?

"That is not the point. The point is that it's not safe to ever leave your door unlocked, let alone while you're sleeping so deeply."

"I know that! I didn't mean to do it."

He sighed then ran his hand over his face, wincing. She grimaced. Shoot. She didn't want to feel guilty. She wanted to stay mad at him. But the guilt won. "I'm so sorry."

"Not your fault. I gave you a fright. I should have woken you up with more care but I was worried you were suffocating."

"Suffocating?" What was he talking about?

"I thought you were ill or something when you didn't answer your door. Then when I walked in here you were almost completely under the covers. I was worried you couldn't breathe."

She stared at him. Was he for real? People didn't worry about things like that when it came to adults, right? I mean, kids, sure, but she was a grown woman.

Although sometimes he acted like she was younger.

And sometimes, she kind of liked that. She breathed out a tired sigh. Her head still ached. So did her hands, knees and side. She just wanted to crawl back into bed.

"Kent?"

"Yeah?"

"I'm fine."

He took her in. "I wouldn't say fine. You have dark marks under your eyes and you're still moving like you're hurting."

"I'm not injured or suffocating, though. I was just asleep. Which I'd really like to get back to doing. So, why are you here?"

He stood up. "I came to check on you, wanted to make sure you were feeling okay after last night."

"I'm good. Just tired. How is Eden?"

"Furious." His lips twitched.

He thought it was amusing that his sister was mad?

"Physically, she's sore and that never puts her in a good mood. Eden is the worst patient ever. But mostly, she's just really angry at Clint."

"Why?"

"Because he grounded her."

"How can she be grounded?" she asked, confused.

"Because Clint is an old-fashioned guy too. He's the head of our family. And until Eden gets married, she's his responsibility. And last night, she put herself in danger. So, she's grounded."

People didn't live that way anymore, did they? Men didn't take responsibility for their twenty-five-year-old sisters.

"Hmm, shocked you into silence, have I?" Amusement flashed in Kent's eyes.

"He can't ground her."

"He can. He did." That was all he said.

"But...but...shouldn't you do something to stop him?"

"Why?" He frowned.

Good question. "Because she's twenty-five?"

"Doesn't matter how old someone is if they're gonna go putting themselves into dangerous situations and they have someone who loves them, someone who wants them to be safe and healthy and happy, someone who is prepared to ensure that, then there's gonna be consequences to reckless behavior. And those consequences need to be harsh enough so that next time that person thinks about doing something that puts them at risk, they stop and think again."

"Harsh enough?" She wasn't certain she liked the sound of that. "He'll hurt her?"

"Of course not," he replied so fiercely that she felt bad for ever suggesting it. "No man would ever harm a woman on Sanctuary. And if they did, they'd find themselves in a world of trouble. But a woman puts herself into a male's care, agrees to follow his rules then breaks them, then she's getting consequences whether she wants them or not. Abby, look at me."

He waited until her gaze hit his to speak again. "I'm expecting you to keep all that to yourself."

She shook her head. "I wouldn't...I'd never say a thing."

He gave her a small smile. "Didn't think you would, sweetheart. Around everyone else, you're quiet as a mouse. I like that you're different with me."

She wasn't different with him, was she?

Oh hell, she was.

"Did you eat something before you climbed into bed?" he asked, sounding concerned.

She shook her head. "No. I was too tired to bother. I felt a bit ill as well."

"When did you last eat?"

"Umm, I had something around ten I think."

He glanced at his watch. "Right, it's nearly five. Here's what's going to happen. You get up. Don't get dressed since you'll be back in bed soon. I'm going to order us some take-out and while we're waiting for it to come, I'll put the new dead locks on your front and back doors. You can rest on the sofa."

Okay, she got that he was a man who was used to taking charge but there were a few things there that she had to address.

He had already turned away and left the room by the time she ordered her thoughts though, so she had no choice but to get up.

Then her bladder let her know she urgently needed the toilet. She set Bun-bun down on the bed. Crap. She couldn't believe that Kent Jensen had seen her sleeping with a stuffed toy. At least he hadn't said anything. Maybe he was choosing to ignore it. He was a good guy. She wrapped a robe around herself and strode into the bathroom. She used the facilities and cleaned her teeth because they felt kind of scummy. The last thing she needed to be was the girl who slept with a stuffed rabbit and had smelly breath.

When she was feeling a bit more alert, she walked out to find him at her front door. "Are you sure you don't want a bag of peas for your nose?"

He glanced up at her with a grin. "Baby, I was a Navy SEAL, I run a security company filled with bad asses. I *am* a bad ass. I promise that a whack on the nose from a little bit of a thing like you barely even stung."

"You're a bad ass?" Her lips twitched at the term.

He gave her a firm look. "Bad. Ass."

"All right then. So do bad asses always put new locks on the doors of women they hardly know?"

"They do when said woman comes to the aid of their sister," he told her. "You planning on arguing with me?"

She thought that over. She was still tired. She was hungry. She had a headache. She was annoyed at him for coming into her house and waking her up, but she also found it kind of sweet that he had been worried about her.

"I don't think I have the energy," she said honestly.

He watched her for a moment longer then his eyes melted into deep pools of deliciousness. It was all she could do not to dissolve in a pile of goo at his feet "Go sit down, sweetheart. Turn the T.V. on and zone out for a bit. I got this."

She stared at him. "Would you like me to order dinner?"

"I'll do it. Anything you're allergic to or don't like?" he asked.

"Only things I don't like are artichokes, raw fish and lemons."

His lips twitched. "Well, I promise that I will keep those things off our pizza."

"Pizza. Yum. I like meat lovers." She bounced up and down in excitement.

He gave her a strange look. And his voice was tender when he replied. "Meat lovers it is, then. Go on. I got this."

Yeah, he had this. She watched him for a minute longer, after all she wasn't exactly used to a hot guy whose jeans molded to his spectacular ass. Things that he didn't accept anything in return for.

He's doing all this because you helped his sister.

It would be nice if it was because he liked her. But she'd take what she could get. She walked into the kitchen and put on some coffee. Then yawning, she strode into the living room and switched on the T.V., searching for something to watch. It wasn't long before she was sipping coffee liberally laced with hazelnut creamer and watching *The Bachelor*.

"Oh man, what is he doing?" she muttered.

"What are you watching?"

She sat up with a gasp, coffee spilling over the edge of her cup. Luckily, it wasn't that hot. Kent walked around the sofa and crouched in front of her. He grabbed the mug from her, looked at her hand. "Are you burned?"

"No, it was pretty much cold," she told him. "Sorry, I didn't hear you walk up behind me. Umm, I'll just go clean up." She scooted forward and thankfully, he stood and moved out of the way. She kept her gaze down as she hurried into the kitchen to wash the coffee off her hand. She wiped at the spill on her top. Could she get more klutzy?

"Was that decaf coffee?" he asked.

"No." She gaped at him. "What's the point of coffee without the kick of caffeine?"

He brought the cup to his mouth and tasted what was left in

the mug. For some reason that felt awfully intimate. Her body throbbed in reaction.

Stop it, Abby. He's here because you helped Eden. Nothing else.

He grimaced. "Not sure I'd even call that coffee. What flavor is that?"

"Hazelnut. Let me guess, you drink yours black?"

"Damn straight. I'm a manly man. Black coffee puts hairs on your chest."

She had to smile at that. "And you want hairs on your chest?"

"You don't like a hairy chest?" There was amusement in his gaze as he stared down at her.

"I...I..." Shit how to answer that? That she didn't really know what she liked since the only time she'd had sex she'd been drunk and it had been a lot of fumbling in the dark followed by pain and disappointment then humiliation.

The doorbell rang, saving her from having to answer. She moved away from the sink but he pointed at her. "I'll get it. Stay put. And no more coffee or you won't sleep tonight."

She heard the murmur of voices and figuring it was the pizza grabbed a couple of plates and some napkins, carrying them into the living room and setting them on the coffee table. Her attention was snagged by an episode of *CSI*.

Kent walked in and set the pizza down on the coffee table. "I can see you've gone from one extreme to the other."

He frowned slightly as he studied the dead body laid out on the examination table. "No wonder you have bad dreams, watching this stuff." He placed the pizza on the coffee table. She reached for the remote, guessing that he wasn't a *CSI* fan. "What do you like to watch?"

"I only watch sports. Baseball, preferably."

She managed to find a game on another channel.

"You don't have to do that," he told her quietly.

She glanced over at him with a shy smile. "I know."

He smiled back and she felt warm inside. It was a small thing but it felt good to make him happy. He opened the lid of the box and her mouth watered. "Oh, wow, that smells good. It's been so long since I've had pizza."

"Why's that?"

She shrugged. "Not much use in ordering it for one." She reached for a piece then stilled. "Oh, let me get you some money for it."

He snagged her wrist as she stood. "Pretty sure I told you already that I'm old-fashioned, haven't I?"

"Umm, yes."

"Which means when you're out with me, I pay."

"But we're not out."

"It also extends to take-out. Sit your butt down and eat."

"What about a drink? Can I get you one?" She felt the need to do something for him in return for all he'd done for her.

"Abby, keep going and you're going to be sitting there on a red ass eating your pizza. I can get my own damn drink if I want it."

She gaped at him. He did not... "Did you just threaten to spank me?"

He looked at her. "Yep. Got a problem with that?"

She swallowed heavily, wondering at why that thought made her feel so hot. "I probably should. A sane person would."

He grinned. "Well, I've never claimed to be sane."

She couldn't be completely sane either. Because she wasn't frightened or horrified by the threat. Instead, she was kind of intrigued...

"Can see the wheels in your head turning, baby, but I can't see you doing much eating and I don't like that. Leave all the serious shit behind. Enjoy your pizza."

"Okay." She picked up a piece and bit into it, making a noise of satisfaction.

"Shit," he muttered.

"What was that?" she asked.

He was watching her strangely, almost as though he'd never seen her before.

"Nothing, just never thought watching someone eat pizza could be so...umm...you got any beer?"

"Oh no, I'm sorry. I don't drink beer." She felt bad for some stupid reason. It wasn't like she'd known he was coming around.

"Don't be sorry. I should have brought some with me."

"I've got pop, milk and water."

He stood with a nod and entered the kitchen, when he returned, he had one glass of water and one of milk. He set the milk in front of her.

"What's this?"

"Milk."

"I know that its milk, but I don't drink it."

He raised both eyebrows. "Then what do you do with it?"

She blushed. "I use it with cereal. I don't drink it out of a glass."

"It's good for you," was all he said. As though that meant she should change her mind about liking the taste.

"I'll just go get some pop." She scooted forward.

"Stay there. That crap will rot your teeth, drink your milk."

"You sound like my nana." Whoops. Why did she say that? She nearly thunked herself on the forehead with her hand. No man wanted to be compared to someone's nana for God's sake.

"I do? She sounds like a smart woman."

"She was."

"It's been a couple of years since she passed, hasn't it?" There was sympathy in his voice that stupidly made the end of her nose sting as she fought to push back tears.

It had been, but she was surprised he knew that. "Yes, just over two years."

She stared down at the half-eaten slice of pizza in her hand and suddenly didn't feel so hungry.

"You lived here with her?"

"Yeah, my mom disappeared when I was a kid. Just up and left. She was there in the morning then when Max and I got home from school she was gone."

"Max is your brother, yeah? He's younger than you?"

"Two years younger. He hasn't lived in Wishingbone for a while. He moves around a lot."

"You're not close?"

"Not really. He pops in when he's in town." Usually to wheedle or steal what money he could from her. That knot in her stomach tightened further.

"Did you ever discover what happened to your mom?" he asked.

"No, I never knew what happened to her. At the time, I didn't think much of it, she wasn't the best mother in the world. She tended to spend most of her time getting drunk and hanging out with her friends. She went through men like they were candy. I'm not even sure who my dad is."

"Oh, baby. I'm sorry."

Fuck. Why was she telling him this? He couldn't possibly want to know and it wasn't exactly painting her in a good light. "It's okay."

He gave her an incredulous look. She shrugged. "All right, so it's not okay."

"What happened?"

"I made Max some dinner. We had a bit of food in the cupboards but not much. We went to bed. When I woke up the next morning, she still wasn't home. We went to school as usual but when we got home...well, she'd never been gone that long before. I wasn't sure what to do. I knew I wasn't supposed to tell people about anything that went on at home but we were running low on food. Max was hungry, so I went to our next-door neighbor. She was nice. She had a boy Max's age and she often gave us cookies and milk after school. She called the cops. Child Protective Services took us into custody. The next day Nana came and got us."

"And none of you ever heard from your mom again? What did the cops say?" He was frowning.

"The police think she took off with her latest boyfriend."

"Oh, baby." He pulled her onto his lap. She tensed up. Umm, what was happening? Why was she sitting in his lap? What was she supposed to do? Where did she put her hands? What if she was too heavy for him?

But he didn't seem to notice her freaking out. Or if he did, he ignored her reaction, pulling her in against him and tucking her head in under his chin. He rubbed his hand up and down her back. Wow, okay, that felt nice. Gradually, she relaxed into him.

She yawned. He was so warm. And he smelled so good.

"Here, eat some more pizza, sweetheart." He leaned forward and picked up a piece of pizza, holding it to her lips. She reached up to take it and he pulled it back. "Uh-uh, I'm going to feed you. You just sit there snuggled into me so sweetly and let me take care of you."

God, those words. They were like a balm soothing the ragged edges of her soul.

She finished off the slice of pizza then shook her head as he held up another piece. "Full."

"You sure? You didn't eat much. I've eaten four times as much."

"You're bigger than me."

"I am. Here." He held the milk up and she sighed, grimacing.

"I really don't like drinking milk."

There was a beat of silence then to her surprise he set the milk down without argument. Instead, he picked up his glass of water and held it to her lips. "I promise I don't have germs."

She took a few sips, realized how thirsty she was and gulped down the whole lot. She tried to move off his lap, thinking to get him another glass but he held onto her. "Didn't say you could move."

"I thought I'd get you some more water," she explained, feeling special that he didn't want her to move.

"I'll get it in a minute. And I'll bring in some wood for your fire. It's starting to get chilly. Where do you keep it?"

She bit down on her thumbnail. He gently extracted her thumb free. "Gotta do something about that."

"About what?"

"What's going on that you don't want to tell me, Abby?" he asked instead.

"Well, okay, I don't have any wood." *Being poor is nothing to be ashamed of. Being poor is nothing to be ashamed of.*

Yeah, she wished she actually believed that. Considering how much shit she'd taken over the years about being poor, it was hard to believe.

"You used it all during winter? It was a cold one this year. You need to order some more though, sweetheart because this house is so old it's probably drafty and needs its insulation upgraded."

She nodded. It wasn't really worth telling him that she didn't have money for wood. That she hadn't had any all winter and instead relied on blankets and hot water bottles to keep her warm.

Although, he was better than any hot water bottle.

"Just relax, baby," he told her, rubbing her back up and down.

"I should clean up the pizza."

"I'll clean it up before I leave. I just want you to relax so we can get you back to bed. When's your next day off?"

"Sunday."

"Tomorrow? That's good. You can get some rest."

"No, next Sunday." She yawned, her eyes growing heavy. She wanted to prolong this. It felt so nice to be touched, held

He grew tense beneath her. "Next Sunday? Seven days away? When did you last have a day off?"

"Last Sunday." Belatedly she realized why he had tensed up and his voice had grown low.

"You're working thirteen days in a row?"

"Umm yeah." Her thumb crept towards her mouth and he gently grabbed hold of her hand, pulling it away.

"You're going to bite your thumb raw. Why are you working those sorts of hours?"

"Because I need the money." And because she wasn't very good at saying no.

"I don't like that."

She sat up with a sigh, trying to climb off him. He pulled her back. "Kent, let me go."

"No."

"Kent," she warned.

"I don't like you working such long hours."

"Well, I don't either. But I need the money. It's my life. My job. Now let me up."

"Well, shit. Don't like that either."

"Kent!"

He drew her back into his arms and she opened her mouth, ready to blast him and that's when he kissed her. And oh boy, was it a kiss. Yeah, she should pull back and tell him off. But was she going to?

Hell, no.

Because Kent Jensen was kissing her. The man who featured in the majority of her fantasies. The man she'd watched from afar longingly for years. He was the sexiest, most gorgeous man she'd ever met.

And the man could kiss.

For a moment she was frozen, unsure what to do. He pulled back slightly. "Kiss me back, sweetheart."

Kiss him back? She'd only kissed one boy and that had been

horrid, his tongue jabbing into her mouth until she wanted to vomit.

This was far, far from that.

But instead of embarrassing the hell out of herself by explaining to him that she had no idea what she was doing, she decided to just follow his lead. She relaxed her mouth, ran her tongue along his. He tightened his hold on her, and a low growling noise escaped from him.

"Fuck, yes, baby. Kiss me." He ran kisses along her jaw. "You have the softest skin."

He took her mouth again as he grasped hold of her ass, squeezing tightly. She gasped, her body going up in flames. His lips were surprisingly soft. The scent of him was masculine. Rich. Woodsy. His arms were strong around her, his body so hard and hot. And she melted.

And just from a kiss.

But then it wasn't just any kiss, was it?

It was *the* kiss. The kiss to end all kisses. The kiss she'd never forget for the rest of her life.

He moved gently to begin with. Everything felt light and sweet from the brush of his lips against hers to the way his hand rubbed up and down her thigh. Her clit tingled, her nipples aching. She'd never experienced arousal like this. Something all-consuming. Something that made her forget everything except his touch.

She groaned against his mouth and he pressed his tongue in to play with her. Their kiss grew wilder. Explosions of heat. Her heart raced and she moved restlessly on his lap. She wanted more. Needed more.

"Where do you want me to touch you? Tell Daddy, baby."

6

F uck it all to hell.

What the hell was that? Why did he just say that? He wasn't a daddy. He didn't want a baby girl. He'd just gotten carried away.

He stared down at her, his hands dropping away. He should say something. He just didn't know what.

What had he been thinking? What was he doing kissing her? He was supposed to be here as a friend. As part of a debt owed.

He was not supposed to pull her into his arms and kiss her for fuck's sake. It wasn't fair on her. It was obvious how innocent she was. The way she'd kissed him back had very clearly demonstrated that. Not that the kiss hadn't been hot. But she'd been hesitant, unsure.

Until the kiss had deepened and she'd stopped thinking. Then it had become far too hot for his peace of mind.

And then he'd fucked it all to hell.

Daddy? Really?

When he was younger, he'd always been attracted to women

with attitudes, with confidence. He'd enjoyed the thrill of the chase.

And none of them would ever have wanted to live on a ranch in the middle of Montana. To yield to his excessive demands around their safety. To cede control beyond the bedroom.

Was that why none of them had lasted?

Fuck. Fuck.

Abby stared up, her lips swollen. Her face slightly flushed. Her eyes, which had been glazed with lust, were now darkening with worry.

"Is something wrong?" she asked.

"I can't believe I just did that. It was a mistake."

Her body grew tense and she scrambled her way off his lap. He let her go. She scooted her way onto the sofa, kicking him in the thigh as she moved.

"Oh crap. Sorry. Shit." She stared at him in horror. "I didn't mean to do that. Honestly. It wasn't on purpose."

"Abby, I know it wasn't. Calm down, sw—" He cut himself off before he could call her sweetheart. He needed to back off. For both their sakes. Because the more he thought of that kiss...the more he wanted to kiss her some more. The more he wanted to take things further. To lay her down on the couch. To explore every inch of her.

She sat in the corner of the sofa and the way she crouched in on herself, as though to make herself smaller, punched him in the gut.

"Abby, I'm so sorry. That shouldn't have happened. I apologize. That's not what I...who I am. What I need." He needed to get out of here. Before he was tempted to pull her back into his arms and comfort her. Which would no doubt lead somewhere else...

Fuck. What was wrong with him? This was Abby. Sweet, kind, innocent Abby. She wasn't the sort of woman that could deal with him. She needed someone who would be gentle with her. Guide her. Nurture her.

Not someone who'd want to tie her to the bed, plug her ass before fucking her. Hard. Fast.

She stared at him incredulously. Those wide, hazel-colored eyes were filled with something he couldn't quite decipher. It wasn't anger, although she was entitled to feel that.

More like disillusionment.

"Not what you need? It was a mistake?"

He nodded. "It was. And I'm so sorry. Can we please just forget it happened? I came here to put on new locks so you are safer and to check on you after the late night you had. My family owes you a debt—"

"No, you don't," she interrupted.

"Pardon?"

"You don't owe me a debt. I didn't do anything. And I think you should leave."

He didn't want to leave things like this. Not with her looking at him like he'd slapped her. "You went running into a dangerous situation to help my sister. Anything could have happened to you. Many people would have stayed hidden or left to get help but you didn't." He gave her a stern frown. "Of course, if that situation ever happens again, that is exactly what you should do."

"You would expect me to leave your sister there on her own with those assholes?" she asked.

An uncomfortable feeling filled him. The thought of anything happening to Eden made him nauseous. But he also had this growing protectiveness towards the woman sitting as far away from him as she could on the couch.

"It won't happen to Eden again."

"I hope not," she said quietly.

"It won't," he repeated firmly. "Sanctuary takes care of its own. Eden is going to find herself much more closely watched." He knew Clint was already beating himself up for not taking a firmer stance with their sister. They tended to indulge her where they could. She'd been through so much in her short life and she was the baby of the family.

"Okay, well, you don't owe me a debt. Or if you did it's been paid with the new locks on my doors. So, you can leave now."

He didn't want to go.

It was ridiculous. He'd just pushed her away. He should be taking the out she gave him and going.

"Abby, it's not what you think," he told her gently. "It was a slip of the tongue. We're just not well-matched."

"That's one way to put it," she said stiffly. "I get it. A mistake. I'm tired."

Except it hadn't felt like a mistake. Not the kiss. Not even calling himself Daddy. An uncomfortable feeling filled him. Why had the kiss felt so intense? Was it just chemistry? Or more?

Was he making a mistake?

He studied her. The cutesy pajamas she wore. He remembered the stuffed toy she'd been hugging when he woke her earlier.

To take things further wasn't fair to her. Not when what she needed wasn't him.

"Abby, how many men have you kissed?" he asked.

She stiffened even further. "None of your business."

He sighed. "I'm betting it's not many."

"Sorry if I wasn't any good."

"No, that wasn't what I meant," he said, his frustration building.

She stood up. "I really want you to go now."

He stood as well. He couldn't insist on staying when she asked him to go. Well, demanded that he go.

"I don't want to leave things with you like this. I'm not saying that your needs are wrong just that they're not for me. I'm not even sure why I—"

"I get it." She stomped her way towards the door. Her ass jiggled slightly. He'd always been an ass man. And quite frankly, hers was magnificent.

He was aware of his erection pressing painfully against his jeans as he stared after her. She opened the door. "Leave, please."

"Abby," he said cajolingly. "Look at me."

She kept her gaze on the floor. He moved closer. He stopped when he stood in front of her and touched her cheek with his finger. A shock like a bolt of electricity went through him when she flinched away.

"Abby." He dropped his hand immediately, gazing down at her in horror. "I would never hurt you."

"Please leave. I want you to go."

He hated the vulnerability in her voice. "Okay, sw—Abby, I'm going. I just want you to know that my family does owe you a debt. And we always repay them. So, I'm going to leave my card with my private number. You call me if you need anything. Anything at all. Understand?"

He pulled his wallet out and grabbed his business card. It wasn't the one he gave to just anyone, but a special one for his long-term clients. He held it out.

She didn't take it.

His frustration grew. He pulled on the control that he'd honed in his years as a SEAL, and a Dom.

"Abby, take the card."

"You don't owe me anything," she said stubbornly.

"Abby, I get that you're upset with me. You have good reason. I'm not the kind of guy you need."

But he could find her the sort of guy she needed. The ranch was filled with Daddy Doms searching for a Little. So why hadn't she been snapped up already?

"More like I'm not the sort of woman you want, right?" she asked angrily.

"That's not what I meant." Only wasn't it? Even he could hear the lack of conviction in his voice.

"Leave, Kent. Before I call the sheriff."

"I'm not going until you take the card and promise me you will call if you need something."

She stared up at him, her jaw set firmly.

"Funny, I did not pick you as the stubborn type."

"Because I'm so quiet and boring?"

He narrowed his gaze. "That's the last time I want to hear you say that about yourself. And don't think I've forgotten what you called yourself earlier."

She just glared at him. "It's not any of your business what I call myself. You came here to pay a debt. It's paid. We both made a mistake, our lips met. Big deal. We're both adults. Now, I want to go to sleep. I'm tired. So please leave."

"Easiest way to get me to go is to take the damn card."

She reached up and snatched it out of his hand. "Fine. I've got it. Now go."

"Promise."

"Urgh!" She threw her hands up in the air and stomped her foot down. Oh, there was most definitely a temper under all that shyness. And that small stomp of her foot would find his lap under different circumstances.

You don't want a Little. You don't want her.

Well, his erection would beg to differ.

Just as well he didn't make decisions based on what state his dick was in.

"Promise me, Abby. I need to know that if you're in trouble that you will call me."

"I don't get in trouble." She yawned and a shiver ran through her. She was standing by the open door dressed in threadbare pajamas. She was exhausted. And he was badgering her.

Way to be an asshole, man.

"Abby, please," he gentled his voice. "Just because we're not suited to each other is no reason for you not to take me up on this. You never know when you might need help. Promise me."

"Fine, I promise," she said with great reluctance.

Funnily enough, the knot in his stomach didn't dissipate the way he thought it would. He took one last look at her, then turned towards the door. "Make sure you lock this behind me," he ordered. "I'll wait on the other side until you do."

She didn't answer. Just slammed the door shut behind him. He sighed. But he stayed there until he heard the quiet click. Then he walked down the steps, towards his truck. A sense of wrongness filled him. It pulled at him, urging him to turn around and tell her that he had made a mistake.

But his mistake wasn't kissing her. It was pushing her away.

Instead, he forced himself into his truck, started up the engine and left. It was for the best. There was no way he could give her what she needed.

ABBY HUGGED herself as she leaned back against the door. Her eyes closed as she heard his truck start up. She'd kissed Kent Jensen. Even though things had gone to shit afterwards, even though he'd been clear to tell her what a mistake he'd made, she'd always have that.

All these years of crushing on him, she'd never once thought he would end up in her house, that he would kiss her. He was gorgeous. Sometimes sweet. Bossy. Protective. He called to every longing inside her. All she'd ever wanted was someone to watch over her. She knew that she was supposed to be independent, strong, she was supposed to be able to take care of herself. To not rely on a man.

But she guessed she was just built differently from most people. Growing up, she'd loved reading books where the girl had an older brother. Someone to watch out for her. To give her advice. To warn off other boys from wanting to date her.

That wasn't to say her feelings towards Kent were brotherly. Far from it.

But watching him with his sister, hearing him talk about the way the women on Sanctuary were protected by all the men, it spoke to that part of her that had always longed for a safe place, a family, home.

Nana had tried her best. She'd loved Abby and her brother. But it wasn't that warm, fuzzy love. She hadn't been the type to hand out hugs or praise. She'd kept a roof over their heads, food in their bellies, she'd clothed them, she'd tried to teach them right from wrong. Although that hadn't really worked with Max. But she hadn't been one to put up with any sort of emotional nonsense, as she'd liked to call it.

Abby moved slowly through the house, tidying up the mess. Nana would roll over in her grave if she didn't clean up before bed. She walked into her bedroom. And froze. All she could remember was Kent kneeling by the bed, his hands on her legs, his handsome face creased in concern.

She'd thought he cared.

Idiot.

He just felt a sense of obligation. She took a deep breath then walked to her bedside drawers, opened the top one and dropped the card he'd given her in. She should probably chuck it in the trash. But she couldn't bring herself to do that.

She sat on the bed, and placed her elbows on her thighs as she cupped her forehead in her hands.

She'd made a fool of herself.

She sucked back a sob. She would not cry. Tears didn't solve anything.

Reynolds don't cry, Abigail.

"Sorry, Nana," she muttered. She grabbed Bun-bun, holding him tight.

I made a mistake. I'm not the kind of guy you need.

She gave a humorless bark of laughter. Right. More like she wasn't what he needed.

Knowing she couldn't sleep in this room and there was only one way to calm the emotions rioting inside her, she got to her feet, still holding Bun-bun and pulled off her duvet and pillow. She dragged them into the small dining room and dumped them by the table. Then she turned a lamp on in the corner of the room. Moving to the linen cupboard, she grabbed a couple of spare blankets. She arranged them on the top of the table so they draped over the edges, completely covering the table.

She pulled the cushions off the sofa and used them to create a mattress under the table. Finally, she picked Bun-bun back up, grabbed her duvet and pillow and climbed into her fort. She lay there and took a couple of slow, deep breaths to calm herself.

As a child, when her mother would bring home a strange man, she'd always hide herself under the bed. Sometimes, Max would join her.

She winced as she remembered some of the noises she'd heard. As a child, she hadn't recognized what they were. She'd often worried that the man her mother had brought home was hurting her. Sometimes they would. There would be the slap of flesh meeting flesh. A cry of pain. Her mother limping the next morning or telling her and Max that the fresh bruise on her face was just because she was clumsy.

Abby was clumsy. She'd never once had a bruise on her face. Let alone multiple times.

Of course, she hadn't realized the lies her mom had told them as a kid. But part of her had still known something was wrong. Hiding herself away had made her feel safer. As she'd grown older and was no longer able to fit comfortably under her bed, she'd started hiding under the covers. When Nana took them in, she'd often let Abby build a pillow fort like this one.

As a teenager, she'd stopped building them. Knowing it was weird and childish. But after Nana died, when things got bad with Max, and when she was stressed or worried, it was the only thing that gave her any sense of safety.

Pushing down the shame and embarrassment she felt, she snuggled into the cushions and grabbed tight hold of Bun-bun.

This wasn't the first time she'd been rejected.

She'd get over it. Like she always did.

7

Kent strode out of the stables. He'd hoped a ride would clear his head. Rid him of some of the temper flooding him.

Yeah, that hadn't worked out.

He kicked a rock off the pathway, sending it flying. Shit.

"Woah, big bro, what's eating you?"

He turned to find Eden watching him. Her blonde hair was tied up in a high ponytail, she was dressed in a sweatshirt and jeans and looked about twelve. She was one of his favorite people in the world. From the minute she was born, when he was eight years old, he'd vowed he would take care of her.

But right now, he wasn't in the mood to talk to her. Or anyone else.

"Nothing," he muttered. "Got to go." He walked towards her, then knowing he was acting like a jerk, he lightly touched her head in apology. "You should have a hat on, it's cold out here."

She sighed. "Where are you going?"

"Back to work."

"Kent, wait."

He paused, then forced himself to turn. Even though he was in a foul mood that was no reason to take it out on Eden. And if she needed something then he'd never forgive himself for not being here for her.

She still hadn't given him or Clint an acceptable reason for why she had been at the Suck 'n Blow. Clint had told her that she was grounded until she came clean. He knew there was a running bet about who would cave first.

Clint would blow a gasket if he heard about it.

Kent had his money on Clint giving in first. Eden could out-stubborn them all.

"Yeah, baby? You need something?"

She nodded and wheeled her chair closer. "I wanted to talk to you."

"Everything okay?" he asked in concern. "Something bothering you?"

"More like someone and his name starts with C and ends with pain-in-my-ass."

His lips twitched. "Strange name."

She glared up at him. "He's making my life hell."

He raised with one eyebrow. "Why? Because he's not letting you get away with whatever you want?"

"Yes," she wailed. "He's always been overbearing but now he's being impossible. Speak to him for me?" She gave him a sweet smile. Which normally worked. She'd always had him wrapped around her finger.

But not this time.

"Nope."

He rocked back on his heels, ready for the explosion. Her head shot up. Her eyes widening. "What?"

"I said no."

"But...but...you never say no!"

He pulled his hat off his head and ran his hand through his

hair. He'd barely slept last night. He'd had a late-night conference call with a businessman in New Zealand who wanted to hire their services for some employees he was sending to the Congo. Then afterwards, he'd worked out for a while to try and exhaust his mind. His body had been begging for sleep by the time he'd showered. Only for him to toss and turn for hours. And when he did sleep the dreams...

Shit.

"Kent?" Eden's voice was soft now. All anger and indignation were gone. "Are you okay? What's going on? Is it something at work?"

"I'm fine," he snapped. Then silently cursed as he saw the hurt look on her face. "Sorry, boo," he said using the nickname for her that he'd had since they were kids. "I'm not sleeping well and it's making me short-tempered."

But this time it wasn't nightmares plaguing him. They weren't the thing that crept into mind when he least expected it.

Nope, that was a pair of hurt-filled hazel eyes, surrounded by the longest eyelashes he'd ever seen.

Eden stared at him worriedly. "Want to talk about it?"

He gave her a half-smile. "Don't think that will help."

"You're always making me tell you about my shit."

He raised his eyebrows at her language.

She shook her head. "I'm not a kid anymore, you know."

"I know," he replied quietly.

"Do you? Does Clint? I mean, really? Grounding me? I'm nearly twenty-six years old! I shouldn't have to put up with this crap."

"You know the way our family works, Eden," he told her mildly. "Clint is just looking out for you. You gave both of us a hell of a fright the other night. You want to tell me what you were doing there?"

She pressed her lips together. Yeah, that's what he'd thought.

Stubborn. He shook his head. "I've created a bad habit by running interference for you with our big bro, but not this time. Because I agree with him. You could have ended up badly hurt, raped, murdered." He crouched down in front of her, in much the same position as he'd been with Abby three nights ago. He winced. He wouldn't think about that right now. "You mean the world to us, Eden. We don't want anything bad happening to you."

She let out a sound of frustration.

"It's only because we love you."

She snorted. Then she sighed. "I love you guys as well. But if I don't get off this ranch soon, I'm gonna go freaking insane."

"No, you won't. There's plenty to do here. Are you supposed to be wheeling yourself around with your sore ribs?"

"They feel better." She bit her lip. "I wanted to go into town and check on Abby. I called her yesterday and she sounded funny."

He stiffened. "She did? Funny, how?"

"I don't know. Just weird. I just...I don't think she has many people watching out for her. Macca told me you put a new lock on her door. Was she all right?"

All right? No, he wouldn't say that.

"I just feel terrible about all the times I've essentially ignored her. I mean, I've never been rude or mean to her, of course. I've always shut anyone down when I've heard them say something mean."

"Who says mean things to her?" he demanded. Fury filled him. How dare anyone be nasty to her?

"Well, mostly they say things behind her back. They call her mouse."

He clenched his hands into fists. He wanted to teach her that she shouldn't allow anyone to put her down.

"I just wish now I'd made more of an effort to get to know her. I just...I feel bad. She helped me when most people would have run the other way. Do you think you could go check on her?"

Yes. "No."

Eden's eyes widened. "What? Why not?"

"I've got a lot to do right now. I'll see if Macca is free to check on her."

Only he didn't want to do that. Not at all. Because the too-charming Aussie already seemed to be taking too much of an interest in Abby. Just yesterday he'd asked Kent if he'd done anything about her car problems or whether he wanted him to install a security system.

He ground his teeth together. He should send Macca to see if she was all right. The other man would be a good fit for her. He was a Daddy Dom like Clint. He was tough, smart, loyal. But he could also be very compassionate.

He'd be a much better fit for Abby than Kent was.

So why didn't he want the other man near her?

"Kent? What is it? You don't like Abby?"

"Of course, I like her. She's an absolute sweetheart. Who wouldn't like her?" He frowned thinking of what Eden had just told him. "I don't like that anyone would put her down. She made a few disparaging remarks about herself..."

"Well, I know she didn't have the easiest upbringing. Her nana was a stern woman. I only saw her a few times, but she wasn't the cuddly, sweet kind of grandma. And Abby's brother, well, you know about him, right?"

"No. I don't."

"Oh. I figured you would. You usually know everything," Eden teased.

"What about her brother?"

"He's bad news. If you wanted something, you'd talk to Max Reynold and he'd get it for you. Didn't matter how illegal it was."

Fuck. Shit.

"What? You're kidding me. How did I not know this?" Eden shrugged, then seemed to think back. "I guess you were in the SEALs at the time. He might have left town before you returned. I can't quite remember."

He still didn't know how he didn't know that.

Maybe because you're too involved in your own life to see what's going on around you?

He'd told himself that he needed to concentrate on business. He'd thrown himself into it. Not just to make it a success. Or to give other ex-military personnel a safe place, somewhere they could work where they were valued. Where they were still part of something. But also, to chase away his demons.

But he knew he hadn't paid much attention to what went on in Wishingbone. He'd only cared as far as it concerned him or the people on Sanctuary.

"So, he definitely doesn't live here anymore? She has nothing to do with him?"

"I don't know Abby that well. But I probably would have heard if he was back." Eden gave him a curious look. "You seem awfully concerned about Abby's brother. Especially considering you won't even go check on her for me."

"It's best I stay away from Abby right now," he said without thinking first.

"Really? Why is that?"

"That is none of your business, boo. Now, did you have breakfast? Because I'm starved. Think Charlie might take pity on me and whip me up some pancakes?"

Eden snorted. "You know she will. But don't think I don't know what you're doing. Something happen with you and Abby?"

"No. Nothing. I'm just too busy to go check on her. I'll send Macca. She's met him before."

Coward.

He ignored the sick feeling that bubbled in his gut at the

thought of how the other man might care for her. It would be a good thing if they developed feelings for each other. Macca was just the sort of man she needed. She needed someone to build up her self-esteem. To make her see how beautiful she was. To protect and guide her.

Yep, he was perfect for her.

And now Kent really wanted to punch his face in.

THE FIRST THING she noticed was that the front door was ajar.

Her heart raced. Her body started to shake. She tightened her hold on the bag of groceries in her hand. What should she do?

Call the cops, Abby.

Right. Right. Only problem was her phone was dead and her neighbors weren't the type of people who'd welcome the cops bearing down on their doorstep.

Maybe she'd just forgotten to lock it this morning. She gulped. Except she knew she hadn't. Was it the guy who'd approached her in the diner parking lot the other night? Had he broken into her house? Her mind went to the card in her top drawer.

No. Nope, not happening. She wasn't calling *him*.

He had made it abundantly clear that he was just repaying a debt the other night. That she wasn't his type. Oh, he'd tried to soften the blow by saying he wasn't what she needed.

But how did he expect her to believe that? He was gorgeous, smart, rich, strong and kind to his sister.

She'd finally managed to read between the lines and figured out what he'd really meant. Then she'd gotten angry. After a few days, that had worn off and now she was just sad. Lonely.

And apparently, the victim of a break-in.

Seriously, what sort of an idiot would break into her place?

Wasn't it obvious from the outside that she had nothing worth stealing?

Her temper stirred. Like she needed this right now? Wasn't the universe sending enough crap her way, now she had to deal with this too? She didn't have the money to replace the door let alone anything else this asshole had taken or destroyed.

She gasped as she remembered the one thing in the house that might be worth stealing.

Her precious T.V.

Her outrage gave her enough courage to push the door open with her foot, step inside and yell out, "if you're still in there, you might want to run now because I've called the cops and they'll be here any minute."

Someone walked out of the living room. Only they weren't running. And they weren't trying to hide who they were. Dark, angry eyes turned on her.

"You better fucking not have."

8

The bag of groceries slipped from her hand. She winced as it hit the floor, knowing the likelihood of her having an omelet for dinner had probably just been destroyed. But that was a fleeting thought, since most of her attention was on the man standing too close to her.

He'd been a cute kid with his dark hair and olive skin. He had a tall, thin build. Although he was leaning towards gaunt at the moment. Worry stirred and she pushed it aside.

He'd never cared about her. Except, for when he was younger. And that was why she couldn't let go. Because every time she tried to pretend she didn't care, she remembered the sweet little boy who'd hold her hand as they hid under her bed while her mother fucked whoever she'd brought home that night.

Abby had often wondered whether her mom brought those men home for fun or if she'd charged them. Then she'd decided she didn't want to know.

They had to have different fathers. Even though neither of them knew who their father was. Abby's hair was a lot lighter, her skin far paler.

None of which really mattered right now, since he'd just broken into her house and scared the living daylights out of her. And made her drop a bag of groceries that were supposed to last her a week.

Shit. Shit. Shit.

"You better fucking not have called the cops!"

Before she realized what he was doing, Max had his hand wrapped around her wrist and was yanking her forward. Her foot connected with the bag, sending food flying.

"Fuck! You're making a fucking mess, Abby!"

"Me?" she snapped back, trying to free her hand. "You're the one who broke into my house, damaged the door and scared the shit out of me. What do you think you are doing! And let go of my wrist, you're hurting me."

"You're gonna get fucking hurt worse if the cops come here." He slammed her back against the wall, kicking the door shut before letting go of her wrist. She cradled it to her chest as it throbbed, knowing it was going to bruise. Hoping like hell he hadn't done more damage. The last thing she needed was to be unable to work.

Max loomed over her and her heart raced. She knew he was capable of violence. It was the drugs. He never really meant to hurt her. Or at least that's what she told herself. With him standing so close that the stale scent of his sweat and the stink of tobacco clogged her nose, and the heat of pure fury in his eyes, it was hard to believe that he wasn't very much intent on doing her harm.

"Did you call the fucking cops?" he spat out. She shuddered as bits of saliva hit her face. Gross.

"No," she muttered. Maybe it wasn't the right thing to say. Maybe she should have said yes and he would have taken off.

He let out a deep breath, taking a step back and running his hand through his scruffy, greasy hair.

"Shit, Abby, you scared ten years off my life." He certainly looked a good decade older than twenty-two. His clothes were stained and hung on his skinny frame. And there was a hunted feel to him. His eyes darted around as though he was expecting someone to jump out at him at any moment.

Definitely on something.

Tread carefully, Abby.

"What do you want, Max? What are you doing here? Are...are the cops after you?" A pretty good assumption considering what he did. And how he'd just threatened her when he thought she'd called them.

"Cops? I don't care about the fucking cops. Bunch of pussies chasing their own tails." He barked out a laugh.

"Then why did you just threaten to hurt me?" she asked. She probably shouldn't ask. Sometimes those sorts of questions tended to backfire on her.

He turned so quickly towards her that she flinched back, having to hold back a whimper of fear. She hated that she was so scared of him. She wished she could stand up to him. Could tell him to get lost.

"Why do you look so scared, Abby?" he asked in a soft voice. And in that moment, he almost sounded like her brother. Like the boy she'd helped raise. But she knew he wasn't. He was dangerous. An addict. And like any addict he'd do what he needed to in order to get his next fix. And if he hurt her along the way then so be it. He gently touched her cheek. "I'd never hurt you, Abs."

She didn't tell him that her wrist was already swelling. Or that he'd broken into her house. She just stood there and wished he'd stop touching her. Because it made her skin crawl.

Wrong. Wrong. Wrong.

"I wasn't threatening you. You're my sister, I'd never hurt you. But I can't be spotted here. There are people after me. Bad people.

Lucky, I found the spare key so I didn't have to wait outside or break in."

Shoot. Why had she put out a spare key after the locks had been changed? She'd put it in a different spot, but he'd obviously had no problem finding it. He strode into the living room and peered through the front window.

"They could be out there, waiting for me," he muttered.

Okay, now he was really freaking out for real.

"Who could be? Is it the same people that say you took something from them?"

He turned, stormed over to her and she wished she hadn't said anything. She bit back a whimper as he came closer. Fuck. She wished she had her baton handy, but it was under her bed where she usually kept it.

Okay, was she really thinking about using a baton on her own brother?

As he got into her space, intimidating her, she realized that she was. At some stage, she was pretty certain he was going to completely lose it and hurt her. Oh, he might feel remorseful afterwards maybe. But the damage would be done.

She had to protect herself. She might not be a fighter. But there was no one else going to do it.

Again, she thought of the card in her top drawer. No. She was on her own. Besides, it wasn't like Max was going to let her go charge her phone, find the card then make a call to Kent.

She licked her dry lips.

"What do you know of it?" he snarled.

"Some...some man approached me after work the other night. He...he said that you have something his boss wants. He wanted to know where you were. I told him I didn't know but that I would find out."

And that had kept her awake and restless these past few nights.

"Fuck! Fuck! Can't believe they fucking came to you!" He paced back and forth.

"What does he want? Can't you give it to him?"

"No, I can't fucking give it to him! It's my pay-day, I just need to work out how to cash in. I just have to hide for a bit. I need cash."

"I-I don't have any money."

She gasped as he grabbed her upper arms in a powerful grip.

"Fuck, Abby! I'm desperate."

"And I'm sick of bailing you out of trouble all the time!" she exploded, surprising herself as much as him. That was probably the only reason she managed to break his hold on her.

"I have to go. These are not men you fuck around with!"

"Then why did you get messed up with them? I'm already paying off Mr. Markovich for you."

Max snorted. "Markovich has got nothing on these fucking guys. He looks like a goddamn teddy bear in comparison. "

Why did she stay here? Why didn't she sell the house and disappear to somewhere he couldn't find her? A sense of rightness came over her. It was the only thing to do. She'd sell and disappear. Couldn't be that hard, right?

It made her feel slightly ill to leave him in a mess. But he brought this on himself. And at some stage she had to decide just where the limit was. How far she was willing to go for him?

Was she willing to die for him? Because she was very much scared that's where this was going to end up, with her being murdered because of his choices. His actions.

Well, fuck him.

Okay, so they were brave words. And she wasn't really sure she had the courage to back them up. But just as she was trying to decide how to get rid of him, because there was no way she was staying in this house with him, she heard a vehicle pull up outside. Max darted to the side of the window and pulled back the screen curtain slightly

"Who the fuck is that? Shit. It's one of those uptight holier-than-thou prick heads from Sanctuary Ranch."

"How do you know?" she asked. Was it Kent?

"It's written on the side of his truck, of course." His voice clearly told her she was an idiot.

Patience. Just get rid of him. Then she could figure out a way to get out of here. How long would it take to sell her house?

Or maybe she should just move and leave it behind? Take her paycheck and go.

It wouldn't be enough to get her far. Probably not enough to buy one of those fake identities. How did someone go about finding a person who made a fake identity? She guessed Max would know.

A knock at the door had her startling. Her brother turned to her. "No one can know I'm here. Got it?"

"What if he wants to come in? Maybe you should leave."

He shook his head. "Need a place to stay for a bit."

Oh God, he was staying? She had to wrap her arms around her, jumping as another knock hit the door, this one a bit more impatient.

"Get rid of him, Abby. Or else."

9

She walked to the door and took a steadying breath. She glanced over her shoulder once to where Max stood. He scowled at her threateningly.

With a shaking hand, she opened the door.

Surprise filled her as she saw it wasn't Kent standing there. Followed promptly by disappointment. She squelched that. She didn't want it to be Kent. He was a jerk. He'd kissed her, then told her it had been a mistake.

So, she should be relieved to see Macca standing there. And that's what she tried to convince herself anyway.

"Macca, hi!" She made certain to keep her injured hand behind the door. Only opening it partway, in the hope he would get the hint that she was busy.

"Hi there, love. You okay?" His voice was easygoing, but there was an intense gleam in his eyes. For once she wasn't focused on his movie star looks or that accent. She just knew she had to get him to leave. Or else.

She really didn't know what 'or else' meant. She'd never thought of Max as a violent person. A liar, thief and jerk sure. But not violent. Only her throbbing arm spoke a different story. And if he could hurt her, his only family, then what would he do to Macca?

"Me? I'm fine. Nothing wrong with me." She bobbed her head up and down, grinning like a Cheshire cat. His gaze narrowed and she realized she probably looked like an idiot.

Laying it on too thick, Abby.

Christ, she was so bad at lying. Seemed Max had gotten all that ability. She toned it down. Less of the crazy head bobbing.

"You are, huh?" he murmured.

"Really, I'm just tired. I was going to go have a nap. Can I do something for you?"

"I was just in town and thought I'd stop by to see if you'd gotten new tires for your car." He raised an eyebrow and gazed at her car pointedly.

"Oh, right. Yes. I've just been so busy working that haven't had time. But I'll get that organized straight away."

"They're dangerous to drive on," he said in a low voice that sent a shiver across her skin. "I don't want you getting into an accident, so do it sooner rather than later, yeah?"

She nodded nervously. Those eyes studied her.

Jesus, Abby. Stop nodding. She stopped so abruptly that her neck muscles protested and she winced. Getting slammed against a wall was doing nothing for her tired body.

"Abby, what's wrong?" he asked in a cajoling voice.

The urge to tell him was so strong that she actually had to bite down on her tongue to stop herself. Ouch. Not a great idea.

"Abby? You're worrying me, love."

She forced herself to relax, giving him a small smile. "You're really sweet to worry about me but I promise I'm fine. Just tired. I really need to get going. It was nice seeing you. Bye."

She shut the door and leaned against it, shaking. Her stomach bubbled. She hated being rude. Especially to someone who'd only ever been kind to her. Hell, she was polite to everyone. Even Gloria. She'd probably never see Macca again after practically shutting the door in his face. Sadness filled her and she glanced over at Max.

Yet again, something else he'd taken from her. It was bad enough he was the reason she had no money, had to work every hour she could. But now he was robbing her of the chance of making a friend. Okay, Macca was just being polite. He had only brought her car back because Kent got him to. But he didn't have to come check on her.

She heard the truck drive away and Max moved to the window, pulling back the sheer curtain. "He's gone. Jesus, thought he was never gonna leave. All that 'love' crap. As if women actually like that shit."

She did. Okay, Macca didn't stir her the way Kent did. She didn't have that flash of attraction. But when he said love in that accent of his, she did melt slightly.

"And where the fuck is he from? England?"

"I think he's Australian."

Max just made a derisive noise. "You got any food? I'm starving."

It was then she remembered the food strewn around the floor. Had Macca seen it? If he had, surely he would have said something.

But still, a nervous feeling developed in her stomach.

KENT GLANCED down at his phone. Why wasn't he calling?

"Somewhere else you need to be, brother?" Clint asked him. He'd come to his brother's place to...well...he wasn't quite sure why he was here. He just felt out of sorts. He couldn't work. Couldn't focus.

"No. Sorry."

He took a sip of coffee. He was seated at the breakfast bar across from Clint and Charlie. She'd made them both some huge sandwiches and herself a much smaller one. She took a big drink of her milk, leaving a white moustache on her top lip. He smiled, remembering how Abby had insisted that she didn't drink milk.

He frowned. Glanced at his phone again. Still nothing from Macca. How long did he take to check on one small female?

"Do you not like your sandwich?" Charlie asked, still wearing the moustache. "I can make you another one."

She tried to climb off her stool, but Clint placed his hand on her shoulder, stilling her. "He doesn't like his sandwich; he can make himself another one. You sit. Eat." He turned to stare at her, then grinned and grabbed a napkin, took hold of her chin with one hand and wiped at her face with the napkin.

"Hey! Stop!" Charlie squirmed around.

"You've got a moustache, sweetheart," he told her gently. "There we go, all clean." He finished by kissing the tip of her nose. "Cute as a button."

She pouted slightly, but Kent could see the pleasure in her face. A strange longing unfurled inside him. He was happy for his brother. More than happy. Since meeting Charlie, Clint had started to change his work-a-holic ways.

"Okay, spill it. You've got a face like a lemon and you're insulting Charlie by not eating the food she made for you."

And nobody insulted Charlie and escaped Clint's wrath. He got it. He picked up one half of the roast beef and mustard sandwich, taking a bite.

"I'm not insulted," Charlie muttered.

Clint sent her a look. "And I better see you finish everything on your plate, little girl."

Charlie screwed up her nose and Kent winked at her.

"You're so bossy," she muttered.

"You get to be bossy when you're the boss," Clint answered back. "And the Daddy. And the big brother."

Kent rolled his eyes. "He's always been like this, sweetheart. For as long as I can remember. Whenever we'd play a game, he'd always have to be in charge."

Charlie sighed. "But at least he doesn't spank you when you don't do what he wants." She went red after saying that.

Kent just laughed. "He would've if he could have gotten away with it."

Clint hugged her close, kissing the top of her head to try to ease her embarrassment. She was still getting used to this lifestyle. Her Little tended to be shy around other people, although she opened up more with Kent than most people.

He glanced at his phone. Where the fuck was Macca?

"Spill it," Clint answered.

"It's nothing."

"Might not be able to spank you, but I can beat your ass in the boxing ring if that's what it takes."

"Like to see you try, big bro," Kent snapped back, riding the edge of his temper. Then he noticed Charlie staring at him with wide, worried eyes. He sighed. "Sent Macca in to check on Abby. I'm waiting for him to call or text me."

Clint frowned slightly. "Something wrong with Abby?"

Kent shrugged. "Not that I know of. Eden just asked me to check on her. She's been trying to call her."

"So, you sent Macca? Why didn't you go?" Clint demanded.

"I'm busy."

"Busy picking apart your sandwich?" Charlie asked.

He raised his eyebrows in surprise, then glanced down at his lunch which he had managed to tear into small pieces. What a mess. "Sorry, sweetheart." He got up and dumped the food. "Guess I'm just not hungry."

"Don't you like Abby?" Charlie asked.

He turned with a small frown. "Why would you say that?"

Charlie shrugged, looking embarrassed. "Doesn't matter."

"Charlie," Clint said in a soft rumble. She peeked up at his brother. "Something you know that we don't?"

"Oh, it's just...I shouldn't say. It's not fair to Abby."

"What's not?" Kent asked.

Charlie glanced at Clint then him. "I've just noticed the way she stares at you when we're at the diner. She, well, I think she might have a small crush on you."

A crush on him? He remembered the feel of her lips against his, tentative and warm. The way she'd let him lead, relaxing into the kiss.

"I kissed her," he blurted out.

Shit.

Charlie's face lit up. Clint just seemed thoughtful. Charlie clapped her hands together, bouncing up and down on the stool. "You did? That's great! Abby is so lovely. She's pretty shy but once you get to know her, she..." she trailed off, her face falling. "Why do you look like that?"

"I'd say because he regrets kissing her, that right?" Clint asked him point-blank.

"It wasn't exactly the kiss I regret. But yeah, I suppose that's partly it." He took a deep breath. "She's a Little."

"I thought she was," Charlie said excitedly. Then she bit her lip. "Oh, you don't want a relationship with a Little."

"No. I'm not a Daddy Dom. And Abby, she's definitely a Little. She needs someone who will guide her out of her shell. She doesn't need someone to tie her up, blindfold her and paddle her ass before fucking it."

"Maybe she needs both," Clint said quietly.

"No. Not Abby." He ran his hand over his face.

"You're attracted to her, though. You kissed her."

"Yeah, and then I made a mistake and called myself her...her daddy. I don't know why I said it. It must have been because I knew it was what she needs. I don't know. But I couldn't lead her on. She's not a casual fling type and I can't be what she needs."

"And you don't think she can be what you need," Charlie said sadly.

"And yet, you send someone to check on her because Eden is worried. You put a new lock on her door. You order new tires for her car—"

"How did you know that?" he asked. They hadn't even arrived yet.

Clint raised an eyebrow, his expression telling him he was an idiot. "I know everything that happens on this ranch. You care about this girl, you're attracted to her, the only thing that doesn't gel with you is that you don't think you can be her daddy and you don't think she can be your submissive in bed. That right?"

"Yeah. I guess."

"Bullshit."

"What?" Kent glared at his brother.

"That's bullshit. Kent, you haven't been serious about a woman for years. Even the girlfriends you did have didn't last long. Why was that?"

He shrugged. "We grew apart."

"They weren't fulfilling your needs," Clint countered. "You may think you only want a sub in the bedroom, but you're nearly as much of a control freak as I am."

Kent snorted. He turned to share that joke with Charlie, but she was nodding. "You are. You just hide that part of you better than he does."

"See no point in pretending to be something I'm not," Clint said. "You can either love me or hate me."

"I'm not a Daddy Dom. I travel all the time. I work crazy hours. I have a lot of responsibility. I can't be responsible for a Little."

"Just because someone is a Little, doesn't mean they're helpless," Charlie countered. She frowned. "I'm not in this lifestyle twenty-four-seven. You know that."

"Every relationship is different," Clint said. "Not everyone could live the way we do. Even though Charlie isn't Little all the time, I'm still the dominant one in our relationship. I make the rules. I enforce them. You know all this. And you might think you don't want that, but I think you do. You can't turn your dominance off at the bedroom door. And that's part of the reason your relationships fell apart."

"Because I was too controlling?"

"I like to think of it as protective," Clint countered. "You're looking at this all wrong. A Little is a responsibility, sure. But being a Daddy Dom, it's all a stress relief. It helps me shut off everything else. I focus on Charlie. What she needs. And it feels right. It feels good."

Charlie sent his brother a small smile.

"I don't know how to do this. I don't know if I want to do this." Why hadn't Macca called?

"If her Little side isn't something you want, then it's better you stay away from her. You have to want both parts."

"I know that. It's why I sent Macca to check on her." His hands tightened into fists. Why hadn't that bastard called him?

"Ah, you're matchmaking. He's a good choice."

Charlie nodded her agreement. "Macca's really sweet. Hot too."

Clint scowled at her. "What are you doing, noticing how hot he is?"

"Oh, so you think he's hot too?" Charlie teased.

"Brat. You are in so much trouble," Clint said with a mock growl.

Right now, he didn't care how sweet or hot Macca was, God help him, he was going to rip him a new one for taking so long. Just then his phone rang and he snatched it up.

"Took your fucking time," he snarled into the phone.

There was a beat of silence. "Didn't realize I was being timed, chief." There was an odd note to the other man's voice. As though he was holding back.

"Well? She okay?"

He fully expected the other man to say she was fine, because if she wasn't then she surely would have called him, right? It had only been a few days since he'd seen her.

"I don't think she is."

It was like a punch to his gut and he froze. "What? What the fuck do you mean? What's wrong with her?"

He was aware of Clint and Charlie staring at him, but he tuned them out as he listened to Macca.

"She was acting funny. Jumpy. Wouldn't open the door all the way, like she was hiding something. And she'd dropped some groceries on the floor."

Dropped her groceries?

"She's clumsy," Kent said slowly, thinking that through.

"I don't think that was it. She didn't even mention the mess on the floor. She was nervous. High-strung. I'm going to stick around and watch her place for a bit. Got a bad vibe."

And Macca's instincts were rarely wrong.

"I'll come in."

"It's no problem for me to stay here," Macca replied. "I'm here already. Wait, she's leaving. I'll follow her. Crap, she's driving in her shitty car with those bald tires. Need to get her new ones. She lied to me about that too."

"What? Lied to you about what?"

"About getting new tires. She's gonna have an accident on those ones."

"I've ordered her new tires," Kent snapped. "You don't need to follow her, I'm coming in."

He knew he should just leave Macca to discover what was wrong with her.

But that felt like it was his job. So maybe Abby wasn't what he thought he wanted. Perhaps he still didn't know if he had it in him to be her Daddy. But he also knew that the idea of her in some kind of trouble made his heart race with panic and his skin go clammy. The urge to go to her was overwhelming.

He cared about her. Wanted to protect her. And he really wanted to kiss her again.

Only you make up the rules for your relationship. It can be whatever the two of you need it to be.

He glanced at Clint. Damn, he hated when he was right. As though his brother could sense his thoughts, he smirked.

So maybe he'd been looking for the wrong thing all this time. Or he'd been searching for a type or relationship when all he needed was a person.

Abby.

"Really, chief—"

"I'm coming in," Kent told the other man firmly. "Thanks for checking on her for me. Follow behind her, keep me updated so I know where to find you both."

"You want her?" Macca asked, surprising Kent.

He didn't reply.

"Because if you don't, you should know I like her. She's cute, funny, and pretty damn adorable. And she sure as shit needs help. So, if you don't really want her, then leave her to me."

"I want her," Kent ground out.

Well, he was all in now.

"You want any pointers, let me know," Clint said, a shit-eating grin on his face.

Perfect.

10

—————

"Where the fuck is your cunt of a brother?"

Abby jumped, her heart racing. She turned away from where she'd been unlocking her car to see the big bruiser from the diner parking lot the other night standing in the shade of a huge tree. He took a puff of a cigarette as he glared at her.

At least she'd put down the bag of groceries. Going back a third time to the store definitely wasn't in her budget.

"Well? You said you was gonna find out an address for me. Where is the bastard?"

"I-I don't know," she stuttered out. What if he'd come to her house? What if he'd seen Max?

Then maybe Max wouldn't be your problem anymore.

She pushed aside the traitorous thought. Max was her brother. She was meant to protect him.

Like he's always protected you? Her wrist still throbbed. He'd terrified her. She was having to dig into the money she'd earmarked to pay off Mr. Markovich to buy more groceries. Did he really deserve her protection?

She didn't know. She only knew that wouldn't be right to give him up to this terrifying man.

"You don't know?" he asked in a low, scary voice.

She shook her head. "N-no. But I'm s-sure he'll call soon. I'll find out w-where he is."

"You better not be messing with me, girlie," he growled. "Or you're gonna pay. I will be back and you better have answers for me or I start to get nasty. And you don't want that."

He turned and walked off. She leaned weakly against the car door. What was she going to do?

"Fuck, who the hell is that?" her brother snapped as they heard a vehicle pull up outside. He stood and stomped over to the front window. Max had nearly lost his mind when she'd told him about the man approaching her in the grocery store parking lot. Not because he was worried about her, he'd been more alarmed that she might have said something.

She was sick to death of paying his debts. Of feeling unsafe. Of lying to kind men who were checking up on her. Maybe she should have said something to Macca and maybe he would have told Kent and...

Nope, can't think like that, Abby. Kent regrets kissing you. He's not going to be interested in your troubles. No matter what he said about calling him if you need him.

You don't need him. You only have yourself to rely on.

Max turned away from the window to give her a strange look. "How much time you spendin' with those Sanctuary dipshits?"

"What?" Hope filled her. "Did Macca come back?"

"It's not Macca. It's that stuck up, thinks-he's-better-than-everyone-else-because-he-was-a-SEAL, Jensen dickhead."

Kent? It was Kent? Butterflies flew through her stomach. Even though she was expecting it, she jumped at the knock on the door.

"Well?" Max questioned.

"Abby! I know you're in there. Open the door please."

"I-I hardly know him."

Max narrowed his gaze. "You're fucking lying to me." He strode to where she sat on the sofa then leaned down. His rancid breath filled her face. "Don't you fucking lie to me." He took hold of her shoulders and shook her. His touch was too tight, and he shook her like a rag doll, making the low-grade headache she'd developed when she first realized who was in her house explode.

"Max, stop! I don't know him that well. I helped his sister, that's all."

"Abby, open the door," Kent demanded.

"I need to go get rid of him."

"Fine. But don't let him in here." Max sat back on the sofa and put his feet up on the coffee table. She wanted to push his feet off. Tell him this was her fucking house and he better fucking respect that.

Yeah, she was all brave inside her head. Instead, she tugged at her sleeves to make sure her bruised wrist wasn't visible and headed towards the door.

Funny, she'd always thought Kent had a lot of patience.

She opened the door and there he stood, dressed in dark jeans and a deep blue shirt. He seemed tired. But still gorgeous as ever.

"About time." He looked at her suspiciously. "What took you so long?"

She stepped out and closed the door behind her. She thought he would step back. Instead he stood his ground, and she found herself nearly pressed up against him. So, she slid to the side and moved to the porch railing. She turned and leaned back against it, keeping her hands behind her just in case her sleeve slipped.

Because she knew Kent would lose his shit if he saw her wrist.

What if that was a good thing? He'd get rid of Max. You could confess it all, the whole mess, ask him to take care of it. He owes you a debt.

No, he didn't. She only did what she would have done for anyone. And their debts hardly matched. Besides, it wasn't fair to drag him into her mess.

She didn't want to be in her mess.

"I was cleaning the bathroom and didn't hear you," she lied. She kept her gaze averted.

"You know that saying, liars, liars, little girl?" he asked, surprising her.

She frowned up at him. "I can't help being short you know."

His eyes widened. Then understanding crossed his face. "I wasn't calling you little girl because of your height."

Then why?

Wait, did this have anything to do with him calling himself daddy the other night? She'd figured that was just some sex thing. You know, something men said.

"And you didn't answer me."

Answer him? About what? Oh right. "Of course, I do. Liar, liar, pants on fire."

"How do you think their pants go on fire?" he asked.

"Um, never really thought about it. Why?" This was a weird conversation. "Spontaneous combustion?"

He snorted. "I prefer to think of it meaning that if you lie your bottom will end up in flames from the spanking that will follow."

Okay, seriously. Now she was really confused.

"Um, what does that have to do with anything?"

"You just lied to me. I want to know why. And I want the truth."

"I wasn't lying."

"That's two," he said in a low voice.

"Two what?"

"Two lies."

"Well, technically, I think that would be one as they're interwoven," she slammed her hand across her mouth. Thankfully the uninjured one. She couldn't believe she'd just said that.

"So, you admit that is a lie. If you were mine, you'd be lying over that porch railing right now, your pants down at your feet getting your ass spanked."

"I...I...you wouldn't!" But she knew he would. It wasn't the first time he'd brought spanking up. And since then, she'd been doing a bit of research. "Are you...are you into BDSM?"

"I am," he replied. "What do you know about BDSM?"

"I watched all the Fifty Shades movies."

"All right. Guess that's a start. Although you know that's a movie, not real life."

"I know." Although sometimes the two things became intertwined in her world. All she had was movies and T.V. shows. "You tie women up and whip them."

"Shit. This is not the conversation I came here to have."

"Sorry." She blushed bright red. "I can't believe I asked you that. That was very personal. Forget I said anything."

"No... it's not that I don't want to tell you about all of that. But not now. I don't want to scare you away."

Scare her away? What did that mean?

"Abby? Abby, are you all right?" he asked, concern on his face.

"Of course." She smiled brightly.

He sighed. "That's three."

She scowled at him. "You are not spanking me."

"Not without your agreement, no. But when I have that, you're in a lot of trouble, little one."

Again, with the little reference. "Well, you won't get that."

"We'll see," he said mysteriously. "If everything is all right then how come we're out here on your porch? Can we go inside?"

"No!" She jumped forward, in front of the door.

He raised his eyebrows. "Everything is fine, huh?"

Shit. Way to act cool, Abby.

"Yes, it is. But the house is a mess. I'm spring cleaning. I don't want you going in there right now."

"Baby, your house is neat as a pin, you don't have enough stuff to spring clean."

Why did she like it so much when he called her baby?

"Well, I've pulled everything from the cupboards and it's a pigsty."

He gave her a disbelieving look.

What to say to keep him out? "I've been sorting through my bras and I don't want you to see them."

She winced. Hell, where had that come from?

He grinned. "Your bras, huh? Sweetheart, I'm far past the age where the sight of a bra sends me into a lust-filled craze. Now, I'm pretty fond of taking bras off," he ran his gaze over her ample chest, "but I can assure you that you don't have to be embarrassed about me seeing them."

Her heart raced. His eyes grew hot. Hungry. She had to be wrong about that, right? He wasn't interested in her. He'd made that perfectly clear the other night when he'd told her how much he regretted that kiss.

It was a mistake.

"Abby, let me in," he said in a low, commanding voice. She actually moved before she caught herself. Damn, his voice was potent. She wished she had that superpower.

She shook her head.

He raised both eyebrows this time. And the look on his face...well, she was surprised she was strong enough to refuse him. Only the thought of Max sitting on her sofa and what he might do to Kent kept her from capitulating.

"Why are you here, Kent?" she asked quietly. "I thought with the way things ended the other night..." Her gaze slid away, unable to meet his eyes.

He tipped up her chin. "That's why I'm here. I made a mistake."

"Another one," she said before she could stop herself.

Kent sighed. "I confess, I'm not a man used to making mistakes often. In my line of work a mistake can be a dangerous thing. But I did make one the other night with you. I reacted badly when I called myself daddy and I—"

"Wait. What?"

Red filled his cheeks and she stared at him in amazement, unable to believe that he could blush.

"Are you...are you saying that's why you stopped? Why you said all that stuff about the kiss being a mistake? Because you called yourself my daddy? But isn't that just something some men say during...well..."

Like she'd know with her lack of experience.

He tucked a lock of hair behind her ear. "For some men, sure. But for me it had a deeper sort of meaning. It meant a role that I wasn't sure that I wanted to take." He sighed. "I'm messing this up. Have you ever heard of a Daddy Dom?"

She frowned, shaking her head.

"All right. So, you kind of know what a Dom is." He raised his eyebrows and she nodded. "Well, a Daddy Dom is a certain type of Dom. They take on a more nurturing role with their submissive partner. There is no one type, of course. Each relationship takes a different path. A Daddy Dom isn't a father, but they can take a parental role. They can be a protector, nurturer, can guide and love. They can set rules and boundaries for their Little to help them."

"How little is a Little? Did that make any sense?"

He shrugged. "That depends on the person. Some Littles enjoy wearing diapers and using pacifiers and some like playing, coloring, like I said, there's no one mold everyone has to fit into."

She wondered if some like building forts and cuddling soft toys at night. So, did all of this mean...

"You're a Daddy Dom?" she whispered.

"That's a tricky question. I didn't think I was. I've never felt that urge to play with a Little. I didn't think I had it in me. As a SEAL I was often out of the country. Even now, I travel a lot. I didn't think it was fair to get into a relationship with a Little. I didn't see it as something I needed. Then I kissed you the other night."

Her breath caught. She gaped up at him. She felt her cheeks heat. "I'm not a Little.

"Oh, baby. You so totally are."

"I don't...I can't..."

"It's a lot to process. I know. But sweetheart, that kiss the other night, it was like nothing I had ever experienced before. I know I acted badly afterwards. I had to get my head on straight. I thought it was unfair of me to start anything with you when I couldn't be what you need. But I had it pointed out to me that maybe I'm just coming to realize what it is I really want and need. These past few days, I haven't been able to get you out of my head."

He studied her for a moment. "I get that you probably have a lot of questions. Maybe we could go inside so I could answer them."

Yes. Wait. No. She shook her head.

Disappointment flashed over his face. Her stomach tightened into a knot. Oh hell, she didn't want to disappoint him. She wanted to see him smile. He smiled a lot, but it didn't always reach his eyes. She wanted to give him that.

But...Max.

Stupid Max. He ruined everything. But maybe he didn't have to ruin this?

Yeah, and how was she going to have something with Kent with all the other shit in her life? It wasn't fair to drag him into that. Even though she longed to tell him it all. She still felt sick from her encounter with Max then the man in the parking lot.

"I just...I've got a really bad headache right now and it's making it hard for me to take this all in."

"Oh, baby. I'm so sorry. Why didn't you say?" He reached around to rub her neck and immediately the tension in her head eased. Even as tension grew in other areas. Oh hell, she had to get rid of him before she did something crazy and invite him inside.

"Could you give me some time? I just need some time to myself to think this through."

He stared into her eyes. It was intense. And she got the feeling he could see through her layers to the truth below.

Crap, she hoped not.

"You're sure there's nothing else going on? Macca said you were acting strange before."

"I'm fine. I just...you know...bras everywhere," she said lamely.

"Abby," he said warningly.

"I'm just really tired," she told him truthfully.

"You still have my card?"

"Yes." She winced as she thought of Max hiding out in her house. She thought Kent would probably consider that something she should have called him about.

"Good. This is what I want you to do. Go inside, get into your pajamas. Take some pain killers and a big glass of water than have a nap. When is your bedtime?"

She shrugged. "Oh, anytime I feel like it."

"Not anymore." He continued to rub her neck as he spoke and it felt so good. "I'm going to give you some time to think this all through. Do some research. Really think about what you want. Because there is something between us. I want both parts of you. And I think this is worth pursuing. But I'm not going to leave you completely alone. One, because I'm worried you might talk your-self out of this with too much time to think. Two, because I want you to have a small taste of the sort of relationship I'm talking about. I can also give you Charlie or Ellie's number if you want to speak to them."

"They're Littles?" she whispered.

"Yes. But that's something private, understand?" he said sternly.

"Oh, I would never tell anyone."

"Good. So, here's what's going to happen. You're going to give me your phone number. I'm going to call you each night at nine. I want you in your PJs, teeth brushed and ready for bed. I'll tuck you in over the phone and say goodnight."

"What? Nine? I can't go to bed at nine. Most of my shows don't start until eight-thirty or later. Even when I'm not working a late shift, I don't usually go to bed until at least eleven."

"Your shows?"

She bit at her thumbnail. "My ah, T.V. shows."

He appeared slightly amused. "Just how many T.V. shows do you watch?"

Now that was a question she didn't want to answer. She shrugged.

"Hmm. Well, you'll just have to record any shows that you can't miss to watch the next day," he told her. "Because nine is your new bedtime."

"And is that your bedtime?"

He ran his thumb across her lower lip. "You're adorable when you pout. And no, it's not. But I'm not exhausted from working too much and going to bed too late."

Well, she thought that was debatable. He seemed like the weight of the world rested on his shoulders.

"And I'm not the Little in this relationship. Daddy is in charge. I make the rules. And I enforce them. Just remember that before you go breaking any."

"But I...I haven't agreed to any of this."

"No. And if you decide this isn't for you then we'll re-evaluate."

Re-evaluate? Did that mean he'd walk away from her?

"But I think it is. And I think the only way you'll know for sure is to experience it. Just a small taste. There won't be any punishment until you agree to this."

"So, if I broke that bedtime rule..."

"Then I guess I'd just have to give you a stern lecture, wont I? You might find that worse."

Yeah, she wasn't sure about that. "But how will you know?"

"Oh, I will know. And I will keep track of infractions."

There was a deep, dark note to his voice that had a mix of trepidation and excitement filling her.

"The next rule is one you already have but I want to say it again. I want your promise to call me if you need me. In fact, go get your cell and put my number in it now."

Nope. She couldn't do that. Couldn't risk him following her inside. "It's dead."

He frowned. "All right. Then charge it, put my number in then text me so I have yours. I'll expect your text within an hour." He lowered his chin, staring at her sternly. "And Abby, don't let it completely die again, understand?"

"Yes." A *sir* hovered on her lips, but she bit it back.

"Good girl."

Her legs nearly gave out on her at those words. Then he leaned in, cupped the back of her head gently with his hand and kissed her. Oh boy, this kiss was even better than the other night. It started off slow. So gentle. Their lips brushed against one another. His were hot. He slid his tongue along the seam of her mouth. She opened her mouth obediently and he deepened the kiss. The scent of him wove a spell. The whole world faded away.

There was just Kent.

When he drew back, she found she was leaning shakily against the door, her legs trembling, feeling slightly dazed.

"Yeah, definitely something there," he muttered. "Just wish I'd seen it before."

Seen what before? She wasn't sure what, but she liked the way he smiled at her, satisfaction and hunger on his face. She'd never had someone look at her like that.

As though she was everything.

"Remember to text me before you go have your nap. And I'll call you tonight." Then he turned away and walked down to his truck. She stared at his gorgeous ass, before he climbed into his truck with a wave.

Somehow, she managed to wave back. She struggled desperately to remember how to walk. Finally, she managed to get herself inside. She felt like she was floating on a cloud. Nothing could get her down...

And then she saw Max.

And her world crashed to a halt.

He grinned at her. It wasn't a pleasant smile. "You always kiss men you don't know that well?"

11

She gave Max a dirty look. "You always spy on private conversations?" Just how much did he hear? He'd turned something amazing into something that felt dirty and wrong.

"Of course. Never know what you might see or hear. Real kinky bastard, isn't he? Sounds like they all fucking are."

"Max, you cannot tell anyone what you overheard." Kent had made it clear what he told her was in private.

Max snorted. "You don't just blab out information, Abby. You keep it, you hoard it, and then you use it when it will get you the most gain."

What was he even talking about? Who was this man sitting on her couch, scratching his hairy armpit?

"You can't use that information against Kent," she said firmly.

He stood and stretched. Then he stared at her in a way that made her feel decidedly uncomfortable. "Didn't peg you for being into stuff like that. Always thought you'd be a missionary-only-under-the-covers-with-the-lights-off type of chick."

"I'm not a chick. I'm your sister."

He shrugged as though that meant nothing. And probably to him, it didn't. So why did she let it mean anything to her? Why did she keep bailing him out of shit? Letting him use her?

Maybe because she was scared what would happen if she said no. That he'd turn on her.

"Why did you even come here, Max? Isn't this the first place those people will search for you?"

"Where else would I go? Besides, this place is so obvious they won't look for me here. Like hiding in plain sight."

She wasn't sure it was such a good idea.

"You know he's loaded, right?" Max appeared thoughtful. What was he planning?

"Who?"

He gave her an impatient look. "Jensen."

"I don't know anything about his finances."

"You know, this is a good thing. Lure him in, get close to him. We might be able to use him to get hold of some of that cash."

She stared at him in horror. "I-I can't do that."

Max glared at her. "Abby, I'm not fucking around here. These assholes, they won't hesitate to hurt me. That jerk will be back. I need to leave and to do that I need cash. It's not like he'll suffer. He's got fuckloads of cash."

She noticed he didn't say a thing about her. About her safety.

"That doesn't mean...I can't do that."

Max took a threatening step towards her. To her shame, she moved back. This was not the boy she used to know. He'd grown harder. Meaner.

Almost...evil.

She couldn't believe he thought she would do that to Kent. That she could do that to anyone.

"Just do it, Abby. Pretend to go along with his sick games. Get him all hot for you and then we'll work out a way for you to get your hands on his cash. Hell, we can always blackmail the sick bastard."

This couldn't be happening. She would never do that, especially not to Kent. The best thing she could do was get rid of Max. "Listen, I have a little cash I could give you."

"I'm on the run, Abby. I need a lot of fucking cash. At least until I can cash in on what I have."

What did that mean?

"These people that are after you, they're going to notice you're here eventually."

"Not if you keep your fucking mouth shut," he told her threateningly.

"You know I won't say anything." She didn't ask him what happened in two days time when that man came back. She was terrified of the answer. Max flopped back onto the couch. He turned on a program about these people who drag-raced cars for money. She bit her lip, wanting to tell him that it was her T.V. and that he wasn't welcome here.

That she had no intention of using Kent Jensen to extort money from him.

But the throbbing in her hand and head prevented her from saying anything more. There was no point in making him angry. Not when she'd end up worse off for it. She just needed to sort out what the hell she was going to do.

This was just all too much for her. And she really wished her biggest problem was the fact that she now seemed to have a bedtime.

KENT USED his credit card to pay for the pile of items in his cart. Shopping wasn't really his thing. But Clint had given him the name of this website, and well, he'd seen so many cute things for Abby, he'd gone slightly overboard.

He tapped his fingers against his desk as he remembered their conversation earlier today. He hoped he hadn't pushed her too far too fast. It was why he'd stepped back and agreed to give her some time. He'd seen the shock on her face. Still, he hadn't been able to resist instituting a few rules.

Parts of this were new to him too. But other parts weren't. Abby was unlike anyone he'd been with before. He couldn't stop thinking about her. Her scent, her smile, the way her eyes lit up when she saw him.

Abby was everything.

And she had needs she might not even know about. Needs he was determined to meet. Now that he'd decided he was all in, he felt impatient. He wanted to push.

Instead, he took a deep breath. His shopping would take a few days to arrive. He could at least give her that long before he turned up on her doorstep. His phone alarm went off. Time to call his girl. He'd received a text from her about fifteen minutes after he'd left her place. All she had said was hi.

She was shy. Careful and quiet. He didn't mind that. And when she got into his arms and let go, she was wildfire.

He picked up his phone and called her. One ring. Two. He frowned. She wouldn't ignore his call, would she?

Well, maybe she would if she decided you were a crazy asshole who had no right to dictate what time she went to bed.

Shit. Shit. Shit.

On the fifth ring, she picked up.

Thank fuck.

· · ·

"H-HELLO?" Abby held the phone tight in her hand. She'd had to fight her way out of the blankets to grab it and she'd cursed herself for not thinking to bring it under with her.

In the end, she hadn't needed to worry about some stupid bedtime since she'd decided to hide in her bedroom soon after Kent left. She'd only left to go to the bathroom or to get something to eat. Max had taken over the living room entirely. She'd glanced in briefly to find empty bags of chips and cans of beer lying on the floor and a haze of cigarette smoke polluting the air. With a pointed cough, which she knew he wouldn't pay any attention to, she'd retreated to her bedroom, gotten into her PJs, grabbed her baton and climbed into bed with a flashlight and book.

Okay, so maybe it was a little silly to think that hiding under the bed covers gave her some modicum of protection. But it made her feel better. She had Bun-bun on one side and her baton on the other. She'd actually slipped off into sleep at one stage, but it had been a fitful one, she'd kept waking up with her heart racing and a feeling of impending doom coming down on her.

And then she'd remember that doom had his ass currently planted on her sofa.

What was she going to do? She couldn't agree to anything with Kent. She had to protect him from Max. From this mess he'd brought to her doorstep. And yet...he was the only good thing in her life right now and she was reluctant to let him go. When the phone rang, she told herself not to answer. To leave it. That it was for the best if he gave up on her.

So, what was it damn well doing pressed to her ear?

She was hopeless.

"H-hello?"

"Hey, baby girl." Kent's rich deep voice reached out to her. He was so confident and strong. She figured he'd never experienced a moment's doubt in his life. He'd never let his own brother push him around. Make him do things he didn't want to do. Have him hiding under the bed covers like a wimp.

"Everything all right?" Worry entered his voice.

Shit. She knew how perceptive he was. She couldn't let on that there was anything wrong.

And what would happen if she did tell him? Kent was strong and smart. He had a team of men who were all incredibly lethal. They'd squash Max like a bug.

It was tempting. So, tempting. But the thing that held her back was shame. She felt so ashamed that Max was her brother. But more than that, she was ashamed of herself. She'd let things get to this state. The first time he'd bullied money out of her, she should have said no. The first time someone approached her to extort money for Max's debts, she should have denied knowing him. Or better yet, called the police.

Okay, maybe it wasn't that easy. But she could have tried. Instead of just letting all this shit happen.

"Fine. Although I still don't think I need a bed time," she added, hoping he would think that was the problem.

His low laugh told her he'd probably bought her misdirection.

"Big Little girls often have issues with bedtimes, but they're the ones who need it the most. Otherwise they get cranky."

"I do not get cranky," she protested then she softened her voice. Not that Max would be likely to hear, but she couldn't trust him. She refused to give him any more ammunition against Kent.

"You sure you're all right?" he asked again. "Your voice sounds kind of muffled. You're not coming down with something, are you?"

"No, I feel fine. I hardly ever get sick. I'm just under the bed covers," she admitted.

"Under the bed covers, huh? The other day you were tucked under so only your hair stuck out the top."

"And you were worried I would suffocate," she teased.

"Still doesn't seem safe to sleep that way," he defended.

"I like it. It makes me feel safe, I guess. Is that lame?"

"Of course, it's not, baby girl," he said soothingly. "If it makes you feel safe then that's what you should do. Although, you know you'd feel even safer if I was there next to you, don't you?"

Her body heated at the thought. She knew she'd feel like she had won the lottery if he was next to her.

"Not sure there's enough room for you in my bed," she teased.

"Well, then, you'll just have to sleep on top of me, won't you? Think I might have you sleep like that anyway."

Just the image of that had her breath coming faster, her pulse speeding up. Yeah, she liked the thought of that. A lot. "Although I don't like the idea of having my feet hang off the end of your tiny bed. So maybe it would be better if you were in my bed."

"I...I..."

"Too soon for that, baby?"

"Umm, yeah, it's not that I, well, I do like the sound of that. But I..."

"I know," he said warmly. "I said I'd give you time to think about all this and I'm going to try hard to do that. Just know that doesn't mean I'm going to let you hide from this. I really think it's what you need, sweetheart. You need a Daddy to take care of you, to make sure you don't work too hard, that you don't stay up all night watching television and drinking pop. That you have a safe harbor to come home to when life becomes crazy. I'd do whatever it took to take care of you, baby girl."

That...that sounded like her dream. Except...

"But what do you need?" she asked him.

There was a beat of silence. "I need to be that for you. I like to be in control. I can be...hmm, not sure I should admit all this when I'm trying to convince you to give me a chance."

"Please," she said quietly. "I need to understand."

What are you doing? You need to push him away. Protect him.

But if she did that, she'd never know what he wanted. What he saw in her that he desired. And it would kill her.

He let out a deep sigh. "All right. You know I was a Navy SEAL?"

"Yes," she replied, wondering what that had to do with anything.

"When I left the Navy, adjusting to life back home, well, it wasn't easy. I was restless without anything to do. Ranching didn't hold much appeal. I was kind of aimless. And I felt like my life wasn't mine to control. I didn't want to go back into the Navy. And yet, I didn't want to be a civilian either. I was in limbo. BDSM was the only thing that kept me grounded. Going to a club, partnering up with a submissive for a scene, that was when I felt most in control.

"Clint has known he was a Daddy Dom for a long time. I never thought I wanted that. But what I thought I wanted, well, it never satisfied me. It never brought this feeling of rightness. Not like I get when I'm with you. When I imagine taking on the role of Daddy for you."

She sucked in a sharp breath. "Are you...are you sure that it's what you want? What if you find it isn't? Or I'm not what you thought I am? Or that we don't match well? What if I'm not actually a Little?"

"This was what I was worried about."

"What?"

"That too much time to think would just leave you with all these worries. Baby girl, I know it seems like we don't know each other well. But I've been coming into the diner regularly for how many years? Our chemistry is off the charts. Our needs match. This feels right. I like to be in charge. I need to know that my woman is safe. That she's taken care of. And I can make certain you are safe. If you trust in me."

She thought about that for a while.

"It won't always be easy for you," he added. "I might give you a rule that you don't agree with. But I will always have your needs foremost in my mind. If you give me your trust, I won't ever abuse it."

"We don't know each other, but sometimes it also feels like I've known you forever. I...well, I've watched you every time you've been in the diner. I've seen how you are with your sister. I know you're a good man. The question is whether I'm good enough for you."

"All right, I'm going to stop you right there and tell you that's the damn last time I better hear that you out of your mouth. Understand me?" His stern voice had her mouth going dry at the same time as her clit started to throb.

She was in so much trouble. Because there was absolutely no way she was good enough for him. And yet she wanted nothing more than to say yes to everything. It spoke to her in a way that nothing else had before.

"Yes, Sir," she said without thinking.

"Very good. Sir is acceptable. But I'd like to hear you say Daddy as well. I want to be Sir in your bed and Daddy everywhere else."

Her breath hitched. "W-what does that mean?"

"I like to dominate in the bedroom. There are certain things I enjoy. Before you start to stress that I'm talking about whips and blood play, I'm not. But I do like to use bondage. I'd like nothing more than to have you naked and spread-eagled face-down on my bed. Your wrists and ankles tied to the corners. Pillows under your hips to prop up your ass. I'd spank your butt until it was blushing. And then I'd spread your ass cheeks."

Oh God. Oh God. Was this what dirty talk was? She wasn't entirely sure. But it sure as hell felt dirty.

"I'd dab some lube on your asshole and push a finger deep inside, preparing the way for a plug. Would you like to be plugged, baby girl? Would you like to take me in your ass? Have you ever had anal sex?"

"I...I think you're going to be horribly disappointed and I think we should just part ways now." She hung up before she lost her nerve. Her heart was pounding and she felt ill. Not from his words, but from the need they had stirred to life.

Yes, she very much wanted what he'd described. She wanted it badly.

But she couldn't have it.

The phone rang. She ignored it. It rang again. She switched it to silent. Last thing she needed was Max coming in to investigate what was going on.

Then it vibrated. She glanced at it and saw he'd sent a text message.

She opened it to see what it said.

Either answer your phone or I'm coming in to talk to you in person.

The message was written out in full sentences. And it made it feel all the more ominous because of that.

The phone rang again and she reluctantly answered it. "Yes?"

12

es? *Yes?* That's how she answered after hanging up on him? He had to remind himself that she wasn't experienced. That this was all weird and different and he was pushing a lot at her. He took a deep breath then let it out.

"That was rude, Abigail Emily."

"H-how do you know my middle name?"

"I just do. And hanging up on me was very naughty. It's disrespectful. I'd never disrespect you that way and I expect the same respect from you."

There was silence. If he couldn't hear her breathing, he might have thought she'd disappeared. Then he heard a hitch in her breath.

Oh hell. Was she crying? Now he felt like a complete ass. Last thing he wanted was to make her cry. Especially when he wasn't there to hold her.

But he didn't want to bend on this. It was important.

"I-I'm so sorry."

"Not yet, you aren't," he muttered.

"What?" she asked.

He reminded himself how little she knew about all of this. Although common courtesy said you didn't just hang up on people.

Something had scared her.

He had pushed too hard too fast.

"Abby-girl, stop crying."

"I'm not crying."

"Abby," he said in a warning voice.

"I'm just sniffling a bit," she said.

"Sweet girl, I'm sorry if I pushed you too hard before. Last thing I want is to overwhelm you, okay? If you need me to back off, you just tell me. Thing is, parts of this are new to me too. So, it's going to be a learning curve for both of us."

There was a beat of silence. "I'm not...I'm not experienced. What if you're disappointed in me?"

"Then I'll have no one to blame but myself. Because as the experienced one, as the dominant one, it's my job to make certain that both of us get what we need."

"It...it is?"

"It is."

"So, you won't get mad at me?"

"Abby, if I ever scare you then you're to tell me. I would never yell at you or touch you in anger. But if that did happen for some reason, you're to walk away and find my brother immediately, understand? No one is allowed to hurt you, including me."

More silence. But there were no more muffled sobs.

"I wish I was there to hold you," he said a little wistfully.

"Me too. Kent, I'm sorry I hung up on you."

"I'm partly to blame. Doesn't mean it's not getting added to your tally."

"My tally?"

"I'm keeping track of your naughtiness. Once you agree to be mine, there's going to be a reckoning."

"Hey! I don't think that's fair."

He grinned, pleased to hear the heat in her voice. She was coming more and more out of her shell. Of course, he might be deliberately nudging her as well.

"Well, now, if you don't want the punishment don't be naughty."

"I've never been naughty in my life."

He left that for a beat. "So, you think hanging up on me the way you did wasn't disrespectful and rude?"

She sighed. "No, you're right it was. I just...I really don't know what you see in me."

"I'm going to have to show you, then aren't I? I'm going to make you see what I see when I look at you. Someone who is sweet. Kind. Brave. Caring. Beautiful."

He could practically feel her squirm, knew she wouldn't be comfortable with his praise, especially with the last part. Guilt stirred. Maybe he should give her more space. More time.

"Sweetheart, if you need me to back off, if I'm coming on too strong, if you want me to give you complete space—"

"No," she interrupted hastily. "No, you were right. Too much space and time and I'll overthink it all. I've done a bit of research. I need to know if this is what I need. I've never really been interested in men or sex. I've never, uhh..."

"Had anal sex," he said, taking pity on her.

"Yeah. That."

Jesus, she was cute. He smiled. "I'm glad."

"You are?" she asked, sounding surprised.

"Yeah, because it means I get to show you how good it is. All of it. I get to prepare you properly to take my cock in your ass."

"Jeez, I can't believe the things you say to me."

He laughed. "You'll get used to it."

"Yeah, maybe in ten years."

He heard her suck in a breath as though just realizing what

she's said. "I didn't mean that...that we'd be together in ten years, I mean that would be nice...oh lord, shut up, Abby."

He felt the laughter rumble up from his gut and he let go. It was the first time in a long time he'd laughed so freely. And it felt great. It felt like a load of tension had come off his shoulders.

"You should do that more often," she said quietly.

"What's that?"

"Laugh. It's a good laugh."

"Thank you, baby. And for the record, ten years sounds like a good start to me. And now, before I scare you off completely, I'm going to say good night. You okay, now?"

"Yes, Sir."

His cock stirred as she called him Sir in her slightly husky voice.

"Good night, sweetheart. Sleep tight. Don't let the bed bugs bite."

"Good night."

SHE CLOSED the car door quietly. If Max was asleep, then the last thing she wanted to do was wake him. He seemed to spend every day sleeping then he was awake all night, eating her food and monopolizing her T.V.

Asshole.

She was tired, she was grumpy and she just wanted her house back. It was horrible when you dreaded going home. She never knew what sort of mood she'd find him in. Mostly, she spent all her time in her bedroom.

How long was he planning on staying? At some stage, he had to go right? That asshole would be back soon and she still didn't know what to say. She was on edge, unable to eat. She'd barely slept these past few days.

The only thing getting her through each day was the phone calls she got every night from Kent. Had it only been two days since he'd told her that he wanted to explore things further with her? Since he'd pinned her to the front door and kissed her?

That was crazy. Sometimes it felt like she'd known him forever. He was amazing. They talked about mundane things like how their days had gone, to their desires and needs. She'd never talked about any of that stuff with anyone before.

But she was still holding something big back from him. And the guilt was eating away at her. If he found out the truth, that she'd been lying all along...

Well, he wouldn't want anything to do with her anymore.

She was reaching for the door before her brain warned her that something was wrong. The door was open, the wood around the lock splintered.

Oh shit.

~

HE KNEW AS SOON as he got to her place, that something was very wrong.

Yeah, the cop car sitting outside was a big fucking clue. As he pulled up outside her place, parking in behind her piece of shit car, he hoped he hadn't made a huge mistake in waiting so long to come back.

Two days. It had been all he could give her. And he'd taken that time to set a few things in place. He'd re-organized some meetings to free himself up. He'd also done a bit of online shopping for some things that might help her feel more at ease with him. To make up for the mistakes he'd already made with her.

But none of that was important if she was hurt...

He jumped out of the truck, not even bothering to shut the door as he raced towards the house. The front door was at a strange angle and he noticed the dent in it as though someone had rammed their boot into it.

When he walked inside, he came to a stop. His heart was racing. He stared around in horror. If there was anything that hadn't been turned over or smashed, he couldn't immediately see it.

He heard the quiet murmur of voices coming from the living room and headed that way. Inside, he could see the couch cushions slashed, the insides pulled out.

What the fuck? The T.V. was pushed over. There was glass and shit everywhere. This wasn't a normal robbery.

"Kent?"

He moved his gaze towards the kitchen where Abby stood next to Ed. He studied her, not going to her immediately, wanting to calm himself slightly. If she'd been here when this person had broken in... he had to swallow against the bile rising up his throat.

Fuck. Fuck.

"What are you doing here?"

She appeared unharmed. Physically, anyway. She had her arms wrapped around her waist defensively, as though hugging herself. Her eyes were wide as she stared at him, her face pale. In shock.

"Abby." He took a step forward and she stepped back. He stilled.

Ed shot him a look, filled with curiosity and something else. "Kent, what are you doing here?"

"I came to see Abby."

"That so?" Ed shot his gaze back to Abby. "You said there was no one you wanted me to call, Abby."

She'd said what?

"Abby, why didn't you call me immediately?" he asked in a low, calm voice. Much as he wanted to lecture her, he was going to have to give her a chance to explain.

Whoever had done this to her house had been either in a rage or searching frantically for something. Everything had been destroyed and she didn't have anything worth taking. So, what had they wanted?

Why hadn't she called him?

"I...I knew you were busy in meetings today."

He frowned. True. But didn't she know that she was more important than any meeting? Obviously not, since she'd chosen not to call him.

"I don't care how busy I am, something like this happens, you call me, understand, little girl?"

She blushed slightly and glanced over at Ed. The sheriff gave him an assessing stare. "Like that, is it?"

Kent nodded. "It is. And from now on, if there's ever any trouble involving Abby, I expect a call straight away."

"I'll note that," Ed said dryly.

"I don't understand what's happening," she whispered.

"I just took responsibility for you," he told her in a firm voice.

"Umm, you what?"

"If you get into trouble, get a speeding fine, get into an accident, something like this happens again then Ed knows to call me immediately. Although, if you're able to I'd expect that call to come from you."

"You can't just accept responsibility for me," she whispered.

"She doesn't know it's like that, huh?" Ed asked, sounding amused.

"We were taking things slow." He looked around. "Timeline just got pushed forward."

"It did?" she asked shakily.

Sympathy stirred. Poor baby, she seemed like she'd reached her limit. He moved slowly closer, not wanting to make any sudden moves and scare her. Thankfully, she didn't shy away from him. He cupped the side of her face with the palm of his hand. "It's okay, baby. You've had a bad scare. You're in shock. Just let me help you, okay?"

"I don't understand what happened." She took in the living room with horror-filled eyes.

He grasped hold of her chin, raising her face up so she was staring at him. Just him. "Just focus on me, baby. I'm going to take care of everything else. All right? Just me."

Her eyes were still too wide. Her pulse was racing. But she kept her eyes on his. He ran his thumb over the smooth skin of her cheek. "That's my sweet girl."

Ed cleared his throat. "Now that that's settled, maybe you can shed some light on the bruises she's got on her wrist?"

13

You're not scared of Kent. Kent isn't scary.

But right at that moment, as he stared down at her bruised wrist, the one she'd forgotten to hide from the sheriff in her shock over the state of her house, she had to work really hard to remember that she had nothing to fear from him.

She swallowed heavily. She couldn't believe this. Any of it. Who had done this to her house? Why? They hadn't taken anything, it just seemed like they'd done their best to destroy everything they could. There wasn't anything left. Nothing.

She had nothing.

And where the hell was Max?

A sob worked its way up her throat and Kent raised his eyes from her bruised wrist to study her face. He still held her hand gently in his large one. His skin was warm, his touch surprisingly gentle, the look in his eyes was banked fury.

"How old is this bruise?" he asked.

Tears swam in her eyes. She shook her head.

"You don't know?" he asked incredulously.

She did. She just didn't want to answer him. Once he knew it all, he'd be so disappointed in her. Disgusted by her life.

And what is the alternative? Keeping this all a secret?

"Abby, if someone is threatening you, we can help," Ed offered.

She sobbed out a breath. "You can't. Nobody can."

Kent shook his head. "Abby. You know who I am. What I do. The teams of men I have who work for me. There isn't much I can't do. And I can most certainly protect you. I will take you to Sanctuary with me, and I will make damn sure that nothing happens to you."

"But you won't want to take me with you once you know," she whispered.

He frowned. "Know what?"

"How I've been lying to you."

Kent didn't explode like she thought he might. He didn't do anything except give her a thoughtful look. Then he turned to Ed. "Give us a minute on our own?"

Ed shook his head. He was watching her carefully as well. "Wish I could, but it's best just to get my questions out of the way now so you can take her home and get her settled. Got two of my deputies coming to help process the scene. They'll be here soon and I'd really like some answers." There was a stern note to his voice now.

Kent nodded. "Me too. Right, get it off your chest, Abby. Tell us the worst of it."

She took a deep breath. There was no hiding from the truth anymore. She had to tell him. "The bruises are two days old. I got them that day that you...that you came here and I wouldn't let you in the house."

Kent's eyes narrowed, but it was his only reaction to her statement. "That's the reason you wouldn't let me in? Why you were acting so odd? Who gave them to you?"

"My brother."

"Max is back?" Ed asked sharply.

"Yes."

"Damn it, Abby. Don't you know there's a warrant out for him? Do you know what kind of trouble you could get in for harboring him?"

To her surprise, she suddenly found herself behind Kent's wide back. He stood between her and the sheriff. And when he spoke, it was in a voice she'd never heard before.

Controlled fury.

"First, don't ever swear at her. Second, don't take that tone with her. Third, she's obviously a victim and there will be no threats of arresting her or anything else. Understand?"

"I...I didn't even think about that. I'm sorry."

Kent turned so he still stood between them, but could stare at them both. "It's okay. You obviously had other things on your mind." He gave Ed another glare.

Ed huffed out a breath. "Sorry, Abby. Do you have any idea where Max is now?"

"No, that's the thing. I think maybe whoever did this was looking for him. He said he was in trouble—"

"When isn't he?" Ed remarked.

Abby nodded. She held her hands together tightly in front of her. "I know. But I think he's in worse trouble than usual. He owes money. He gambles and he doesn't know when to stop. And he's using. I think he was high when he did this." She pointed to her wrist.

"You should have told me," Kent told her. "When I arrived, you should have told me he'd hurt you and that he was in your house."

"I was scared."

"Of me?"

She shook her head. "Of him. Of what he would do to you. He's not the brother I grew up with. He's mean. He's violent. He said these people wouldn't hesitate to hurt either one of us to get what they wanted from him. I'm not sure what that is. Usually people just want money. Not that I can afford to pay anyone else off. All of my spare cash goes to Mr. Markovich."

"What?" Kent whispered.

HOW HAD he not known any of this was going on? How had he missed it all? She had a bruised wrist, for fuck's sake. Clearly, her brother had been threatening her. Mistreating her.

And she hadn't said a word to him.

Fuck it. He should never have left her that day. He'd known something was going on, but he'd never imagined it would be something like this.

"You've been paying off Max's debt with Drew Markovich?" Ed asked incredulously. "Wait, is that why you were at the bar the other night when Eden was attacked?" He turned to Kent. "Markovich owns the Suck 'n Blow."

Kent nodded, still unable to find his voice. He knew that. He also knew that Drew Markovich was a dangerous, ruthless bastard. And she'd been paying him off? Visiting the damn Suck 'n Blow every week? Anything could have happened to her.

"I go there once a week to give him the money. One of his goons approached me months ago. They forced me into a car and drove me to him. He told me that Max had used me as a guarantee on a loan. I tried to tell him he couldn't do that. I mean, I'm not responsible for my brother. But he said...he said when he caught up to Max, he'd start taking off body parts unless we came to some arrangement. I believed him."

"Fuck. Fuck." Kent ran his hand through his hair. Why hadn't he questioned her further about what she was doing there that night?

Maybe because he'd been too busy thinking about his own personal crisis. Which suddenly seemed so stupid in the face of what she'd been going through. He started to pace up and down, he had to do something with all the restless energy inside him.

"Luckily, he lets me pay it off as there was no way I could come up with the cash Max owed. Not without selling the house." She rubbed her arms and he caught sight of the horrible bruise surrounding her wrist in shades of yellow and green and he felt ill. "Of course, I still might have to do that."

"Markovich is threatening you," he snarled.

"What? No. Well, not anymore. He's actually quite a reasonable man to deal with," she said.

"Never heard that said about Markovich before," Ed said. "He must like you."

He didn't like the idea of that much either. He didn't want her around a dangerous character like Markovich at all.

"No, it's the other people Max owes something to. That night that Eden was attacked, when I was leaving work this man approached me in the parking lot. I'd just fallen over and he appeared out of nowhere. Said Max had something that belonged to his boss and they wanted to know where he was. I told them I didn't know. He got so angry and I was scared he would hurt me so I said that Max called me each week and that next time he called I'd find out where he was."

She rubbed at her head as though she had a headache. But he couldn't offer her any sympathy or help until she got this all out.

"And you didn't think to tell me?" Ed asked the question Kent wanted to.

Abby shook her head. "He made it clear I wasn't to tell anyone. And I didn't think there was much you could do. If I told you and he found out, well, I'm rather fond of my toes and fingers where they are."

"He threatened to chop off your fingers and toes?" Kent roared, making her jump.

"Well...no...not in so many words. But isn't that the way these things go? At least it always is in the movies."

Kent had to bite his lip to prevent himself from pointing out this wasn't fiction. It was real. Truth was, with people like the ones Max was obviously mixed up with, things could very rapidly escalate to violence.

"What happened after he threatened you?" Ed asked, making notes as she spoke.

"The first time?"

"First time?" Kent whispered. This just got better and better.

She gave him a guilty look. Oh, he so wasn't going to like this.

"Yes," Ed said, sending him a look.

"Afterwards, I went home, got changed and headed out to Suck 'n Blow and, well, we all know how that went. Then a few days later, I came home to find the door ajar. Max had found my spare key and was inside the house. He got angry with me, because he thought I'd called the police."

"Which you should have done," Ed said firmly.

Kent scowled.

"He slammed me against the wall and twisted my wrist. He said he was in trouble and needed to hide. That he needed cash to go on the run. I told him I didn't have any, but he wouldn't leave. And I was scared of him. I'd dropped the bag of groceries, so I went out to get more. That's when that scary man approached me again, in the parking lot of the grocery store. He wanted to know where Max was, but I lied and told him I still didn't know. He said he'd be back and that he'd get nasty if I still had no answers for him." She glanced at Kent. "I couldn't tell you about him. I was scared of what he'd do to you if you knew he was there."

He stopped pacing to stare at her with exasperation. "Baby, I was a Navy SEAL. I own a security company. Every day, I train, I work out, I go to the shooting range. Do you seriously think Max could do anything to hurt me?"

"I...I didn't want to take that risk."

He shook his head. Damn it. He knew she didn't know him well. Not then. But over these last few days they'd spoken each night. He'd texted her during the day. She could have told him any time.

"He...he wanted me to use you."

"What? Who?"

"Max. He listened in on our conversation on the porch. I'm so sorry. He might use what he heard against you. For blackmail, he said. If you wouldn't...if you wouldn't..." she closed her eyes as though she couldn't bear to look at him while she said what she had to, "he wanted me to get close to you so I could rob you, or something. I don't know. I know I should have pushed you away. I shouldn't have been talking to you on the phone or agreeing to anything. I lied to you. I kept things from you. But please, you have to know I would never have done it. I wouldn't have let him black-mail you, either. I'm so sorry. Please, you have to believe me. Please."

She was nearly hysterical as she stood there and begged him. Tears dripped down her pale cheeks, her eyes were wide and glassy. Still in shock. And here he was, pacing angrily up and down the room instead of taking care of her as he fucking promised he would.

Fuck.

He strode to her and she flinched back. Shit. Shit.

"Baby, Abby-girl, I would never hurt you. Not ever."

"I...I know. It was just reflex. Sorry."

The sound of a car door slamming made her jump. "That will be my men," Ed said. "I'll go meet them and give you as long as I can. You'll take care of this," he said to Kent.

Kent just nodded.

Ed disappeared out the front door, shutting it behind him. Kent took in a breath then glanced around, searching for a place where he could sit. He gently took hold of the wrist that wasn't bruised and walked with Abby into the dining room. The chairs in here were solid and still in one piece. He turned one upright and set it down. Then he sat and reached for Abby once more, pulling her over.

She went reluctantly, tears still spilling down her cheeks. He basically had to lift her onto his lap.

She sat there stiffly. "What are you doing?"

"I'm trying to comfort you," he told her. "Lean into me. Put your face against my chest." He rubbed his hand up and down her back in slow, soothing movements.

"Why are you being nice to me? You should be yelling at me. Telling me I'm a terrible person."

"Should I?" he murmured. "Why?"

"Because I lied to you, kept things from you, because my brother wanted me to use you for money."

"But you didn't, did you?"

"No. Never. I wouldn't ever. Please, believe me."

"I do, sweetheart."

"W-what?"

"I believe you. I know you wouldn't do that. You're too honest. Someone who could risk themselves to save another person they barely know, couldn't turn around and blackmail someone. Not when I know how much you like me."

She snorted. "Don't get too carried away. I tolerate you."

"Oh, tolerate huh?"

She nodded her head, but she gradually relaxed into him. He kissed the top of her head. "This doesn't mean that you're not in trouble for lying and keeping things from me. I distinctly remember telling you that you were to contact me if you needed me or were in trouble."

"I was scared Max would hurt you."

"He couldn't hurt me."

"You don't know what he's capable of." A shiver rocked her body. "He doesn't fight fair, Kent."

"When something is important to me, neither do I."

He wasn't certain if she believed him or not and in the end it didn't matter. Because it was the truth. And he had no intention of letting her brother hurt either of them.

"There's going to come a time when you and I will have a chat about all of this, keeping promises, telling me when you are in trouble so I can take care of you. Not telling me when you've been hurt or threatened or forced to pay off a debt you don't owe. But that time is not now. All I want from you right now is to trust me."

"I do."

A throat cleared and he glanced over to where he knew Ed had been standing the last couple of minutes. Abby jumped in his arms and he thought she might try to climb off, so he held her gently against him.

"My guys are here," Ed said, walking forward. "Abby, I'm going to need a description of the guy who threatened you."

"It was so dark. I didn't see much of him. He was tall. Had dark short hair. That's all."

"Think you could look at mugshots for me? Be good to know who we're dealing with and I'm thinking that he might have something to do with what went on here."

"I-I guess."

"Not tonight, she can't," Kent said firmly.

"She's going home with you?" Ed asked.

"Yes."

"Wait. What? I am?"

Kent leaned back and grasped hold of her chin, raising her face to his. "You are. You can't stay here. It's a wreck. And it's not safe. I'll get someone here to deal with the door. And I'll arrange a cleaning crew."

"I can't let you do all that."

"You're not letting me do anything. I'm doing it. And I'm taking you home so I can care for you properly. Okay?"

She took in a breath and then nodded slowly. "Yes. Okay."

"What about Markovich? Want to press charges against him?" the sheriff asked.

She shook her head. No way. Ed sighed. "Figured that was gonna be your answer. Do you have any idea where Max is now? What this guy might have wanted from him?"

"No. He wouldn't tell me, he just said it was his pay-day and he wasn't giving it back. I don't know where he is now." She rubbed at her head and he reached up with his other hand and massaged her neck gently.

"All right. You think of anything else, you let me know. I'll be in touch about coming in to look at those mugshots."

Kent lifted her off his lap. "Let's get some clothes packed for you and grab Bun-bun."

She gaped up at him, devastation clouding her eyes.

"What is it, baby?"

"They...they destroyed Bun-bun."

14

—————

His heart actually hurt for her.

He glanced over at where she sat in the passenger seat of his truck. She seemed so small and delicate. When she'd told him that they'd destroyed Bun-bun, he could actually feel her pain. He'd hoped there might be some chance of resurrecting her stuffed rabbit, but when he'd seen it, he'd realized it was hopeless.

Who the hell slashed open a soft toy like that? And all of her clothes were destroyed. Someone had gone through her small wardrobe. They'd done their best to destroy everything she owned.

He pulled up outside one of the small clothing boutiques on the main street of Wishingbone.

"What are we doing?" she asked, turning to him.

Poor darling, she was so exhausted. Soft trembles rocked her body. He wanted to get her home, fed and into bed as soon as possible. But he also knew it would make her feel better if she had something to wear when she got up in the morning. He had a few things she could wear, but if she wasn't comfortable with what he'd bought for her, he wanted her to have something she could put on.

He wanted her comfortable in his place. With him.

It was then that he realized this felt completely right to him. He'd had relationships last for months and never once had the urge to ask his girlfriend to move in with him. But with Abby, he was imagining...forever.

"We're going to do some shopping for you."

"Oh, right, yeah." She frowned. "Um, I can't afford to shop there, though. Normally, if I need something, I just go to Walmart."

"Walmart is on the other side of town. This is closer."

"No, well, I guess we could go to the secondhand shop that's along the next block."

"We could." He climbed from the truck and came around to her side. She was still sitting there, seatbelt on, staring at him in confusion. "Why are we getting out? Are we walking there?"

He reached over her, his arm brushing against her breasts as he undid her seatbelt. She shivered. "Oh."

Kent bit back a smile. He reached up and lifted her down. He wished he'd brought the booster seat with him that he'd purchased for her.

There'd be time to introduce that later. He set her on her feet reluctantly, but made certain to brush her body against his. Probably wasn't very fair of him. She certainly wasn't up to any play. But he loved the feel of her against him. He loved doing things for her. Like undoing her seatbelt, lifting her in and out of his truck. And he was definitely going to enjoy spoiling her.

If anyone could use some spoiling, it was Abby.

How little she had appalled him and now that he knew where all her spare money went...it was horrifying. No wonder she worked as many hours as she could. He cursed himself for having his head up his ass and not actually thinking about what all the clues added up to.

"No, we're shopping here."

She tugged at his hand. "Kent, I can't shop in there."

He stopped with a sigh and turned to her. Gently he cupped the back of her neck with his hand. "Baby girl, you're not paying for anything. I am buying you what you need."

She tried to shake her head but couldn't with his hand holding her still. "I can't let you do that. I don't know when I can pay you back."

"You're not letting me and you're not paying me back."

"No."

"You're very cute when you try to out-stubborns me. But it's not going to work. Nobody out-stubborn me. Well, except for Clint. This is happening. I want to do this for you. I need to."

"I don't want to take advantage—"

"Baby, stop." He placed a finger on her lips. "I offered. I don't offer to do things I don't want to do. I have to do this. It makes me feel like I'm looking after you."

"I don't need your money."

He leaned down and kissed her forehead. "I know you don't. But this is important to me, so you're going to let me do it."

She sighed. But she walked towards the shop with him without arguing. "Are you sure Clint can out-stubborn you?"

"Hard to believe, isn't it?" He held open the door for her. But she just stared up at him, clinging to his hand. "Not ready to let go, baby?"

She shook her head.

"All right, then you don't have to. Just keep hold of me, I'll steer you through."

15

Just keep hold of me, I'll steer you through.

As they drove through the gates that led to Sanctuary Ranch, those words kept running through her head. She resisted the urge to stare at the bags filling the backseat.

She'd almost had a *Pretty Woman* moment in the shop. Especially when she'd seen the look on Clarissa's face when she'd seen who Kent Jensen was buying up a storm for. Clarissa was one of Gloria's friends. And she'd never even spoken to Abby.

Yeah, that had been kind of fun. Seeing the way the other woman's mouth had gaped open.

But the thought of Gloria brought up another problem.

She turned her gaze away from the window. Night had now fallen, and she couldn't see much beyond the truck's headlights.

"I have work tomorrow. Late shift. Can you drive me in?"

"We'll talk about it tomorrow, sweetheart. For now, I want you to try and relax. Forget it all for a while."

"I don't think that's possible."

"I can think of one way it can happen." He reached the peak of a hill and down in the valley, lights blazed.

"Wow, how many people live here?"

"Probably not as many as you'd think," he replied. "My place is up by security headquarters, it's a bit of a rough ride so you'll need to hang on." He took a turn before he reached what she thought must be the main house due to the size of it. Wow, he wasn't kidding when he said it would be a rough ride. She held on tight to the sides of the seat beneath her as she bounced around.

Kent reached across her at a particularly rough spot, placing his arm over her to hold her in place. That was unbelievably sweet even if totally unnecessary.

"Shouldn't you keep both hands on the wheel!" She tried not to sound too demanding when really what she wanted to scream was, *keep both hands on the damn wheel!*

Kent chuckled. "Don't worry, I've driven this path so many times I can do it with my eyes closed."

"Well, don't!"

"Baby, I would never. Especially not with something as precious as you with me."

Oh boy, the things he said to her. They spoke straight to that place inside her that felt unnoticed. Insecure.

He even slowed down slightly, although she wasn't sure that made the ride any better. When they finally pulled up outside an A-frame log cabin with lights burning from the front windows, she felt like her head was close to rolling right off her neck.

"Wait in here while I go light the fire and turn up the heat," he said, not turning the truck off. "I'll also carry in all your stuff."

"I can help," she offered.

He shook his head. "No, I don't want you catching a chill. Just stay in here. I mean it." There was a stern note to his voice.

She nodded her head. Honestly, she was too tired to argue even if she wanted to. The manners her nana had drilled into her dictated she offer to help, but she was pleased just to wait in the warmth. There was a chill that had settled deep inside that had more to do with the wreck her life had become than the weather outside.

"Abby, what if I said there was a way you could let all your worries go for a while and just be?"

"I'd say it sounds impossible."

"Not impossible. But you'd need to let your Little side out. Your Little doesn't have to worry about big girl stuff. She just needs to worry about obeying Daddy. And if she doesn't, Daddy will deal with that. I know it's fast and I know you're probably not ready. But if you want me to take over, to take that role for you, then just know there is nothing I want more right now. I'll give you some time to think. Stay here."

He'd give her some time to think? She gaped at his back as he strode up the steps onto the large porch at the front of the A-frame. Another time she would have been more intrigued by his place. But right now, her mind was caught on his words.

The last thing she wanted right now was to think.

And yet, as exhausted as she was, wasn't that exactly what would happen as soon as she was on her own? But how did she let her Little out?

She startled as the back door to the truck's cab opened and he reached in to grab all the bags in one sweep.

"I can hear you thinking from here, sweetheart," he told her quietly. "It's all going to be okay, Abby. Nothing happens you don't want to happen."

She watched him walk into the house once more, this man who insisted she stay in the warm truck while he trudged back and forth in the cold. Who called her each night, telling her amusing stories about his day even though she was sure that he spent much of his day doing things that weren't funny at all.

He'd told her he would take care of her.

This time she saw him come back out of the house and walk to her side of the truck. He opened the door and in his arms was a thick blanket. "Gonna wrap you up in this and carry you in, sweet girl so you don't get so cold."

And that's when she knew what her answer would be.

"I'll do it."

"What?" he asked as he reached across her to undo her seatbelt.

"I want to try what you said. I want to let my Little side out. I don't want to think or worry or stress. I'm just, I'm not sure how to do that."

"Leave that to me. I have an idea."

KENT GLANCED over at where Abby lay on the sofa in front of the crackling fire. She had a blanket over her. He slid the grilled cheese onto a child's bamboo plate that had a picture of a monkey on it. The matching cup was filled with water, knowing how she felt about milk. He'd cut the grilled cheese into quarters already. He slid his own sandwich onto another plate and grabbed a beer from the fridge.

Then he juggled everything as he carried it into the living room. He had yet to expand on his idea to help her Little side take over. First, he wanted to feed her. Besides, this might help some.

When he reached the couch, he could see that she was half-asleep. Her cheeks now had a bit of color in them. Her eyes were sleepy as she gazed up at him.

"Oh hey, you didn't have to go to any bother," she said.

"No bother, it's just grilled cheese but I thought comfort food might be good after a day like you've had. I'm afraid it's about the extent of my culinary skills, besides working a grill that is."

She smiled as she sat. "I like to cook. It was just never really worth it for one person."

She ran her fingers through her hair which had slid free of the ponytail she'd had it tied up in. It lay in soft curls around her face. The scent of strawberry wafted out to him as he placed the plates down then settled in next to her. He grabbed her plate. She studied it curiously.

"Is that a monkey?"

"Yep. I thought it was cute."

Her grin widened. "It is."

He picked up one quarter of her sandwich and blew on it. Her eyes widened as she watched him. He brought it to his lips...as though he was testing the temperature. Then he handed it to her. "Perfect temperature, little one."

She took the piece of sandwich in awe of what had just happened. She couldn't remember anyone checking the temperature of her food for her before she ate it. She had a bite, even though she wasn't really that hungry. In fact, she felt a bit nauseous. He was right, though, it was the perfect temperature and as she ate her stomach settled. When she was ready, she reached for the plate which he'd put on the coffee table.

"Uh-uh, let me." He grabbed it, going through the same ritual. By the time the sandwich was eaten, she was feeling full, sleepy, content and completely cared for.

She leaned back with a yawn. "Thank you."

"You're welcome, sweet girl." He stood and gathered up the plates, handing her the cup of water. "I want you to drink all that, okay?"

She nodded and drank it down thirstily.

"Now, do you want a bath before bed?" he asked.

"Actually, I'm so tired I think I'd just fall asleep in it," she told him.

"Can't have that," he said firmly. Then he reached out a hand to her.

She was so tired that she knew she should go to bed and yet she also didn't want to be by herself.

"Could we watch television for a while?"

He shook his head. "You're exhausted. You need your sleep. Don't worry, I've got some ideas to get you to relax. Come with me."

She took hold of his hand and he led her to a staircase. "Your house is gorgeous."

"Thanks. I like it. There are three bedrooms upstairs, the master has its own bathroom, so you can have this one to yourself." He opened a door and she glanced in on a truly beautiful bathroom done in gray and cream, complete with sunken tub. She sighed.

"Okay?"

"I'm regretting telling you that I didn't want a bath. That looks amazing."

He smiled at her. "You can have one tomorrow night. Now, for your room." He walked through an open doorway across the hall and turned on a light. She followed him in, blinking in surprise. It was a large room with a big window taking up most of one wall. He walked over and pulled the drapes across. The bed had a soft pink bedspread on it. Laid out on the bedspread were a few pairs of what appeared to be onesie pajamas. Lying against the pillow were four stuffed toys. A giraffe, teddy bear, dog and cat.

None of her bags were anywhere to be seen.

"I put all your stuff away," he explained. He turned on the lamp by the bed. The lampshade had stars cut out of it.

In one corner of the room was a pink velvet chair in almost the same shade as the bedspread.

"Did you decorate this room?" she asked

"Ahh, no, Eden did. She reckoned I might need it one day. Never realized what she meant. But I, umm, bought these, for you." He picked up one of the garments from the bed. Yep, it was a pair of onesie pajamas with rainbows all over them. "Didn't know which one you'd like. There's a unicorn and a dog one, too."

She cleared her throat. "I like all those things."

He beamed at her and she was glad she hadn't told him she didn't want them or that he shouldn't have gotten them.

"I bought you these, too." He waved a hand at the soft toys.

Her eyes widened. "All of them? For me?"

"Ah, yes. I thought Bun-bun might like some company. Is there one in particular you'd like to sleep with?"

She stared at them all, but the reminder of Bun-bun just made her feel funny. She bit at her thumbnail. "I don't...I'm not sure."

He rubbed at the back of his neck for a moment. "Hmm, I have an idea. Why don't you go use the bathroom and put these on? There's a spare toothbrush in the cupboard under the sink. Help yourself to whatever you need, I'll be back in a minute."

He disappeared out of the bedroom so quickly, that she stood there for a full minute before she recalled the task he'd given her.

Brush teeth. Get into PJs. She could do that.

Ten minutes later, she stepped into the bedroom and found him sitting on the bed. He'd turned off the main light and the lamp by the bed cast shadows of stars around the room.

"You might want to turn it off so it doesn't wake you up," he said, standing. He reached for the covers and pulled them back. "You look really cute in your PJs, little girl."

"Thank you." *Daddy* hovered on her lips, but she couldn't quite say it.

"Did you use the toilet?"

"Umm, yes." She blushed.

"Brushed your teeth?"

"Yes."

"Good girl. Climb into bed now. Daddy will tuck you in then I've got something for you." The bed was high and she felt like a little girl as she climbed in. She lay back with a sigh of pleasure.

"This bed is really comfortable."

"I'm glad. Want me to read you a story?"

"I guess so."

"Would you like some company while you're getting a story?" He pulled something out of the drawer by the bed. At first, she was going to reject this toy the way she had the others. But she noticed it seemed a bit more worn. She reached out to touch it. Then she took hold and brought it close to her.

"His name is Boss Hog; he was mine when I was a boy. I thought he would guard you well."

"He smells like you," she exclaimed.

"Well, I'm not sure how since I haven't hugged him in over twenty years."

She smiled at the thought of a young Kent going to bed with Boss Hog.

"He's perfect, Daddy, thank you."

Kent froze and she stared up at him worriedly. "Everything okay?"

"Everything's fine, sweet girl. That was just the first time you've called me daddy. I liked it."

"Oh. Good." She hugged Boss Hog tight as she snuggled in. He tucked in the side of the bed and then settled down on the bed, facing her. He grabbed the book on the nightstand. "You like *Winnie the Pooh*?"

"I love him," she said. She noticed her voice had gotten distinctly more childish, but she didn't care. She settled in and relaxed as he read the story. He wasn't even halfway through when her eyes drifted shut and the last thing she remembered was him brushing his lips across her forehead.

16

The man grinned at her evilly. In his hands he held a huge pair of pliers.

She tried to move, tried to get away, but she was stuck. All she could do was sit there in horror as he drew closer and closer.

"Now, which finger should I take first?"

SHE WOKE SUDDENLY, sitting up in bed, her heart racing, her skin clammy with sweat. Where was she? She gazed around the strange room in fright. This wasn't her bedroom. She raised her hand to wipe her face and realized she had a tight hold on a stuffed hedgehog.

It rushed back to her. Her trashed house. Kent. Coming to his place. Grilled cheese and bedtime stories.

Safety. Acceptance. Caring.

She was safe. It had just been a bad dream. She should go back to sleep. Last thing she wanted to do was wake Kent. But as she lay back, she knew she wasn't going to be able to sleep.

She picked up her cell phone. She'd remembered to charge it

last night before she'd gotten ready for bed. It wasn't even two a.m. She lay there for at least five minutes, staring at the ceiling. This wasn't going to work.

Maybe she could get up without disturbing him. Perhaps watching some T.V. for a while would help. She climbed out of bed, still holding onto Boss Hog and tiptoed her way down the stairs. She didn't want to turn on a light and risk waking Kent so she had to be very quiet.

Last thing she needed was to fall and break a leg. Once she got to the living room, she switched on the light and grabbed up the remotes, turning on the T.V. before climbing onto the sofa and pulling the blanket she'd used before over her.

"What do you think you're doing?" a sleepy voice asked.

She screeched, sitting up with a fright as she stared at where Kent stood, leaning against the doorframe. He wore a pair of low-slung pajama pants.

And nothing else.

Oh, my lord, the man was ripped. She'd never seen a finer looking body in her life. Wide shoulders, a light smattering of chest hair then down his magnificent abs. And then her eyes moved lower.

"Abby? Abby, my face is up here."

She raised her eyes with a snap to his face. A grin danced at the corner of his mouth.

"I'm so sorry," she said, mortified. "I don't know what I...I mean, I didn't mean to...oh hell."

"Abby-girl, it's okay. I like that you were looking. Hope you liked what you saw."

"Oh, I did," she said fervently.

His grin widened. "Good. So, want to tell me what you're doing up at two a.m. with the T.V. on?"

"I'm so sorry, I didn't mean to wake you."

"I'm a pretty light sleeper."

"I'm so sor—"

"Abby, stop saying you're sorry. It's okay. I'd rather wake up than not. I wouldn't like to think of you needing me and me snoring away in bed."

"Oh no, you snore?" she teased.

"Brat." He walked forward and sat next to her. Then to her surprise, he lifted her, blanket and all, onto his lap. "All right, talk. What's going on?"

She squirmed around on his lap. He let out a low groan. "Baby, you got to stop moving like that."

She froze. "I'm sor—" She bit that off as he sent her a sharp look. "I didn't mean to make you uncomfortable."

"Just being around you makes me...uncomfortable." He winked down at her.

"It does?" she said breathlessly. He really did want her that much?

He raised an eyebrow. "Being around me doesn't turn you on?"

"Oh no, it does. It really does. And I wish I didn't just say that so emphatically." Her gaze dropped away. She was such a dork.

He placed a finger under her chin and raised her face. "I like that you don't hide what you're thinking. That you're not one of these women who pretends something she doesn't feel. Or likes to play games. I just want Abby. Smart, sweet, kind Abby."

"Oh." She melted even more. "I don't think anyone has ever said anything that nice to me before."

"Then that's a crime. Now, tell me why you're up."

"I had a nightmare."

He raised one eyebrow. "Didn't I tell you to come get me if you needed anything? Want to tell me why you instead snuck downstairs, in the dark, when you could have tripped and hurt yourself, to turn on the television?"

"Yes...but...well, I thought that was just something people say. Not that you actually wanted me to do it."

"Abby, two things about me. I don't offer to do things I don't want to do and I don't say things I don't mean, okay? Believe it or not, I'm not that polite."

She grinned at that. "Okay. Sorry."

"I'm sorry you had a nightmare, baby. Tell me about it."

It wasn't a request. She took in a deep breath, trying to calm the nerves dancing around in her stomach. "It was that man, the one in the parking lot of the diner. He was smiling at me, but it was an evil smile. And he was walking towards me with this huge pair of pliers and then he said, which finger did I want him to take first? That's when I woke up."

She felt a tremble work its way through her. Then he pulled her even closer, running his hand up and down her back. "It's okay, baby. Nobody is going to get to you. No one will hurt you. Not with me around."

But what about when he left?

She buried her face into his chest to try and prevent herself from thinking about that moment. She just had to take as much of him as she could while he was here.

"No wonder you couldn't get back to sleep. But I wish you had woken me up."

She shrugged. "I figured I would watch T.V. until I felt sleepy again."

"You can't stay up half the night watching T.V., though."

"I'll keep it down. I don't even really need the sound if you think it will bother you."

He sighed. "I'm not worried about me."

Her? He was worried about her? He really was an amazing guy. "You don't need to worry about me. I often wake up and can't get back to sleep. Or can't get to sleep in the first place. I'm used to watching T.V. and falling asleep on the couch. Or I was, until Max arrived. He took up residence on the couch even though there are two perfectly good bedrooms. I couldn't watch any of my programs."

"Terrible," he replied.

She leaned back, staring up at him suspiciously. "Was that sarcasm?"

"No, baby. I think it really is terrible the way he just took over."

"T.V. helps me sleep. Makes me feel less alone, I guess. I don't stress or worry when I'm watching it."

"Is there anything else you do that stops you from worrying or helps you sleep?"

"Oh...umm..." She couldn't tell him about that, could she?

He already knows everything else. The man bought you onesie pajamas, the type with feet attached and a back flap. He gave you his stuffed childhood toy. He's not going to be horrified.

"I like to build forts," she blurted out.

"What?" He blinked.

"Blanket forts. I put a few blankets over the dining table then pull the cushions off the sofa and put them under the table and then climb in. I know it's silly, but it makes me feel safe."

And now she was wondering if she shouldn't have told him.

"Hush, it's not silly. It's actually a great idea. Except I don't have a dining table and I'm not really keen on either of us sleeping on sofa cushions. I do have an idea, though." He stood and glanced down at the blanket still tucked around her. "Will you be cold if I take that?"

"No, I'll be fine. Here. What are you doing?"

"You'll see. Stay here. I'll come back for you."

She watched with curiosity as he left. What was he up to? What was this idea he had?

Fifteen minutes later, she was watching a rerun of *Friends* when he returned. He reached for the T.V. remote and switched it off. She sat up from where she'd been lying on the sofa and took the hand he offered.

"From now on," he said as they climbed the stairs. "When you're Little Abby and I'm Daddy you don't take the stairs on your own at night, understand?"

"Umm, yes."

He didn't lead her to her bedroom as she'd thought he would. Instead, he steered her to his bedroom. And what she walked into was like some sort of magical dream.

"How...how did you do this?" She moved closer to the bed. Kent had actually put the mattress on the floor, rigged up some poles over it, then draped a couple of large blankets across the poles.

But he hadn't stopped there. Around the entrance to the blanket fort, he'd put up some fairy lights.

"Camping supplies. The fairy lights are something Eden bought. She said you can never have enough fairy lights. You like it?"

He sounded almost unsure. Unlike the confident man she had come to know.

"I love it." Abby walked to him then slipped her arms around his waist. For a moment he stood stiffly then he wrapped her up in his embrace and held her tight.

"Good," he told her. "I didn't want you to sleep on your own in case you had more nightmares, so I thought it was better to do it in my bedroom. You can sleep in here with me."

You can sleep in here with me.

Christ, thought this one through well, didn't he?

He stared down at Abby who was still nestled up against him and wondered how the hell he was going to manage to get to sleep.

Get it together, man.

He cleared his throat. He needed to be strong for her. She was coming into his bed because she'd had a nightmare because of her shitty, shitty day.

She didn't need him trying to get into her pants.

"Do you need the bathroom, baby?" he asked her.

She nodded with a yawn. He let her go and stepped back. She just stood there. Poor baby, she was dead on her feet. He turned her and gave her a small nudge towards the bathroom. When that didn't work, he gave her ass a small slap.

"Hey!"

Yeah, he should have known that would get her attention. She rubbed her ass. "You spanked me."

"Sweetheart, in no way was that a spanking, that was a tap to get your attention. Go use the bathroom and then come to bed. We both need sleep."

A FEW MINUTES LATER, she shuffled her way back into Kent's bedroom from the ensuite bathroom. The only lights on were the fairy lights and it looked romantic. She glanced down at her onesie. Yeah, she wasn't exactly dressed for any sort of seduction. Not that she'd even know how to start trying to seduce someone.

No doubt she'd make a complete mess of that.

"Abby, stop stalling and come to bed," Kent growled.

She jumped slightly, and chewing on her thumbnail, approached the fort he'd built.

For her.

Had anyone ever done anything so nice for her before? As that thought hit her, so did everything else. This past week had been absolute shit. Not all of it. Not Kent. But she felt torn about that. She had no right bringing him into her life. She should have been upfront from the start and told him she didn't have time in her life to start anything with him.

Tears dripped down her cheeks. She hated that she was crying again. What was wrong with her? Her body rocked with sobs as she just stood there, unable to move. Where was Max? Who had wrecked her house? What was she going to do? She had nothing.

Maybe you should just leave.

Kent poked his head out of the tent and saw her. The frown on his face smoothed out.

"Oh, baby. It's all hit you, huh?"

"I don't know what's wrong with me. I c-can't stop s-shaking."

He crawled out and walked to her, gathering her into his arms. "You... you shouldn't be nice to me."

He pulled back, gazed down at her. "And why shouldn't I be nice to you?"

"B-because I'm a t-terrible person."

He made a noise of disbelief and pulled her in close, tucking her face into his chest as he rocked her gently. "Baby, I don't know anyone better than you."

"T-that's not t-true. Or you k-know some truly a-awful people."

He rubbed his hand up and down her back. "Why don't you tell me why you're so terrible, hmm?"

"I l-lied to you. Kept t-things from you. And a-all because I was s-selfish."

"I'm pretty certain you don't know how to be selfish so you're going to have to explain that one."

She took a deep breath. "I d-didn't tell you a-anything about M-max or the m-money I was p-paying off. Or that I-I might h-have to sell my h-house and leave."

She felt him stiffen but she wanted to get this out.

"I t-told myself it was to p-protect you. But mostly it was b-because I didn't w-want to l-lose any t-time with you. See, I'm horrible and s-selfish."

"Okay, there's a few things there we need to address and three in the morning probably isn't the best time to talk about them. But here's what you need to know. One, you wanted something for yourself. That's not selfish. Two, I'm not happy about you keeping any of this from me. You know what I expected. But I also know that what's between us is new and scary to you so I'm going to take that into consideration when I work out your punishment for that."

She sucked in a breath at that, but didn't protest. She deserved to be punished.

"I know you haven't agreed to a relationship like that with me. With me as the head, with your agreement to be my Little and my sub, however you're obviously carrying a lot of guilt, which isn't healthy. And you need to let that go. A punishment can do that. It can wipe the slate clean. And you can forgive yourself. I want you to think about that. But lastly..."

He stepped back and placed his hands on her shoulders. Then he leaned in, his face stern. "You are not going anywhere, understand me? I didn't just meet you only to lose you. I don't know where this is going, but I know where I hope it does. And for that to happen you need to be here. Preferably in this house. With me."

"You want me to live here?" Her sobs had long since dried up, now she was trembling for an entirely different reason.

"I know that's fast. But when I want something, I go for it. I don't mess around. But I would never force you. You're here for now, where I can watch over you and keep you safe. That's what's important. All right?"

"All right." She licked her lips. "I want you to do it now."

"What? Baby, we don't have to—"

"Please. I want it now. I feel so guilty about not telling you the truth. It's like this lead ball in my tummy. Please, I want it over with now."

He watched her for a minute then he nodded. "All right, we'll do this now. But you know there's a few things to address. Not just you keeping things from me. I believe there were a few lies and you hung the phone up on me."

"Oh yeah." She gulped. Shit.

"Sure about this?"

If it would make her feel better then yeah. "The slate will be clean?"

"Yes, all will be forgiven."

"Then yes, I'm sure."

"All right then. Come with me." He held out his hand and she slid hers into it. Then he led from the room and into the spare bedroom she hadn't seen before.

"I don't want to do this in the room I gave you. That's your safe place and there was nowhere for me to sit in our bedroom since the mattress is on the floor."

Oh. Right.

Our bedroom? Wow.

He sat on the bed and patted his lap. "Over you go."

She stared at him nervously.

"Don't worry, baby. For this first spanking, I'm only using my hand. Normally, for such a bad transgression I'd use the paddle or belt. But I'm going easy on you."

Shit. This was easy?

But since she really didn't want to experience either the paddle or the belt, she laid herself across his lap. He adjusted her, moving her forward so her fingers brushed against the floor and her ass was up higher. Then he opened the back of her onesie.

She tensed up.

"Hmm, maybe I should make it a rule that there are to be no panties worn under your onesie," he stated as he slid them down over her ass. "Make it easier to bare your bottom."

She didn't think that sounded like a good idea at all. She braced herself for the first slap. But instead, when he touched her ass it was to rub it. She gradually relaxed as that was all he did.

That's why it was such a surprise when the first slap landed. She yelped and jumped.

"Easy, baby. There's plenty more to come."

Smack! Smack! Smack!

Holy shit! That damn well hurt. It wasn't long until her butt was stinging and tears were dripping down her cheeks onto the floor below her. But he kept going, laying spank after spank against her defenseless ass. She tried to wiggle off, unable to help herself. But he held her steady, keeping up that same rhythm.

Spank. Spank. Spank.

She sobbed. "Daddy, stop!"

"Not yet, baby girl."

He had to stop. She was dying. She reached back with her hands to protect her poor flaming ass, but he just grabbed her wrists gently in one hand and continued to lay into her bottom.

"No more. No more."

"Yes, more. We have to get rid of all that guilt." Smack. Smack. Smack. "I want you to remember this the next time you think about lying." Spank. Spank. Spank. "Or you think about disobeying me."

He moved his hand lower, to the tops of her thighs. It felt like her skin was on fire. How the hell would she ever sit again?

"And you will never keep anything from me again, understand?"

She howled as another barrage of spanks descended. Shit! How did she ever think she wanted this? It was horrible.

And then she realized he had stopped. That he was rubbing her bottom gently while she sobbed and sobbed.

"That's it, baby girl. Let it all out. Good girl. It's all done now. All is forgiven. Abby is a good girl."

He carefully turned her over and held her on his lap. She hissed and winced, trying to get off his lap, but he held her there.

"Uh-uh, sitting on a sore bottom is a consequence of being naughty," he told her.

She sniffled and cried. "It hurts."

"I know. It's meant to." He wiped her cheeks with his fingers. "I don't ever want you keeping things from me, understand?"

"I understand. I'm sorry."

"All is forgiven, baby." He picked her up and carried her into his bedroom. He set her down in the bathroom and grabbed some tissues to clean her up. Then he pulled up her panties and set her onesie to right before giving her a gentle, loving kiss.

"I want you to promise to put this stuff about moving out of your head."

"I'm just so tired of worrying about everything." She yawned. Her bottom still throbbed, but now she felt lighter. The heavy ball of guilt was gone and she really wanted to just go to sleep.

"I know, baby. But you don't have to move for a clean slate. You can have it right here, with me."

He tucked her back in against his chest. It was so easy to rest against him. She loved when he held her. "But how do I do that with all this Max stuff?"

"By letting me deal with it."

She shook her head. "That's not fair."

He sighed. "That wasn't actually a request."

"Kent..."

"Fine. By letting me help you deal with it. All right?"

He pulled her back to give her a serious look. "Agreed?"

"You're sure?"

"I'm sure. This is what I do, I take care of problems for people."

"I thought you ran a security company?"

"Yeah, and most of that is helping people deal with a problem they've got. They're sending employees into war-torn areas and need protection. Someone they love has been kidnapped for ransom and they want them rescued. Someone needs a specialized security system. Someone else is getting death threats and needs a bodyguard. Problem solving is my thing. So, let me help. I'm good at it."

"Wow, I didn't realize that a security company did all that."

"JSI does."

She yawned and rubbed her hand across her face. "I'm sorry."

"Come on, baby. You're about to crash again. You've had one hell of a day."

"One hell of a week," she corrected as he led her to the fort. She climbed in and settled down on her side.

He moved in behind her, and pulled her close so he was cradling her from behind. Wow, he was like a furnace.

"Kent?"

"Yeah, baby?" he asked.

"Thank you. For everything. I don't know what I would have done without you today."

HE WOKE up with her bottom pressed against his cock. He was so hard it physically hurt, but he was reluctant to move and risk waking her up. He carefully leaned up on one elbow and stared down at her as she slept.

Her mouth was open slightly and she was snoring softly.

That was freaking adorable.

Poor baby, she'd absolutely crashed. He'd lain awake for a bit longer, wondering what he could do to fix all the problems her asshole brother had created for her. One thing he did know was that she wasn't going to continue paying off his debts. Or having anything more to do with whoever else was after her brother.

He felt ill at the thought of all the things that could have happened to her. She wouldn't be allowed in such dangerous situations again.

Ease up, man. She hasn't agreed to anything.

She would, though. What she wouldn't be doing was leaving. He had to fight hard not to hug her tight to him. She needed her sleep. He'd have to make certain she had a nap this afternoon. Of course, first he'd have to convince her to call into work sick. He gently moved away from her and slid down the bed to climb out. Surprisingly, sleeping in a blanket fort hadn't been weird like he'd thought it might be.

He yawned as he made his way into the bathroom. He might need to take a nap himself.

ABBY OPENED the door to the bathroom. She'd woken up with a foggy brain and this feeling that she was forgetting something. Unable to get back to sleep, she figured she'd get up and have a shower. Maybe that would wake her up and help her remember. She stepped into the bathroom, still half-asleep.

A rush of warm, steamy air hit her first.

And then he hit her.

Not physically, of course. He was several feet away, standing in the shower, his body partially visible through the door to the shower.

And oh, what a body it was. Hard, chiseled, tanned.

Abby, don't just stare at him. Move. Turn around. Apologize. Get out of there!

How could she leave when the man had a backside like that? What would it feel like just to reach out, open that door and squeeze...just then he turned around and she got a full-on frontal view of his entire package.

Oh Lord. She gulped. She'd never really studied a cock before. She'd seen them on T.V. and in the dirty magazines that Max used to hide under the bed, but she'd never really stared at one like this.

That one time she'd fumbled around with Joey McBride in the back of his pick-up didn't really count. It had been dark and she hadn't even had time to really touch him before he'd rolled her onto her back and thrust inside her...

And that was a memory she really didn't want right now.

"Abby? Abby, you okay?"

She then realized he'd turned the shower off and was stepping out. Shit. Shit.

She did the only thing she could think of.

She slammed her hand across her eyes. "I'm so sorry! I didn't mean to look!"

17

H e had to bite back a laugh.

Yep. Freaking adorable. She stood there with her hair a wild mess around her head, dressed in her onesie, with her hand covering her eyes like a little girl caught doing something naughty.

Hmm, but the look in her eyes had been all hunger and heat. She wanted him.

"No need to hide your eyes, baby. You can stare all you want."

Two of her fingers parted and one eye peeked out at him. "What? Really?"

He grinned at her. "I'm not shy. Like what you see?"

"Like? Are you kidding? You're a freaking Greek God. I'm practically salivating over here." She slammed her other hand across her mouth and covered her eyes up once more. Her face was entirely covered by her hands.

He couldn't stop the laugh that erupted.

"Baby, drop your hands."

She said something that was muffled by her hand. He glanced

at the towels which were hung on the rail. He should probably wrap one around himself to make her more comfortable. But screw it, he needed all the tools he could put his hands on in order to get her to agree to a relationship with him. Maybe it was a bit manipulative...but if she liked his body that much who was he to deny her from staring, and touching, her fill. Stepping forward, he gently grasped hold of her hands. He frowned at the bruises on her wrist.

Never again. Never again would he allow any harm to come to her.

He drew back her hands, kissing her bruised wrist gently. Her eyes were still closed and he leaned forward and placed soft kisses on each eyelid.

He saw the tension melt from her. She sighed. He kissed the tip of her nose then brushed his lips across hers. She whimpered in protest when he moved his lips away. She raised her face. "More."

He raised an eyebrow at the demand. "More, what?"

"More kissing, please. I like when you kiss me." The words came out in a rush, and she blushed slightly.

"That's good. Because I love kissing you. First, though, I'm going to need you to open your eyes."

He waited. She opened one eye, stared up at him. Then the other.

He rewarded her with a proper kiss. He grasped hold of her chin, holding her in place as he drew her lower lip between his teeth and tugged at it gently before pressing his lips against her soft ones and teased her with his tongue.

Heaven.

"There, that wasn't so hard, was it?"

"I...I didn't mean to walk in on you."

"If I didn't want you to then I would have locked the door."

"You wanted me to walk in?"

"Anytime you want to come join me in the shower you are most welcome."

"I've never showered with anyone before," she confessed.

He'd bet there was a lot of things she hadn't done before. He ran his thumb across her lower lip. Her mouth parted and he slipped his thumb inside. "For the record, I love kissing you."

Her eyes widened.

"There are other places I can kiss you that you'll enjoy even more." He slid his thumb from her mouth with a grin.

"Like...like my breasts?" she questioned.

"Like your breasts." He cupped one through the onesie. Hmm, that was entirely too much material between them. "But I was actually thinking of somewhere else."

Her breathing was coming rapidly as she stared at him. "My tummy?"

Damn, she was delightfully naïve.

"Lower."

"Oh." By now her pulse was racing.

"Anyone ever eaten you out, Abby?" he asked. He knew she didn't have a lot of experience, but had none of her sexual partners shown her how good oral sex could be?

"Eaten me out? You mean put their mouth on my...on my..."

"Pussy?" he supplied. "That's exactly what I mean."

"Oh well...I..."

Poor baby she was bright red and struggling to answer him. He took pity on her. "How many sexual partners have you had?"

She narrowed her gaze. "Are you going to answer that question as well?"

"Nope," he said honestly. "But I'm willing to bet it's probably a lot more than you've had. The number doesn't matter, Abby, but you are expected to be honest with me."

She sighed. "One."

"Tell me about it."

"I can't tell you," she squeaked.

He raised an eyebrow. "Baby, you don't need to be embarrassed. I just want to know what your experience is."

"Well, you know that expression 'wham-bam-thank-you-ma'am'?"

"Yes," he said slowly.

"It was that. Without the thank you. Basically, it was me and Joey McBride in the back of his truck, parked up on the outskirts of town."

"Oh fuck, and that was your first sexual experience?"

"First and only." She averted her gaze from his. "So, now that you know how ridiculously inexperienced I am, are you sure you still want to be with me?"

Did she seriously think he would turn her away because her entire sexual experience was an awkward fumble with Booger McBride?

"Baby girl, I want nothing more than to throw you over my shoulder, carry you into my bedroom, tie you to the bed and spend all day showing you exactly how amazing sex can be. I want to eat your pussy until you scream, suck your nipples until you squirm, hear you beg, feel your mouth around my cock. I want to explore every inch of you then start all over again."

She snapped her head up to gape at him, her mouth wide open. "But? There's a but, right?"

"But I don't want to take advantage of you. You're in my house, my bed, I'm a dominant guy. It could be easy for me to overwhelm you. I want your head clear and for you to be very sure before you get into my bed, well, you know, other than to sleep. Because unlike every other sexual encounter I've ever had, I'm not going to let you go once you're there. Okay, that sounded a bit creepy stalker. I promise I'm not going to lock you in the basement. I don't have a basement. And now I'm rambling..." He took a deep breath and shook his head. "Damn, I've never been this nervous in my life."

"You're nervous?" Her face softened as she stared up at him in surprise.

He nodded. "I'm nervous. I don't want to say something that might scare you away. This is intense. I get it. It's only been a week and I already want everything. I want you in my bed, but more than that I want you in my life. And I'm trying really hard not to push and I think I'm failing at that and I..."

She reached up and placed a finger against his lips. It was then he realized his cheeks felt hot. What the hell was he doing? What happened to confident and suave? Shit. He hadn't acted like this much of a fool since he was a teenager...all it took was one Little with big eyes and the sweetest smile and he became a bumbling idiot.

"I really mean that much to you?"

He lightly nipped her finger then drew her hand away, taking a deep breath. Time to take charge again. Center himself.

"You do."

"I've never meant anything to anyone before. I mean, my nana loved me, but...I mean, not that you love me or anything...I just...God, I want to shut up now."

He shook his head. "I think we both need a cup of coffee and some breakfast."

"Really?" she asked. She bit at her lip, staring up at him shyly. "Because I was thinking that throwing me over the shoulder and tying me to the bed stuff sounded kind of nice."

ice? *Nice?* Was that really the best she could come up with?

How about hot? Amazing? Intriguing? Fucking unreal?

Nope. Best she could come up with was nice. But Kent didn't seem to notice or didn't care. His eyes flared; hunger filled his face.

"Yeah?"

"Yeah," she whispered. "If that's what you want too?"

"I think I've already made it clear that it is." He grabbed her around the back of her neck. Okay, she never thought that she'd go for a dominant guy. But she melted whenever he took charge.

"You want me," he muttered. "First thing you're gonna do is lose the onesie."

Okay, that was straight to the point. She guessed a onesie wasn't exactly sexy. She didn't own anything sexy. She didn't own any clothes anymore. She pushed that thought from her head.

Except, there was just one problem with losing the onesie.

"I'm practically naked underneath," she muttered. All she wore were some cotton panties

He grinned. It was a wild grin. Wicked. Ravenous. "Good."

Nope. Not good. Cause while he might look like a Greek God, she did not.

But how did she tell him that?

He knows what you look like. He's not blind. Yeah, but seeing her in clothes and seeing her nearly naked were two completely different things.

"You're already thinking too much. Gonna have to fix that." He cupped her face, raising it. "You did some reading into Daddy/little girl relationships?"

"Y-yes."

"What about into BDSM?"

"Yes, that too."

"Good girl. Abby, in the bedroom, I like to be in complete control. Can you submit to me? Can you trust me to know that I won't hurt you?"

She took in a breath. How did she feel about that?

She knew she could trust him. She wouldn't be here if she couldn't.

"I don't know what I like or dislike."

"Then we'll find out together. I'll never push you more than you can take. I'm not hardcore. You'll have a safe word if you get scared or you're in any sort of pain."

"W-what exactly do you plan on doing?"

"Nothing too scary, I promise. Choose a safeword now. Something you wouldn't say during sex."

"Huh. Okay. How about tutu?"

"Tutu is good. How do you feel about being bound?"

"I want to try. I trust you."

"I'm so thankful you do. Later, we can discuss any other limits.

But what you do need to know is this means you're agreeing to be mine. I'm not doing this casually."

Happiness filled her. How was this not a dream? "Me either. I want to be yours."

A slow grin crossed his face. "Even though being mine means you follow my rules and submit to my discipline if you break them."

"Are you trying to talk me out of it?" she demanded, feeling a bit disgruntled.

"Nope, just don't want you to claim ignorance when you find yourself over my knee getting your butt paddled."

Well, shit.

"I'm going to struggle to ever hide anything from you, aren't I?"

"Nope. Because you're never going to hide anything from me. I'm going to know you inside out."

"And will I know you inside out?" she asked.

"Everything I can tell you. There are some things about my job that will never touch you. And that's not negotiable," he said firmly. "So, I need the words. You're gonna be mine, you're gonna follow my rules and accept my discipline if you're a naughty girl, both as my sub and my Little."

"Yes."

"No, I mean I really need you to say the words."

Oh crap. "Who knew you'd be such a talker?"

He grinned. "I'm very good at contract negotiations and I like things to be very clear and out in the open. So?"

She couldn't believe she had to do this. "I'm going to be yours; I'll follow your rules and...accept your discipline if I'm a naughty girl as your sub and your Little."

She still didn't know exactly what all that would entail. But excitement and need far outweighed the nerves.

"So, do we get to have sex now?" she blurted out. Fuck. Why did she go and say that?

"Oh no, baby. We're not having sex."

They weren't? What the hell?

"We've going to have out-of-this-world fucking sex."

"Oh. That sounds nice."

Nice. Again, with nice. What was wrong with her?

Suddenly he lifted her over his shoulder. She squealed and he slapped his hand down on her onesie-covered ass.

"Kent!"

"That's Sir to you, sweets. Or Daddy." He walked into the bedroom and placed her down next to the mattress on the floor. He pulled away the roof of the fort. "Lie down, baby. Now."

She obeyed the command in his voice, laying on her back. He knelt next to her, reaching for the zipper of her onesie.

"Wait, Kent, I mean, Sir!" She grabbed hold of his hands.

He raised an eyebrow. "Yes?"

"I just...I mean...are you sure we have to take this off?" Okay, that sounded silly even to her.

"I'm not fucking you in it," he told her bluntly. "So yes." He reached for the zipper; she grabbed his hands again. Fuck. Shit. What was she doing? Of course, he had to take it off. "Can I get under the covers?"

"You got a problem with being naked?"

"I've got a problem with my pouchy stomach and huge thighs," she blurted out.

He scowled. "Abby, you're fucking gorgeous. This shit about your body, it's all in your head. And I know that means that no matter what I say, you're probably not going to believe me, so I'm going to have to show you. But first, I'm going to need to get this onesie off you. Okay?"

"Okay," she replied nervously, letting go of his hands. "I'm sorry, I'm just nervous and I'm not really sure what to do and I want to make this good for you."

He smiled at her gently. Then he ran his finger down her face.

"You don't have to worry about what to do or making this good for me. That's my job. I'm in charge. All you worry about is doing what I tell you and that will please me greatly. Can you do that?"

"Yes, I think so."

"Yes, Sir."

"Yes, Sir," she repeated shyly.

"I like hearing you call me Sir."

"You do?" she asked breathlessly as he undid the zip and tugged off her onesie, revealing her breasts. He sucked in a sharp breath. "Oh hell, yes. I do. Damn you're beautiful."

She was? She didn't think so. But the way he stared at her...okay, maybe he was right. She probably wouldn't believe the words out of his mouth. But when he gazed at her like she was a Christmas present he couldn't wait to unwrap...well, she found herself slightly less worried about being naked in front of him.

And she liked that she was pleasing him. She wanted to do more to take away that frown from his face. To make him smile. From their conversations, she gathered he worked a lot. And his work sounded stressful and sometimes dangerous. The more she could do to ease that stress, the better.

He drew the onesie off each arm and then grabbing it, tugged it down her hips.

He ran his hand down her stomach then cupped her panty-covered mound. Her heart raced. "Fuck me, baby. I need you so bad."

She glanced down at his cock and saw the truth in his words. She bit her lip. He'd grown longer, thicker. The head was a purplish-pink color. She'd never thought of a cock as beautiful before, but she had that fleeting thought before he dragged the onesie off her ankles and threw it aside.

Then before she could grow nervous or think about hiding herself, he laid himself over her. His forearms held him up so she didn't have to take his entire weight. He leaned in and kissed her.

This kiss was hot. His tongue was demanding, he nipped at her lip, he kissed his way along her jawline to tug at her ear. He laid a kiss behind her ear and she swore she felt it all the way down to her clit.

Her breath grew raspy. She wrapped her arms around his neck. She should do something, give him pleasure in return, she just didn't know what.

"You're thinking too hard," he said as he laid tiny nips down her throat.

"I don't know what to do," she groaned. "How to please you." Because when it got down to it, that's what she truly wanted. To please him.

"Obeying me, pleases me. Not holding back pleases me. But I've got a way of helping you let go." He rolled and she made a noise of protest, reaching for him.

"Don't leave."

He glanced back. "I'm not leaving baby. I'm just getting something." He crawled off the mattress then stood and walked over to the closet and she made a low noise of pleasure as she watched his ass. Oh God. Who knew he'd have such a gorgeous ass?

He turned and grinned. "Like what you see?"

"Uh-huh," she replied, not even bothering to pretend she wasn't checking him out. Who wouldn't stare when such deliciousness was presented to them? He bent down to grab something from the wardrobe and her heart raced so hard she thought she might have a heart attack.

"If I die, I'm gonna die happy," she muttered.

"You're not going to die, sweetheart. Although I'm glad the sight of my butt sends you into cardiac arrest."

She just shook her head with a laugh as he set a large, brown leather bag on the mattress. "What's that?"

"This is my big bag of tricks."

"You're a magician?"

He laughed. "Not quite." He drew out a light blue rope. "Feel this."

She touched the rope gently. "It's so soft."

He nodded. "It's jute rope. Soft but very strong." He glanced down at her wrists and frowned. "Only we won't be binding you today with that wrist. Damn."

He seemed like he was growing mad all over again.

"It's okay, it doesn't really hurt anymore." Much.

He shook his head. "Unacceptable that you were hurt at all. I don't want to risk it. One day I'm going to bind your entire body. A lot of subs get a feeling of peace from it. Security."

"Really?" she asked.

"Yes, but for now I want you to put your hands behind your head and keep them there."

She followed his instructions.

"Good girl. Does that feel okay? Not hurting your wrist in that position?"

God, who was this man? If she could have built the perfect man, she thought it would have been him. "I'm good."

"You're more than good." He winked at her. "But tell me if that changes, baby. Don't move them without my permission."

He ran a finger down her cheek. "So beautiful." He moved his finger lower and circled her nipple. "I'm going to have fun introducing you to all sorts of pleasure, my sweet girl."

He ran it down her stomach. "Spread your legs." His voice changed. Became lower, more demanding and she could do nothing else but obey.

"That's my good girl." He slipped her panties to one side to run a finger along her slit. Then he drew his finger free and placed it in his mouth. "Yum. Even more delicious than I had imagined."

"I can't believe you just did that." She gaped at him.

"Oh, baby. I am going to love corrupting you."

Not as much as she was going to love being corrupted, she was pretty sure. He lay alongside her, cupping her breast with her nipple. "I wish I wasn't in so much need of you, I want to explore you slowly, relish it, drive you to orgasm over and over. But I'm so fucking in need of you, and we don't have the time right now. Once we do, expect to spend the day in bed with me loving on you, fucking you, taking you."

"We could make the time for that now, Sir."

He grinned up at her. "Greedy girl. I like it."

He leaned in and took her nipple into his mouth...and oh, save her. It was like fireworks going off in her blood. Her clit throbbed. Her body went tense, her hips rising as though seeking his touch as he sucked on the tight nub.

"Kent! Sir!"

He lapped at the nipple and she could swear the room spun. She'd never felt anything like it. So this was what all the movies and T.V. shows had been trying to depict? This overwhelming sense of pleasure and need and...and hunger.

"Please! Please!" she cried out.

"My baby needs me as much as I need her," he muttered as he moved his mouth lower.

"Yes. Yes!"

He sat and tugged off her panties, throwing them out of the fort. He stared down at her. "Beautiful. I need to see more. Touch you. Taste all of you. Spread your legs further apart. That's it. Sir wants to feast."

Oh fuck, he did not just say that. But then he settled himself on his stomach between her legs...and oh hell, did he feast. First, he spread her open and leaned his face in close, breathing in deep.

Shit. Shit. He was sniffing her? What if he didn't like her scent?

"Damn, baby, that's a fucking aphrodisiac."

Okay, he liked the scent of her. That was good...that was, oh holy shit. He took a long, slow lick of her. He started at the bottom then moved up until he flicked lightly at her clit.

Yes! She let out a low cry as he lapped at her clit. Slow then fast. Then slow again.

Torture. Pure torture. Then he pushed his tongue lower again, against her entrance. And then he drove his tongue inside her. She gasped, her hips driving up as he fucked her passage with his tongue. He placed his thumb on her clit, rubbing it back and forth as he drove her higher and higher. It felt like the build-up went forever and then she crashed. She dove over the edge. Wave after wave of release swamped her as the world faded to nothing around her. Just him. Only him. The movement of his tongue slowed; the touch of his thumb grew lighter until he drew back completely.

She whimpered, not wanting him to leave. But he didn't go far. He rolled onto his back then lifted her onto him. "You can move your arms now, baby."

She blushed as she realized they were still behind her head. She pretty much collapsed on top of him. Resting her head on his chest. His heart beat fast and sure beneath her head.

She sighed happily.

"How you doing, baby?" he asked as he ran his hand up and down her back.

"Good," she said huskily.

"I'm glad. You really lose yourself in an orgasm, don't you? It always so intense for you?"

"I don't know," she admitted.

"I know you didn't get any pleasure from your encounter with Booger McBride." Oh crap, he did know Joey's nickname. "But surely, you've given yourself pleasure before. Don't you masturbate?"

"Not very often," she whispered. "I mean, I try every now and then but...oh God, am I really talking about how often I masturbate?"

He chuckled. "Yep. And don't expect it to be the last time.

There is nothing that a Little girl can't say to her daddy or that a sub can't say to her Dom."

He pressed up slightly and she felt the head of him knock at her entrance. "Fuck, I want nothing more than to take you bareback." He rolled her onto her side then reached back into the drawer, she guessed to get a condom.

"You can if you want," she said shyly.

He froze and turned back to her. "You protected against getting pregnant?"

She nodded. "I'm on the pill for my period pain. And oh God, now I'm talking about period pain...what is wrong with me?"

He kissed her as she stared at him in mortification. "There is nothing wrong with you. Nothing you can't say to me, baby. And who do you think is going to be taking care of you when you have your period?"

Umm, well, she hadn't actually given that any thought. But okay, she needed to stop being so squeamish about these things.

"Are you sure? I can wear a condom if you want. I want you protected."

"I'm sure."

He leaned in and kissed her. God, she loved when he kissed her. Then he rolled her gently onto her back, pressing himself between her legs. She wrapped her arms around his neck as the head of his cock entered her, stretched her.

"Fuck, baby, you're like a goddamn glove around me. Christ, how am I meant to last when you feel this good and I'm not even fully seated inside you. This is going to end embarrassingly quickly."

"I don't care, Sir."

"Well, I do. Can't have you thinking sex is always wham-bam."

"This has far exceeded any of my expectations," she told him.

He laughed. "Well, good."

"Oh, that maybe didn't sound right."

"No, baby. It sounded perfect." This time when he kissed her, it was lighter, gentler, then he moved his hips, pressing forward, seating himself fully.

And she was so full. It felt amazing. Despite that spectacular orgasm he'd just given her, she found herself greedy for more. He pulled back. Then thrust forward. Slow at first. So slow. She wiggled beneath him, wanting more. Needing it. But he wasn't going to be rushed.

"Sir, please!"

"You need something, sweetheart?"

"More, I need more."

Sweat slickened her skin, her breathing came in ragged pants. There was something waiting for her. She was on the cusp of something great. He shifted slightly, and his shaft brushed against a spot inside her that had her tightening around him.

"Sir!"

"Like that, baby?"

Like? Like? It was so far beyond like. "Please! More!"

"Oh, it would be my pleasure."

AND IT WAS. He drove himself deep. Fuck, he hadn't been lying before, she was like a soft, silky glove around him. So tight, he had worried for a moment he might hurt her. But there was no pain in her face, just a growing, glowing pleasure that he got to bask in the light of.

He rubbed himself against that spot that made her eyes widen and her breath quickened. He moved faster. He couldn't hold back much longer and he wanted her coming with him. He reached between them to rub at her clit.

"You're going to come when I do, baby."

"Sir! Sir!"

Kent rubbed at her clit. He felt her tighten, knew she was close.

Then she screamed, bucked and came around him, her pussy rippling, drawing forth his orgasm. His own shout of pleasure filled the room, rocked his very soul. He drove deep, never wanting to move again as he collapsed on top of her. Then realizing he was resting his entire weight on her and no doubt making it hard for her to take a proper breath, he forced himself to roll to her side.

"Fuck, baby."

"Oh wow."

"Wow, huh?"

She rolled with a giggle to face him. "Oh yeah. Want to do it again?"

He groaned. "I've created a monster."

"I didn't know sex could be that good. I finally understand what everyone was talking about."

"Everyone?" he asked as he gathered her close.

"Well, everyone on T.V. and in movies."

"Ahh." He kissed the top of her head.

"So," she said, "what else have you got in that magic bag of tricks?"

19

She studied the wardrobe full of beautiful clothes and felt like a fraud.

What was she doing here? Doubts filled her head, making it ache. She shivered slightly. The towel Kent had wrapped around her after their shower together was now damp. Yep, after having absolutely mind-blowing sex with the most gorgeous man on the planet she'd showered with him.

Naked.

Well, naked was the normal state to have a shower in, after all. She shook her head. She was a mess. For a brief period, she'd managed to forget the state of her life. When Kent took charge, it was like the stress melted off and then when he'd touched her, when he drove her up to that peak, and she'd crashed...

There had been nothing else.

But now reality was back. Truth was, she could ignore it all she liked but this wasn't going to just go away. What was she going to do?

She sat on the bed, still wrapped in the damp towel and stared around at the beautiful room she was in. It appeared even more gorgeous in daylight. This whole house was spectacular. She was in Kent Jensen's house. She'd slept in his bed. In his arms. She was about to get dressed in the most wonderful clothes she'd ever seen in her life.

And none of it seemed quite real.

Was she...was she really his girlfriend? Stress flooded her, making it hard for her breath. A weight pressed against her chest. She didn't deserve any of this. She wasn't anything special.

Why her?

Abby, stop. You're here. He wants you.

He'd made that clear. And she wanted him. More than she could have ever imagined. In ways she'd definitely never imagined.

She grabbed Boss Hog, hugging him against her. Yeah, her life was a mess. But she also had something good for the first time ever. And she wasn't going to let her self-doubts get in the way, was she?

Well, she was going to try not to.

HE GLANCED at the stairs for the hundredth time. What was she doing?

He shouldn't have let her leave his sight so soon after taking her into bed. When she'd ducked off to get dressed, he'd felt like she needed a bit of time to herself. But giving her too much time could backfire on him. He just hoped like hell she wasn't going to attempt to pull away from him

Well, if she did, he'd just drag her back. Because he wasn't letting go. Maybe he hadn't thought he'd want this sort of relationship, but once he made up his mind about something that was it.

Just as he was about to go up and get her, she appeared in the doorway.

"Hi," she said shyly.

Relief filled him. All right, she didn't look like she'd spent the last twenty minutes devising a way to leave.

"Hey, baby girl. Everything okay?"

"Sort of." She gave him a wry smile. "I guess as good as it can be with everything that's happened."

"I get that." He held out his hand to her. She walked slowly over and slipped her small hand into his. He drew her close and kissed her lightly. "It will be okay. I promise."

She leaned her forehead against his chest. "I know I should tell you I can handle this on my own. But the truth is, I'm totally out of my depth and have been for a while."

"There is nothing that says you have to handle this yourself. It doesn't make you weak or less to ask for help, Abby."

She leaned back. "Do you ever ask for help?"

"All the time."

She narrowed her gaze. "Are you lying to me?"

"Nope. I know when to ask for help." He thought about that. "Most of the time, anyway. My big brother is a nosy bastard who is known to pester me until I tell him what I need help with. Some of my guys can be the same," he said, thinking of Zeke the other night. "But there are times when I don't ask for help even though I should, when I bottle things up. That's usually when the nightmares get to me."

"You have nightmares?"

"Yeah. I was a SEAL, baby. I saw some truly awful things. But some of the worst things that happened were when I got home."

"What do you mean?"

He sighed. "This really isn't a conversation to have before breakfast. Come on." He led her to a breakfast bar stool and lifted her up. He glanced down at her feet with a frown. "Where are your socks?"

"Oh, we didn't buy any."

"Right. That was an oversight. We'll get you some. And some slippers."

"I don't need them. I'm fine," she said quickly. Too quickly.

He reached down and grabbed one of her feet in his hand. She squealed and had to grab hold of the counter to keep herself from flying backwards. "Kent!"

"Sorry, baby. Your feet are freezing. Of course, you need socks and slippers. We'll get them later. Along with a few other things you need that we didn't get. Like hair ties and bath things and any other girly stuff my baby needs."

She rolled her eyes but smiled.

"Wait here. I'll go get some of my socks for you." He raced upstairs and grabbed a pair of warm socks for her. He strode back into the kitchen and then crouched in front of her. "Foot," he demanded.

"I can put them on myself."

"Foot," he repeated.

She poked her foot out and he slid the sock on. He let that foot go and she held out the next foot before he could ask for it. Strange the sense of satisfaction you could get from making sure your baby had warm feet.

He moved back around the kitchen counter and popped some bread in the toaster. "There anything you're allergic to?"

"No. Nothing. You didn't have to cook for me again."

"Got to make certain my baby is well fed. She needs her energy." He leered at her playfully, delighting in her giggle.

He buttered some toast then cut it into fingers. He placed a boiled egg in an egg cup and cut off the top before grabbing a teaspoon. "Here you are baby. Toy soldiers."

She stared down at the plate he put before her like she'd never seen food before.

"You've never had toy soldiers before?" he asked.

"No."

"Well, you're in for a treat. You grab a piece of toast and dip it in the runny egg yolk, see?" he demonstrated then held the piece of toast to her mouth. "Open up for Daddy."

Her breath caught but she didn't protest, opening her mouth so he could feed her.

"That's my good girl," he said warmly.

She smiled then took the piece of toast from him and dipped it once more. He grabbed his own plate and they ate in comfortable silence. The peace felt nice. No stress. No worries.

When she finished her cup of coffee, he got up and poured her another one and she smiled her thanks.

"Shoot," she muttered, pushing away her plate as she glanced at the clock. "I didn't realize it was so late. I need to get to work, can you take me? Oh no, what am I going to do about a uniform? Both of mine were wrecked. Gloria is going to be furious."

He frowned at that last statement. Surely Gloria should be more worried over Abby than a couple of uniforms.

"I don't want you going in to work today," he said calmly.

"What?" She whirled towards him. "What do you mean you don't want me going to work? I have to."

He shook his head. "It's not safe."

"Not safe? But I'll be surrounded by people all day. Besides, we don't know that I'm in any danger."

"Abby, your brother is missing. Your house was torn up. You've been threatened. You're also no longer paying off your brother's debt to one of the most dangerous men in the state. I don't care if you're going to be surrounded by people all day or not. The only way I could assure myself of your safety was if I was to spend all day watching you and I can't do that."

"But I...I can't just take the day off."

"Sure you can, just call Gloria and tell her what's going on."

"Wait, what do you mean I'm no longer paying it?"

"I mean, you're not paying your brother's debts to Markovich anymore."

"But I have to."

"Why?" He grabbed up their plates and took them to the dishwasher.

"I can do that." She came up behind him. "You cooked. I should clean."

"I got this, sweetheart. Why don't you go call Gloria and tell her you won't be in?"

"I can't, Kent. I need the money. I can't just stop paying the debt. Mr. Markovich will get angry."

"Let him. I'm furious with him. It was never your debt to pay in the first place. He had no business taking money from you. I get that he doesn't have any morals or scruples but his days of taking you for a ride are over. And so are the threats being made against you because of Max's fuck ups. From now on, his shit doesn't touch you."

"That sounds great in theory, but—"

He turned to her and grabbed her lightly by the upper arms. "It's not a theory, it's reality. I promise you that. Now call Gloria, tell her you won't be in."

"Kent, she won't like it."

"I don't care."

"Kent! This is my job."

Okay, he could see they needed to have a chat about this. "Did you agree to be mine just a few hours ago?"

"Well, yes, about that..."

"Oh no, you're not taking it back."

She frowned at him. "I wasn't going to take it back. I was just going to say that if you change your mind—"

"I'm not changing my mind, Abby."

By now she had his shirt clutched in her hands. "But if you do—"

"Abby," he growled.

"Because I know I'm not good enough for you, so if you do—"

"What did you just say to me?"

"That if you change your mind—"

"Not that. The other part. About you not being good enough for me."

"Oh. That." Her cheeks flushed red. "Well, it's true, isn't it? You're gorgeous, smart, handsome, look at your house. My house is its poor, several times removed cousin from the wrong side of the tracks. Just like me...wait, Kent! What are you doing?" she squealed as he grabbed hold of her and lifted her onto the counter. He laid her on her stomach with her legs hanging over the edge.

"Kent! Put me down."

"Nope," he said grimly as he secured her flailing arms, pinning her wrists to her lower back. Then he grabbed hold of her sweatpants and pulled them down her legs. Next he grabbed her panties, tugging them under her ass.

"Kent, what are you doing?"

"I'm giving you something you desperately need, little girl." He smacked his hand down on one cheek and she let out a yowl. He shook his head at her dramatics.

He gave her other ass cheek a slap.

"No, I don't! I don't need this." She kicked her legs, trying to wriggle away.

"Oh yes, you do. You need a hell of a lot more than I have time to give you right now too." As he spoke, he continued to smack her ass with a steady rhythm. Smack, cry. Smack, cry. She was going to lose her voice if she kept up that sort of noise. And he might have to soundproof the entire house. He shrugged. If that's what he had to do, he'd do it. Because he didn't intend to give up spanking her. He also didn't intend to go easy on her.

"I do not ever, ever want to hear you put yourself down like that again. You're not to speak badly about your body, about your mind or about where you come from. So what if you don't have as much money as I do, does that make you less than me?"

"N-no," she sobbed out. By now her ass was a nice pink color, but he was going for a deep, dark red.

"That's right, it doesn't. So why would you say that? Does having money make me a better person? Does it make me smarter? Kinder? More loyal? Well?"

"No, Daddy!" she cried out.

He moved his hand lower, down to her thighs. "You are just lucky that you have to call your boss and say you can't come in or I would be getting out my paddle right now."

Her cries grew even louder.

"But don't worry, that will be coming later when we deal with your punishment for not coming to me when you were in trouble."

He laid two last smacks to the place where her ass and thighs met. She lay on the counter, sobbing her heart out.

Aww, poor darling. Even though it wasn't at all a hard spanking, she sounded like she was dying. He let go of her wrists, checking her bruised one and hoping he hadn't injured her.

"Baby, is your wrist okay? I didn't hurt it, did I?" He helped her slide off the counter, cursing himself for not remembering about her bruises.

"My...my wrist?" she managed to get out between sobs.

"Yes." He took gentle hold of her hand, turning it to study her wrist.

"Why are you worried about my wrist when my ass is on fire?" she wailed.

"Because you earned that hot ass. Denigrating yourself is one of Daddy's big no-nos. In fact, I think now is a good time to go through Daddy's rules."

"Wh-what?"

"My rules for your behavior. Remember, you agreed to follow my rules," he pulled her close, hugging her with one arm while he reached around and patted her ass gently with his other hand, "and accept my punishment for breaking them."

"But I-I didn't know about that rule."

He raised his eyebrows. "I'm certain that we had a conversation that night I took you home after the incident at the Suck 'n Blow where I told you that putting yourself down was always going to land you in trouble with me, did we not?"

She shook her head. "I-I guess we did." She reached around to rub her ass but he grabbed her wrist, very gently.

"No rubbing allowed after a punishment spanking."

"A punishment spanking? Doesn't that imply there are spankings that aren't for punishment?"

"There are. There are fun spankings. Or spankings given to release some sort of tension."

"A fun spanking, huh? It sounds like a thing you say to kids to get them to do something. Eat your sprouts, they taste sooo good." She made a face.

He laughed. "Not keen on sprouts?"

She shook her head, as she sniffled and rubbed at her dripping nose.

"Here, baby." Kent grabbed a couple of tissues from a box on the counter and she reached out a hand to take them. But he brushed her hand away and wiped her tears then he held the tissues up to her nose. "Blow."

Oh no.

She just stared at him.

"Blow, Abigail," he said in that low, stern voice that made butterflies flutter in her tummy.

She blew.

He wiped her nose. She checked his face for any sign he found that gross, but his expression didn't change. He opened a drawer and grabbed a pen and paper. He held out his hand to her. "Come, we need to have a chat."

A chat? She didn't want a chat. She wanted to go ice her hot ass. She was cursing the fact that she didn't have a tiny bottom right now. A big ass meant more fat to cushion the blow, right? Only there was also more surface area there for him to cover with that paddle he called a hand. Seriously. That thing should be outlawed. She glared at the offensive appendage.

"Abigail, do you need to spend some time in the corner?"

What? He wasn't serious, right? She gaped at him.

"I'd have sent you there straight away after your spanking but this conversation is important and I didn't want to skip it or rush through it. But if you need some more time to reflect on your spanking and your reason for it..."

"I don't," she said hastily, reaching for his hand and taking a step forward. She tripped and fell against him.

"Whoa, easy, baby. Just walk with small steps."

She glanced down as he helped her stand and she saw that her pants and panties were down around her feet.

Holy shit. How had she not realized she was standing in front of him half-naked? She bent down to grab her pants.

"I didn't say you could put your pants back on, little girl," he said in a low voice that had her freezing.

"I...I can't walk around half-naked." Especially not with her red ass on display.

"Nobody is here but me."

"But what if someone walks past a window or comes to the door? I look like a baboon," she wailed.

He stared at her for a moment then he shook his head with a laugh. "Baby girl, you do not look like a baboon." He tipped up her chin placing a light kiss on her lips. "You look like a naughty girl who has been properly punished. But if anyone comes to the door, you have my permission to pull up your pants."

"Well, thank you very much," she said sarcastically.

"You're welcome," he said seriously.

Lord, help her from killing him. Please.

20

Her prayers must have been answered, because she somehow managed not to attempt to squeeze his throat until he couldn't breathe while he led her, with her taking small steps, over to the sofa. Once he was there, he sat and pulled her onto his lap.

She squirmed. "Can't I do this standing up?"

"Nope. One of the consequences of earning a punishment is having to sit on your hot bottom after. Now, let's talk about your rules and then you can call your boss." He set the notepad on her lap and started to write something along the top.

Daddy's rules for Abby.

Oh crap. She got the feeling she was in trouble.

"When it comes to safety, I am in charge, understand? You will obey any and all safety rules. These are a guide, not the definitive list."

Wonderful.

"First, you need to tell me when you want to leave the ranch," he told her.

"Well, since I need you to take me because I don't have a car that part is kind of a given," she pointed out. "Oh, unless I ask someone else, I guess."

"If you ask someone else, the first thing they will do is check with me."

She frowned; not sure she liked the sound of that. "I'm a prisoner?"

"Of course not. But even when you do have your car, which you won't be driving again until it has new tires and has been checked by a mechanic to make certain it's safe, I expect to know when you're leaving the ranch."

"I'm a prisoner." She stared at him, horrified.

"Of course not." He appeared appalled. Then thoughtful. "It's something both Clint and I agree on. We like to know when people leave and arrive. It helps us keep everyone safe."

"And that's important to you, keeping everyone safe," she said quietly, having some insight into him now.

"It is. Remember how I talked to you before about things getting bad after I left the service?"

She nodded. He ran his hand up and down her leg, gazing off into the distance. "Well, I was really one of the lucky ones, even though I didn't feel at home here on the ranch. Which was weird considering the happy childhood I'd had here. But it felt like there was nothing here for me. I wasn't born to be a rancher. But at least I had Clint and Eden. A friend of mine, he didn't have anyone. He went home only to have his old man get into a drunken rage and kick him out. All his friends apart from me and one or two others were still in the service. He went down to a bar and got drunk then he drove his truck off a cliff."

"Oh God, Kent." Her heart ached for him.

"Yeah, I know. If he'd just had a safe place to go to when he got out. People that understood. If I'd just reached out to him."

"Oh no, you can't blame yourself. You were struggling too."

"But I was in a much better place than he was. Physically and mentally. I should have been there for him."

"But you didn't know."

"I didn't even know he was struggling. I felt that if I had just called him, I could have prevented it. I know in all likelihood that wasn't true, but I'm a guy that likes to take care of those around him. I felt like I failed."

"That's not true."

"Maybe not. Maybe yes. But it gave me the impetus I needed to do something. I started JSI. I hired mainly all ex-military. Some I knew, some I didn't. The only people I hire who live here are ones who share the same views that Clint and I do about relationships. But I have people who live in other places that work for me. And I have organizations that I support that are set up to help ex-armed forces. I can't help everyone, but I can do my bit."

"Oh, Kent, you're doing much more than your bit." She leaned her head against his chest. He kissed the top of her head.

"All those people I help? Who work for me? Not one of them is more important to me than you, baby girl. So, you tell me, if you're in trouble, do you think I won't do everything I have to in order to protect you? That I won't spend every day keeping you safe? Don't you think that a few rules about safety are worth peace of mind for me?"

She didn't really need to think about it. She stared up at him. "Of course, they are. All right, what's next?"

She really was a sweetheart. He didn't fool himself for one minute into thinking she was going to take to all of his rules so easily, but safety was the big one for him.

"When you leave the ranch, I need to know where you're going and when you'll be back. I understand this seems controlling..."

"It's okay, Kent. Really. I can do that."

"If you think you'll be late, you need to call and tell me."

"Sure, that's just common courtesy. I'll expect the same in return."

He smiled and kissed her forehead. "Of course, baby. I travel a lot and that always comes with delays but I will always let you know as soon as I can."

She frowned. Was she upset at the idea of him being away from her? He couldn't help the surge of satisfaction at the idea. Because, Lord knew, he didn't want to be apart from her. And he had some ideas of how he could change that, but he wasn't going to bring that up right now. He knew he had to move slowly so as not to scare her off.

"All right," she said quietly.

"I think I've made it clear that there will be no talking badly about yourself." He noted that down on the piece of paper.

She wrinkled her nose. "I'll try."

He lowered his chin, staring at her sternly. "You will do more than try, understand?"

She nodded.

"Yes, Daddy." She squirmed on his lap, but he held her still.

"Calm down, baby. We're not finished yet. Next rule, obeying the law."

She stiffened. "What do you mean? I always obey the law." Her eyes widened in horror. "Do you think I'm like Max?"

"Shh, sweet girl," he said soothingly. "That's not what I think at all. I know you're nothing like your brother."

She relaxed slightly. "Then what did you mean?"

"I meant things like when you're driving that you will stick to the speed limit. No texting, always wear your seat belt, no jaywalking."

"No jaywalking, right." She giggled. Then her smile died. "Oh, you were serious."

"I am serious. You get caught jaywalking or taking risks

crossing the road and I'm going to think that you need more supervision."

She had a stupefied look on her face. He thought that might just be enough for now. There was just one more thing.

"If Max contacts you, then I want to know immediately. Same goes with anyone associated with him, Mr. Markovich or those other people. I don't intend to let you out of my sight for long until this is settled, but this rule is very important and I need your promise."

"What will you do if one of them does contact me?"

"That's not for you to worry about."

"But I am worried. I don't want you doing anything that will end with you hurt or in jail."

He rocked her slightly back and forth. "I appreciate that you're worried about me, little one. But I can assure you I've dealt with people far nastier and more dangerous than these people are."

"I just feel like all I'm bringing to this relationship is problems," she muttered.

He leaned her back to stare into her face sternly. "Hear me well, these issues are just a blip on the radar. I know everything seems terrible and insurmountable to you, but I'm going to take care of them and then we can concentrate on you and me. Besides, these problems have gotten you right where I want you." He grinned at her.

She rolled her eyes. "Half-naked and on your lap?"

"You got it, babe. So, that promise?"

"I promise."

"I promise, what?"

"I promise to tell you if Max or Mr. Markovich or that other man call or approach me, Daddy."

"Good girl." He kissed her lightly. "I'm proud of you, by the way."

She blinked. "You are?"

Poor baby, she appeared so shocked. Had she not heard that very often?

"None of this is easy. This shit with Max, your house, me."

"You?"

He nodded. "I know this sort of relationship probably isn't what you ever had planned and I can be demanding, especially when it comes to safety—"

She reached up and placed a finger against his mouth. "Oh Kent, don't you know?"

"Know what?"

"You're the one bright spot in my life. It's the only thing getting me through all this other crap." She sighed. "I just hope you don't come to regret any of it."

He hugged her tight. "I can assure you, I won't." Then he glanced at the clock with a low curse. "Abby, you better call your boss. Best to give her as much time as possible to get someone else in. Although she could try doing some of the work herself."

She didn't want to. She wanted to sulk and refuse. But she knew it had to be done. Damn, she hated talking to Gloria, though. She did not take bad news well.

She snorted. "Fat chance of that happening."

He lifted her off his lap and sat her on the sofa. Ouch! She leaned to the side to take the weight off her sore bottom. Then he stood and walked over to grab his phone off the counter. "Here, use my phone."

"Um, I'll just go upstairs. Can I pull my pants up now?"

"You can make the call here. Pants stay where they are."

She wrinkled her nose then glared at him.

"You can always make the call from the corner," he said mildly.

She sighed. Then dialed the number for the diner which she luckily knew from memory. Okay, was there a weirder situation than standing half-naked in the kitchen of a man you'd just spent the night with, your panties down around your ankles, your red ass on view, while you called your boss?

If there was, she couldn't think of it.

"Yo, Wishingbone Diner, Ann-Marie speaking."

"Hi, Ann-Marie, it's Abby."

"Abby-girl, you're the talk of the diner today. Everybody's gabbing about how your house got tossed and that you were rescued by that huge hunk of spunk, Kent Jensen. That true? Did he really carry you from your house then take you shopping for a whole new wardrobe?"

"Um, well, that's not quite true."

"Oh," Ann-Marie sounded disappointed. "Figured it wasn't. So, what you want?"

"Can I speak to Gloria?"

"Girl, you do not want to speak to her right now. Her panties are in a bunch over all the attention you're getting."

She winced. That was just wonderful. Kent raised his eyebrows questioningly.

She shook her head. "Please, Ann-Marie, put her on."

"Fine, your funeral."

"What?" Gloria snapped down the phone.

"Um, Gloria, it's Abby."

"Abby, bunch of rumors being spread around about you. Think you better come in early so you can put them to rest. Also, Rachel needs to leave soon so you can cover her shift. So, see you at one."

Her shift didn't start until three. Suddenly, she didn't feel so bad about calling in to take the day off. Gloria had no problems with making her start early or work late or work thirteen days in a row.

"Actually, I'm not coming in today."

"What do you mean you're not coming in today?" Gloria screeched. "You can't just call in and tell me you're not coming in!"

"You've heard about what happened to my house—"

"So what? So, you got a few broken things? I got a business to run! I can't run it if my fucking staff are all fucking unreliable little bitches—"

Kent plucked the phone from her hand. His lips were set in a firm line, anger had tightened his body.

"Abby will not be in today and you will refrain from calling her such names in the future, understand?"

There was silence on the other end. No doubt, Gloria was in a state of complete shock. Abby couldn't feel sorry for her. How dare she call her unreliable? She never took a day off, she was always there early. She worked damn hard and this was the thanks she got? If she had any other prospects for work, she'd tell Gloria where to shove it.

"Well, when will she be in?" she heard Gloria say.

"When I can be assured of her safety, and only after you give her an apology for the way you just talked to her."

Abby gaped up at him. What was he doing? While she might dream about telling Gloria she was quitting, she actually needed this job.

"An apology?" Gloria let out a cackling laugh. "She's not getting a fucking apology from me. Tell her she's fired. I might consider changing my mind if she comes begging, but it'll be for less pay and worse conditions."

Oh shit. Crap.

"That will happen when hell freezes over. Good day. Oh, and don't expect anyone from Sanctuary Ranch to use your diner again."

He switched off the phone on Gloria's screeching.

"Oh God, Kent, what have you done?"

21

Kent was furious.

Otherwise, he might have found the way Abby paced up and down the room, unmindful to the fact that she was half-naked really quite cute. She'd kicked off her pants and panties so she could move more freely.

But he was too angry. He couldn't believe the way Gloria had spoken to Abby. Far as he was concerned Gloria should have been thanking her lucky stars to have an employee as hard working as Abby.

His girl was far too good for that place.

"Kent!" Abby wailed.

He glanced up, saw the very real panic on her face. Right. Her job. Money. Her house. Shit. No wonder she was in a state. Her whole world had collapsed around her.

"Abby, come here," he said in a low voice.

She shook her head, tugging frantically at her hair.

"Little girl. Get over here. Now. You do not want me coming to get you."

"I can't lose my job," she cried as she walked towards him.

He sat and pulled her back onto his lap, hating the way she was shaking. "You loved it that much, then?"

If she did then he'd do whatever he needed to in order to get it back for her. Hell, he'd buy the diner if that's what it took. Actually, that wasn't a bad idea...

"No, I hated it."

"So why are you upset?"

"Um, I think that's pretty obvious."

"You want to watch your tone, unless you want to find yourself being introduced to my paddle. And considering the punishment you have coming; you do not want that right now."

She grew stiff in his arms and he waited for an explosion. Then she suddenly crumpled in on herself. She curled herself into a ball right there on his lap. Drawing her legs up, she buried her face in her knees and sobbed.

"Baby, what is it? Abby, tell me why you're so upset? Was it my threat to spank you?"

Fuck, he'd never felt so unsure or out of control of a situation in his life.

"I'm so sorry," she wailed. "You're being so wonderful and I just snapped at you. I was such a bitch."

"Oh, baby. You could never be a bitch."

He gathered her closer, rubbing her back again. "Hush, now, Abby-girl. You're going to dehydrate yourself soon."

"I've never cried so much in my life!"

"Come on, now. You're worrying Daddy." He stood and carried her into the kitchen, setting her on the counter. She immediately tried to get off. He placed his hands on her thighs.

"Uh-uh, Daddy didn't say you could get down. You need to learn to stay where you are put."

Her mouth dropped. "You did not just say that to me."

"I did."

"But my bottom is bare! It's unhygienic."

He snorted. "That's why they invented disinfectant cleaning spray."

"I'm pretty sure that's not the reason it was invented," she muttered.

He tapped her nose. "Be a good girl and stay there." He walked to the tissues and grabbed a few then wiped her face clean. "Blow."

He knew from the red that filled her face that she didn't appreciate him taking care of her in such an intimate way. Too bad. He wanted to do it. And he was the one in charge. Besides, there were far more intimate things he intended to do with her. He spread her legs and stepped between them. Her eyes widened as he pressed up against her.

"Now that we've established that working in the diner isn't your dream job, you want to tell me what you'd really like to do?"

She started fidgeting.

"Abby? What is it? Or would you rather not work at all?" He knew it made him sound old-fashioned but that would be his preference. He'd keep her by him as much as possible in order to assure her safety.

But he knew he couldn't make that decision for her. He didn't want to smother her in his protection.

"I've always wanted to write children's books. I know that's silly—"

"Why is that silly?"

"I mean, I don't have any experience. But I took creative writing courses at the community college, I didn't graduate because I had to leave to come back and take care of Nana. So, I guess I'd like to finish them then try writing. I don't know if I'll be that successful, but that's what I want to do."

"Then that's what you'll do," he told her. "After we've sorted everything out, you can enroll in college again or look into doing courses online perhaps and we'll go from there."

She stared at him in shock. "Kent, it's not that easy."

He raised an eyebrow. "It's not?"

"I have no money."

"I do."

She sighed. "I'm not letting you pay for college."

"You are. There is no 'letting me' as far as I'm concerned. I've made the decision, it's happening."

"This is not a dictatorship."

"Hate to tell you, baby, but in a lot of ways it is. You get your opinion, but I have the ultimate say. This is what you want, I'm going to make it happen for you."

"We're not talking about some clothes and a few stuffies, Kent. This is college courses and I'd have to find a job while I'm studying to support myself which may not be that easy and I—"

He placed a hand against her mouth. "Listen to me. I'm going to pay for the courses. And I'm going to support you while you go. I want you to be happy, this will make you happy."

She tugged at his hand and he drew it away. "I don't want to use you. I don't want you spending all your money on me."

He laughed. "Baby, I've never worked so hard to spend my money on someone. I'm starting to think I need another rule where every time you argue with me, I get to spank you ten times."

"I'm not arguing with you about money."

He kissed her lightly. "You are."

"Well, crap," she muttered. Then she fell silent, obviously thinking. He walked over and grabbed the pad of paper he'd left of the sofa, ripped off the top piece with her list of rules and pinned it to the front of the fridge.

"Well?" he asked.

"Thank you," she said simply. "That's a really kind thing for you to do."

"Baby, I have plenty of money, but what I really want is for you to be happy. Okay?"

"Okay."

He kissed his forehead. "Thank you. Truth is, I'm glad you're not working at the diner anymore. Gloria was using you, those hours you were working were crazy. I won't have someone taking advantage of you like that."

She smiled.

"Now that's the way I always want my baby to look. Happy and content." He ran his hand up her thigh, towards her naked pussy. He pushed her legs apart wider so he could stare down at her glistening pussy lips.

"Did this pussy get all wet while my baby was being spanked?" he murmured.

"Daddy!"

"Did it?"

She whimpered.

He ran a finger through her slick folds. "Not answering when I ask you a question is very naughty, by the way. And naughty little girls don't get to come."

She groaned. "Yes! Yes, it made me wet. Is that weird?"

He stilled his finger. "Baby, no. Everyone has different needs or desires. What you want is what you want. It's not wrong. So, I don't want you to think that way, all right?"

"All right."

"What do you need? Tell me."

"I can't believe you're going to make me ask!"

He chuckled. "I'm such a mean Sir. Just as well that's balanced by an indulgent daddy, hmm?"

She eyed him. "Indulgent, huh?"

"Yes, I'm very indulgent. You're going to be one spoiled little girl. Luckily, I'll balance that out with plenty of spankings." He thrust two fingers inside her and she cried out.

"Take your top off," he demanded.

"Oh man, oh man," she muttered as she whipped off her t-shirt. She wasn't wearing a bra. He leaned in and took her nipple into his mouth, suckled on it.

She cried out, her pussy tightening around his fingers. Oh, his baby liked having her nipples sucked. He moved to the other breast and lapped at her nipple with his tongue.

"Lie back, arms behind your head. No moving."

With a whimper, she did as he said. She was laid out on the counter like a feast waiting for him to sample. He slipped his fingers free and she cried out. "No, please, Sir!"

"You still haven't told me what you need. There's going to be some punishment for that."

"No...wait...I'll tell you!"

"Too late, sweetheart. Lie exactly there or I'll introduce you to the hairbrush." He strode to the curtains and pulled them. The door was locked already, but he didn't want anyone approaching and seeing his naked girl. That sight was for him and him alone. His possessiveness was raging. He knew it was highly unlikely he would ever take her to a club. Or if he did then he wouldn't allow her to strip down.

Not that he could see her being okay with that anyway.

He raced up the stairs and grabbed his bag. Even though he'd just had her a few hours ago, his body was pumped with adrenaline and his cock pressed demandingly against his jeans. He also reached into the back of the closet for another bag. This had things he'd especially bought for her. Time to see how his baby reacted to having her bottom played with.

He walked back downstairs to find her exactly in position. Hmm, he was going to have to buy some pretty clamps for her nipples, maybe with some stones that matched her hazel-colored eyes.

He set the bag on the floor. Reaching into it, he grabbed a blindfold and slipped it over her head. "What's your safe word, sweetheart?"

"Tutu."

"Very good. Use it if you need to. Don't worry, I'm not going to do anything that will cause you pain. But some things will feel a bit different. I want you to keep your hands above your head, okay?"

"Yes."

"That's my good girl." He grabbed a bottle of lube and the anal plug as well as a Wartenburg wheel. Then he strode to the fridge and scooped some ice out, putting it in a small bowl that he sat on the counter next to her. "Time for some sensation play. Feel this?" He ran the wheel down the inside of her arm.

"Y-yes?"

"Hurt at all?"

"No, Sir."

"Good." He ran it down her other arm. "You tell me if that changes." He ran it across her chest then up one mound. She stiffened as she realized what was coming but then groaned as he lightly ran it against her nipple.

"Sir!" Her nipple was stiff, peaked.

"Like that?" he asked.

"Yes," she cried as he moved to her other breast and did the same. After the wheel did a pass over her nipple, he leaned down and lapped at it with his tongue.

"Oh! Oh!"

He grabbed a piece of ice and placed it in his mouth then suckled on her nipple again. She half-sat with a scream. "Oh God!"

"Lie back," he said in a low voice, pulling back until she obeyed him. "If you can't keep still, I'm going to have to tie you down. And that will make this torture go longer." He ran the wheel across her other nipple, then took the hard tip into his cool mouth.

"Sorry, Sir. Sorry."

"It's okay, baby. You're trying, I know."

Another piece of ice went into his mouth. The wheel ran down her soft stomach, pouchy, huh? He remembered the derogatory word she'd used and didn't like it one bit. So he paid particular attention to her tummy, running the wheel back and forth and chasing it with cool licks of his tongue.

Her soft cries filled the room, her hips rising and falling as though she was begging him to get to the finale. He would. But in his own time. He ran the wheel across her bare mound, then the top of each thigh. Another piece of ice in his mouth, but this one he crunched down on before he spread her lower lips and drew her clit into his mouth.

Her shocked scream drove his own need higher. He suckled on the tight bundle of nerves, flicked at it with his tongue then just pressed against it as he heard her breathing speed up. He didn't want her to come just yet.

"Oh...oh...I need."

"I know you do," he told her in a rough voice. "But you're not to come just yet." He picked up the lube and the butt plug. First, he spread the lube over the small plug that had a tapered end. Then he put a generous dab on his finger.

"I want you to raise your legs to your chest and then hold them there, understand?"

She took in a breath, but didn't say a word as she did as he ordered.

"What a good girl you are," he praised her. "A very good girl to obey Sir like you are. I'm going to reward you very soon. But first, I'm going to play a bit with your ass."

He spread her ass cheeks, studying her puckered entrance. She gasped out a cry. "Sir, no!"

"Oh, you have that wrong. It's Sir, yes please."

"I can't. I don't..." She shook her head back and forth.

"Who is in charge?" he demanded.

"You are."

"Are you using your safe word?"

"No."

"Then you don't get a say, do you?"

"Oh jeez," she muttered.

He decided to put her out of her misery. She was building this up to something in her head and he thought she would be surprised when she discovered that it wasn't scary or awful. He placed his finger against her back entrance.

"Relax," he told her.

"Easy for you to say."

He gave her two sharp smacks on the ass. "Watch your tone."

"Sorry, Sir," she said hastily.

"That's better." He started to press his finger into her hole. She resisted at first, until he rubbed her clit with the thumb of his free hand. Back and forth. Up and down, he moved his thumb as he pressed his finger deep inside her ass.

"Oh. Oh."

"Feels good, doesn't it? Don't you feel silly now?" He finger fucked her ass while tapping at her clit lightly. Her pussy was slick with her desire and his cock throbbed relentlessly. All he could imagine was his cock in her ass, impaling her. Owning her.

Not yet. Prepare her first.

He drew his finger free and she actually groaned in protest. He grinned. His baby liked ass play. That was good. Very good. He reached for the plug and spread her cheeks once more. Next time she was naughty, he might just have her stand in the corner with her bottom poking out, a plug in her ass and her hands spreading her cheeks wide.

Oh, hell yeah.

He pressed the plug against her puckered entrance and she stiffened. "What's that?"

"This is your very first training plug. I have several so we can stretch you until you can take me in your ass. Don't worry this one is very small."

"I think small is a relative term," she squealed as he slowly but relentlessly pushed the plug inside her.

He twisted it slightly then pushed. Then twisted it again. When it was fully seated, he drew it out once more and started the process all over again. Her head thrashed back and forth. His thumb returned to her clit, flicking at it faster and harder until she arched up.

"Sir!"

"Come, baby. Come for me. Come with my plug deep inside your bottom."

She groaned as she shuddered and came. Fuck, that was a sight he would never get tired of. Her face filled with pleasure, her body trembling, her breath coming in sharp pants. He couldn't wait any longer, he had to be inside her. He grabbed her hips and turned her before undoing his pants. He couldn't even wait long enough to fully undress. He took hold of her hips and pressed himself inside her.

"Yes! Yes!" she cried out. Her pussy convulsed around him as he drove in deep. He pulled back, thrust his way back into her tight sheath. Holy hell. He wasn't going to last again. This was getting embarrassing. Maybe next time he'd have her suck him off first and then he might last more than a few minutes. He grasped hold of her ass cheeks, spreading them wide to stare down at the pretty plug decorating her asshole.

"Damn, that is a beautiful sight, baby. You taking my cock, my plug stretching your ass so one day you'll take me there. This gorgeous body spread out for me. I fucking love it."

I love you.

He didn't say the words, though. It was too soon. But he felt them deep inside. He loved his woman. This big Little girl. The sub. Her sweetness. Her spice. All of her.

He gave one final thrust before coming with a deep groan that shook him to the core. He laid kisses across her back as he fought for his breath, his cock still semi-erect inside her.

So, this was what love was? This overwhelming need to be with someone, to keep them safe, to never want to imagine your life without them.

Yeah, this felt right.

22

Abby glanced over at her phone as it rang. Unknown number. She frowned. Things had been quiet on the Max-front. No messages or calls from him or the people after him. Why had they destroyed her house? Anger over her not telling them where Max was? Or something else?

Kent walked into the kitchen, where she was sitting at the counter. He glanced down at her phone. "Answer it. On speaker."

She nodded, and answered the call.

"Abby? About fuckin' time. Abby, you there?"

Max. Her heart pounded. "Max? Where are you?"

Kent remained silent. But she saw him pick up his phone and text someone.

"I'm not telling you that. Did you tell them I was staying with you? Huh? Did you know they nearly caught me? I had to race out the back. No cash. No ID. I been on the run for days, stealing shit, nearly getting caught. Fuck, Abby, did you tell them?"

"No, of course I didn't. I thought maybe they came to the house to find out if I knew where you were."

Beat of silence. "Okay. Fuck. Maybe. Whatever. I need cash. Now."

"I don't have any cash."

More silence. She looked up at Kent. He gave her a grim look back.

"I need cash, Abby. However you got to get it. You still hanging out with that rich prick from Sanctuary?"

"She's living with him," Kent replied.

Only a few seconds ticked by this time. "Fuck, Abby, you got to warn me if I'm on speaker. Who else is fucking there?" His voice got squeaky high.

"Nobody else is here. It's just me and Abby," Kent said quietly. "Where are you?"

"Why? So you can send the fucking cops after me?"

"Might be the only thing that saves your life."

"Not happening, asshole. I need cash, that will get me out of this mess. You're rich."

"Kent is not giving you money, Max."

"He will if he wants me to keep quiet about his weirdo fucking lifestyle. Think all your fancy clients will stick with you if they find out you're a freak?"

"I think that nobody is going to believe a drugged-up idiot who bullies and abuses his own sister," Kent replied sharply.

"Don't talk to me about my sister, pervert," Max shot back.

"Stop," Abby begged. "Max, what do they want from you? Can't you give it back?"

"No, I fucking can't. Look, I took some information. Put it on a flash drive then I lost the damn thing when I had to run. But they won't fucking believe I lost it. You got to send me cash."

"I can't, Max. I'm sorry." Tears dripped down her cheeks. "Please, just tell me where you—"

Before she could finish the sentence, there was a dial tone then nothing. She looked at Kent in shock. "What happened?"

He shook his head, picked up her phone and tried to dial back the number. No answer.

"I don't know, baby."

"He's in so much trouble. Why would he steal from such bad people? I know I shouldn't care, he doesn't care about me, but I can't help it."

"Of course, you can't, Abby-girl. Because you have a big heart." Kent came around the counter and pulled her into his arms, rocking her. "It's going to be all right. I've let Ed know he called. He wants us to come in so you can look at mugshots and give him an update. We can't do anything more. If you send him money, he'll just get into more and more trouble."

"I know," she whispered. She tightened her arms around him. "I'm sorry I've brought such trouble down on you. I can't believe he threatened you like that."

"Hey," he told her, pulling back to stare down at her. "This isn't your fault. And I don't want you to think for one moment that it is. We're going to sort this. Together."

"I CAN'T GO into the police station with a butt plug in my ass," she wailed as he pulled up outside the police station.

Before coming into the sheriff's office, after Max's call, Kent had made her strip off her panties so he could push another anal plug deep inside her.

"Of course, you can," he said reasonably as though it was something a person did every day.

"They're gonna know."

"How will they know?" He undid his seatbelt then turned and undid hers. "Hmm?"

"I don't know, what if they have x-ray machines you have to walk through?"

"Baby, this is Wishingbone, there aren't any scanners at the police station. And even if there were, the plug isn't metal so you have nothing to worry about."

She thought she had plenty to worry about. She chewed on her thumbnail. He pulled her thumb free. "You're going to wear the plug because every time you move, it will remind you that I am with you, that you're not alone."

"A normal boyfriend would just hold my hand."

He chuckled. "I can do that too. Wait there. I'll come get you."

Oh, he didn't have to worry about that. She wasn't going to attempt to climb down with this thing up her butt. What if it fell out? Mortification filled her.

Kent opened the door and reached up for her, lifting her down. Then he took hold of her hand and closed the door. "You're worrying too much."

"I've got a lot to worry about."

He leaned in and brushed his lips against her ear. "No, you don't. All you have to worry about is obeying me. Pleasing me. Understand?"

She understood he was extremely arrogant. But somehow, that arrogance actually helped settle her. So when they were finally seated at a desk across from one of the deputy sheriffs, she thought she was acting pretty normal.

Ed walked up to them and shook her hand then Kent's. "Thanks for coming in. Jace will take you through some mugshots. You'll both be pleased to know that we got the guys who attacked you and Eden the other night. So that's one less thing to worry about. And your house has been released, so you can get back in to tidy it up."

"I'll get some people onto that," Kent told her. She decided not to argue. She didn't want to step foot in that house right at this moment.

"So Max didn't give any clues about where he is?"

Kent went through the entire conversation with the sheriff, who gave her a reassuring look at the end of it. "Don't stress too much about this, okay? We'll find your brother and these guys."

Okay, so maybe she wasn't pulling off the 'everything is normal' thing as well as she thought. Ed gave her hand a final squeeze, grinning as Kent growled and glared at him.

She slipped her hand free and nudged Kent. "You can't growl at the sheriff," she scolded as Ed walked away.

"He held your hand too long."

She rolled her eyes at his possessiveness. But she had to smile as well.

Fifteen minutes later, she no longer felt the urge to smile. "Him. It's him." She pointed a shaking finger at the photo of the man who'd approached her in the parking lot of the diner and grocery store.

"You're sure?" Jace, the nice deputy asked.

"Yes. I am."

Jace called Ed over. He stared down at the shot with a frown. "Well, shit."

"What is it?" she asked with alarm.

Ed glanced at Kent. She didn't understand the look they shared. "What?"

Kent nodded at Ed. "Tell us both."

"That's Dirk James. He's an enforcer for a crime family in Seattle. Bad news. How did Max get mixed up with the Bartollis?"

She had no idea, but Max had a knack for getting himself into the worst sort of trouble.

"All right, we've got something to work on. Thanks for coming in, sweetheart. Why don't you go and get some rest, you're exhausted."

Rest? How could she rest?

"I'll take care of her," Kent said quietly. "Thanks, Ed."

Twenty minutes later, she gazed out the window as Kent parked the truck. What were they doing at Walmart?

"What are we doing here?" she asked. She could barely remember leaving the police station. She guessed Kent had helped her. She was still in shock over learning how much trouble Max was in.

Much as she hated him sometimes, she didn't want to imagine him in pain or...or worse.

She bit back a cry at the thought.

"We're going to get you a few things to help you relax," he told her.

"I don't need anything. I want to go home. I mean, your home."

"You were right the first time, it's your home too." He undid his seatbelt.

"I'll wait here." She didn't want to deal with people right now. She didn't want to adult right now. She bit her lip, she wished she knew how to free her Little. She wished she could ask Kent for help doing that.

She didn't realize she was chewing on her thumbnail until Kent rescued it from her mouth.

"You're not waiting here. You're not leaving my sight. Come on. You're so stressed you're going to make yourself sick."

He climbed out of the truck then came around and didn't give her any choice but to get down. She dragged her feet as they went into the store, but he didn't seem to notice or if he did, he didn't say anything. He kept a tight hold of her hand as they walked inside.

"Stay close to my side," he ordered her as he picked up a basket, letting go of her hand. He moved down the aisle, picking up a few items and putting them in the basket. There were hair ties, bubble bath, bath toys. Things she might have been more interested if she had the energy to spare.

They reached the aisle filled with nail polish and she stopped, staring at the colors. It had been a while since she'd painted her nails. She didn't notice Kent getting further away.

"Abby? Abby!" She heard him call out.

She turned to him, surprised to see worry and a bit of anger in his face. "What?"

"What did I tell you about sticking by my side?" He gave her several sharp taps on the ass that made her jump. They stung, but didn't really hurt. However, they did cut through the fog in her head.

"Kent!" She glanced around, thankfully they seemed to be on their own. "You can't do that in here."

"Who is in charge?"

Oh shit.

"You are. But we're in public!"

"If you're naughty then I'm going to address that where and when I see fit."

"I'm...I'm sorry I was just looking at the nail polishes."

He took a deep breath, let it out slowly. "Just stay with me, okay? Here, you hold this basket then I can have a free hand to hold yours."

He led her around the store, adding a few nail polishes to the basket she held. By the time they reached his truck, she was yawning. He helped her inside, doing up her belt.

"Close your eyes, baby. Try to get a bit of rest. I was going to put you down for a nap today, but it's so late now I'll just put you to bed early."

"I don't need to go to bed early!" She was slightly surprised at the childish note to her voice.

"Well, luckily, you don't decide things like that. I do. Close your eyes. Rest."

She sighed and obediently closed her eyes. Images of Max rushed through her mind, each one more terrifying than the last. She opened her eyes with a gasp.

"Abby-girl? What is it?"

"I can't rest. When I close my eyes, I keep thinking about every bad thing that could be happening to Max. I mean, I know he brought it all on himself, but he's still my brother. I don't want him to get hurt or die."

"I know you don't, sweetheart." He squeezed her thigh. "You can't keep thinking about it or you will drive yourself insane."

"It's hard not to think about it." She rubbed at her temples.

"Headache?" he asked.

"Little bit."

"Probably stress and exhaustion. When we get home, I'll run you a bath. Afterwards we can snuggle up and watch a movie. What's your favorite movie?"

"Um, *Fast and Furious*?"

"I was thinking more along the lines of *Beauty and the Beast*."

"Oh, I do like *Tangled*."

"*Tangled* it is. Just let me take care of you, baby."

SHE SAT on the sofa and stared at the show on the T.V. screen not really seeing it. Kent was upstairs drawing a bath for her. She chewed at her thumbnail worriedly. Where was Max? Was he okay? Please, let him be okay.

She had this horrible feeling he wasn't, though.

"Abby?" A hand landed on her shoulder, making her startle with a scream. She whirled to find Kent standing behind her. "Damn, baby, you're jumpy."

"Sorry. Sorry." She placed her hand against her chest as her heart threatened to leap out of her chest.

"No, I'm sorry. I should have thought..." He sighed. "Come on, sweetheart. I've got a bath ready for you. Let's help you relax."

She stood and walked towards him, taking his hand. "I don't think I can relax."

"We'll see."

She followed him up the stairs and into the main bathroom. He'd drawn her a bath filled with bubbles.

"This looks nice. Thank you."

"Thank you, Daddy," he prompted.

"Thank you, Daddy," she said shyly.

He reached for her top to pull it off. She took a step back. "I can do that."

"Nope, Daddy is taking care of you tonight. Completely."

"Oh," she said. "And that means I can't undress myself?"

"Nope," he replied. He pulled off her clothing, throwing it into the corner of the room.

"You shouldn't throw clothes like that," she scolded.

"I'll pick it up later, Miss Tidy Pants," he teased her.

She knew he was trying to lighten her spirits and granted him a small smile.

"Well, it was tiny but I'll take it," he said.

Once she was naked, he grasped her around the hips and lifted her into the bath. He'd taken the butt plug out as soon as they'd gotten home, much to her embarrassment.

"Oh, this feels so good," she said as she sat. The warmth of the water soothed her tight muscles.

"I thought my girl would enjoy a bath. You just lie back and let Daddy wash you."

He grabbed a cloth and soaping it up, began washing her arms and shoulders. He moved down to her breasts, running the cloth across each nipple making them harden. A tremble rocked her, but he didn't linger, moving down her stomach then down to each foot.

When he rubbed the cloth over the bottom of her feet, she giggled.

"My girl is ticklish," he commented, doing it again.

"Stop, Daddy," she laughed.

"That's better," he said with a smile. "I don't like seeing you stressed and upset."

"I don't like it either." He placed the cloth higher up her thighs and she took in a sharp breath as he washed her pussy, running the cloth between her folds and against her clit. "Oh."

"Does my girl need an orgasm?" he asked in a husky voice.

"Maybe," she muttered.

"Just maybe?" He drew his hand back. She grabbed for his wrist, holding it there.

"No, definitely."

"Thought that might be the case. Just lean your head back and rest." He ran his finger around her clit slowly as his other hand plucked at her nipple.

"Oh. Oh. More," she cried out. He moved his finger harder, faster.

"I want you to come for me. Nice and hard. Let me hear you scream."

Her groans filled the room as she arched her hips up, shudders rocking her body as she finally reached that peak and crashed. Her body slumped into the water as lethargy swept through her.

"Now, she's relaxed," he muttered.

She opened her eyes and smiled up at him dreamily. "You're really good at that."

"Why thank you, little one," he replied with a grin. "Now, if you have the energy, please sit up so Daddy can wash your hair."

"I can do that," she protested.

He just gave her a look.

"Okay, Daddy," she said, sitting.

"Here are your toys to play with." He dropped in a rubber

ducky, an octopus that could squirt water from its mouth and some cups. She grabbed the cups first and filled them up then tipped them out as he wet her hair then lathered it up with shampoo. She stared at the octopus and a naughty thought filled her mind. Kent massaged her scalp and she moaned in delight.

"Close your eyes while I rinse," he commanded.

Water washed down her face as he washed her hair. Then he grabbed the conditioner. She waited until he'd given her another scalp massage. Seriously, the man could make millions from his fingers. They had endless skills. Then she ducked the octopus under the water and squeezed it until it was full of water.

"Okay, time to get out now." He grabbed a towel and when he turned back, she hit him full in the face with the water squirting from the octopus's mouth. Gales of laughter erupted from her at his shocked face. She laughed so hard, she slid under the water. Two firm hands grabbed her, lifting her as she sputtered between giggles.

"Oh Daddy, you're all wet."

"And you're a little brat," he muttered as he set her down on the tiled floor. She shook herself like a dog, spraying water all over him.

He cursed as she giggled even more. A towel was wrapped around her body then another around her head, which ended up covering half her face.

"Trouble maker, you've gotten me all wet."

"Sorry, Daddy," she said, pushing the towel off her face.

"Wish I could believe that you were. You need a reminder about respecting Daddy."

"I'm sorry, Daddy. You're right, I should always respect my elders. And you're really old."

"You're lucky you're so cute, that's all I can say." He dried her off then towel dried her hair before picking her up and carrying her into her bedroom. He set her down next to the bed then gave her a firm smack on the ass.

"Ow!" She pouted as she reached back to rub her throbbing cheek. "That hurt."

"It was meant to." He moved to her closet and chose another onesie. "Need to move your stuff into my room." He crouched before her. "Hold onto Daddy."

She held onto his shoulders while she put first one foot then another into each leg of the onesie. This one was pink and had cats wearing tiaras on it. "Come on, I left your hairbrush and other stuff downstairs."

"My hairbrush is in the bathroom," she told him. It was one of the few things that had survived the destruction of her house.

"I bought you a new one today, remember?"

Yes, and unlike her lightweight plastic thing, the one he'd bought had been a heavy, wooden one.

He led her downstairs and put a cushion on the floor in front of the sofa. "Sit here, baby." He grabbed the big bag of stuff he'd bought and set out the nail polish, hairbrush, a notebook, colored pencils and stickers. "Here, you can draw Daddy a picture while I do your hair."

"You're gonna brush my hair?" She turned in surprise as he settled on the sofa behind her.

"I sure am." He grabbed the hairbrush and started combing her hair. She glanced at the notebook with a shrug. Might as well give it a go. It wasn't long until she was completely occupied with drawing a picture of the beach, the rhythmic feel of the brush going through her hair relaxing her.

"That's a really good picture, baby girl. You're quite talented."

Happiness filled her even though she knew he'd say that if she'd drawn something utterly awful. "Thanks, Daddy."

"I'm going to put it on the fridge next to your rules."

She screwed up her nose at the reminder but carefully ripped out the piece of paper and handed it to him.

"Why don't you sit on the sofa now," he suggested.

She realized her hair was practically dry as she climbed onto the sofa. Kent returned quickly and searched through Netflix for *Tangled*. Then he moved to sit on the coffee table and pulled her foot up onto his lap.

"Daddy? What are you doing?"

"Painting your toes."

"But daddies don't paint toes."

"This daddy does."

She watched him for a moment, certain he was going to muck up and spread nail polish everywhere or only paint half her nail. But she was surprised to see him perfectly paint each individual nail.

"You're really good at that."

"Of course, I am. I'm the daddy of a little girl, aren't I?"

"Have you painted a lot of nails before?" she asked, surprised.

"No, but I painted Eden's after her accident when she was in the hospital for a long time."

Eden had been partially paralyzed from the accident that killed both his parents. It was so sweet to think of him painting his younger sister's nails.

He moved to her other foot and she turned her attention to *Tangled*. When he finished with her feet, he moved to her fingers, painting those as well. She started to yawn and he sat down next to her, arranging her so her head was on his lap. She tried to stay awake through to the end of the movie, but her eyelids just grew heavier and heavier until finally darkness swamped her.

KENT GLANCED up as the door opened. Only one person had a key besides himself so he knew who it was. When his brother stepped inside, he held a finger to his lips, gesturing down to Abby who was fast asleep, her head resting on his thigh.

"Well now, that's a cute sight," Clint said in a soft voice, sitting in an armchair next to the sofa. He glanced at the T.V. with a smirk. "Never saw you as a *Tangled* fan."

Kent raised his middle finger at him. "You knew what it was straight away."

"One of Charlie's favorites. They'd probably like to watch it together."

Kent nodded. It would be good for Abby to get to know Charlie and Ellie. Eden too. He gathered she didn't really have friends. Poor darling. She'd been rather isolated because of her brother's choices.

"So, a little birdie told me about some trouble you've been having. Want to explain why you didn't tell me?"

He didn't ask who the little birdie was. He'd long since ceased to question how Clint seemed to know everything that went on around Sanctuary and to anyone who lived here.

"Been a bit busy with everything going on."

"I can see that." Clint glanced down at Abby. "You moved quick."

"I could hardly let her stay in that house. Besides the fact that it was trashed, she's not safe there."

Clint nodded. "Agreed. It's the right choice. What are you planning to do once she's safe?"

"Keep her."

"Good. Now run through everything that's happened. I want your take."

Kent went over it all, leaving nothing out. His brother just listened. It was something he was good at, just stopping and listening. Especially when it came to either of his siblings.

"Don't know that there's much we can do about Bartolli. You've put the word out that she's under your protection?"

"Yeah. Hopefully, it keeps him from coming after her. I've also got Corbin looking into him."

"But we can do something about Markovich."

"Planning to." He glanced at the clock. "I've called some of the boys for a meeting about Markovich. Let them in while I put her to bed?"

"I live to serve."

Kent rolled his eyes at his older brother. "I also have something I need you to take to Charlie. I'll grab it as well." He carefully picked Abby up, carrying her to his bedroom. He managed to pull back the covers then laid her down. He'd moved the mattress back onto the bed earlier. He placed a kiss on her forehead after tucking her in. Then he moved from the room. When he returned downstairs, he heard the low murmur of voices. In the living room sat Macca, Bain, Donovan, Zeke, Corbin and Jed.

He grabbed everyone a beer then sat. "Corbin, get anything on Bartolli?"

"Yeah, the family is bad news. Run by Fergus Bartolli. Owns several strip clubs, as well as other businesses, but most of his money comes from drugs and human trafficking. Apparently he's a lecherous old bastard with a taste for young girls."

Kent grimaced. He studied the photo of Fergus Bartolli. He looked like an overweight frog with thinning hair and a huge mole on his lip. Next to him stood a barely legal, leggy blonde who towered above him by at least a foot. She seemed scared as she leaned as far away from him as she could.

"That's his latest wife, Angie. Rumor has it, she was given to him by her father. Payment for a debt owed."

"Jesus Christ," Clint muttered.

"Managed to tap my contacts to see if I could find out whether he's the one who has Max. Nobody seems to know if Bartolli has him, but apparently he's got a real hard-on for him. Someone downloaded a whole lot of documents from his computer. Included in those documents were the names of a number of Bartolli's clients. Who don't want their names getting out."

"When Max called, he said he'd lost the flash drive he had the information stored on," Kent said with a sigh.

"They won't stop coming for him," Clint said. "It's as much about setting an example to others as getting the information back."

Kent nodded.

"So, what do we do about it?" Bain asked with a frown.

"Let's send a couple of guys in undercover to his clubs. See if they can ferret anything out, but tell them to do it quietly. Last thing I need is Bartolli catching on that we're watching him. Corbin, you keep doing some research, see if you can discover anything more. I've got a bad feeling about Max."

"And what about Markovich?" Jed asked.

"He's a different story," Kent said darkly. "I'm going to call him and arrange for a meet."

"Think he'll come?" Zeke asked.

"He will since Clint has been making things difficult for him. I hear he's been having trouble with his licensing and alcohol suppliers."

Clint just smiled.

"Let me go call him now." Kent grabbed his cell phone then called the number he'd had Corbin track down earlier. Five minutes later, he ended the call with a scowl. He walked back into the living room.

"He won't meet?" Clint asked.

"No, he'll agree to it, if I bring Abby with me."

Clint raised his eyebrows. "What? Why?"

"Reckons he wants to check she's all right. What fucking right does he have to worry over her? He was taking her money! I'm not taking her. It's too dangerous."

"We can keep her safe, chief," Zeke said. "And it doesn't seem likely he'd hurt her. She's been meeting with him for months now every week."

"From what I've heard, he rather likes Abby," Corbin added.

Kent scowled at the other man.

"What's the plan?" Macca asked.

"Meeting is for two nights from now. At the rest area off the main highway five minutes out of town. You all know where I mean?"

They all nodded.

"Macca and Jed, I want you there earlier, scout the area then take positions where you have the most visibility. Take your rifles."

Both men nodded.

"Donovan and Zeke will be with me. He'll expect me to bring people. Bain, you'll wait in the truck in case we need a quick getaway."

"I'm going too," Clint said.

"Actually, I had a bigger favor to ask you. I hoped you and Charlie might take care of Abby for me."

"You're giving me babysitting duty?" Clint looked aghast.

"Please. She means everything to me. I'm trusting her safety to you. She'll be comfortable with Charlie and it's best they're not left on their own."

"Fine," he grumbled. "But if they try to make me watch *Frozen*, I'm locking them in the bedroom for the night."

Whatever. The big softie would play it for them as many times as they wanted.

"Sure you don't want her to go?" Zeke asked.

"No. She's not going. That's my final say."

"Good call," Clint told him. "She's got no business there."

23

"Time for a nap, Abby-girl."

Abby glanced up with a pout from the glittery, messy creation on the coffee table. There was glue everywhere. She was even certain that she'd smeared some on her eyebrow.

She glared up at her daddy. "I don't wanna nap."

His face started to grow stern until he obviously got a look at her face. Then he burst into laughter. "Baby, you're a mess. Did you get any glue on the picture?"

"Yes, see?" She pointed down to the picture she was making. She was finding it easier and easier to let her Little side out. It also helped her let go of a lot of the stress she was carrying. Sometimes it didn't always work. Sometimes those worries crept back in, but for the most part she was stress-free while she was Little Abby. And it was amazing.

All she had to worry about was Daddy and his rules. And that really hard spanking hand he had.

"That's a beautiful picture, sweet girl. But it's time for a nap. Let's go get you cleaned up first. You can't go to bed like that, you'll stick to the sheets." He guided her upstairs with a hand at her lower back.

She dropped her bottom lip out. "I really don't need a nap, Daddy. I just got up."

"And I kept you awake half the night instead of letting you sleep," he replied. "Little girls need their sleep."

She sighed and opened her mouth to argue more as they reached the bathroom sink. He gave her a stern glare in the mirror. "Do you remember what happened yesterday when you argued too much about having a nap?"

Crap. She did. She'd ended up getting her butt roasted then had to spend ten minutes in the corner contemplating why she had been such a naughty girl.

"I hate contemplatin'," she muttered.

"I'm sure you do when you have to do it with your bare, red bottom sticking out of the corner."

She still didn't want a nap, but she let him clean her up without complaining. She didn't even moan when he washed her face and she hated that.

"You sulking, sweetheart?" he asked mildly.

"No." Yes.

"Hmm, I think you are and I have a cure for a girl who is sulking. Go into the bedroom. Take off your pants and panties then lean over the edge of the bed, chest flat to the bed, ass in the air."

She slapped her hands against her bottom. "No spankin'."

He lowered his eyebrows. "Are you in charge here?"

"No, Daddy," she muttered. She walked into the bedroom, dragging her steps.

"If you're not in position when I get there, I won't be happy," he called back.

Man, sometimes having a daddy was really hard. And she didn't think he was all that indulgent, either. In fact, he'd been rather stern today and she'd thought yesterday was bad enough.

She frowned, thinking that over. Could something be worrying him? Maybe about her safety. Kent had been working mostly from home, even though his office wasn't that far away from the house, he claimed he wanted to watch over his girl to make sure she behaved.

Well, she certainly wasn't getting away with anything. As she got into position, she made a note to ask him if everything was all right. If he knew something she didn't.

"Good girl," he said as he entered the bedroom.

A buzz of happiness filled her.

"Reach back and pull your bottom cheeks apart."

She stiffened. No way. She couldn't do that.

"Abby-girl, you heard me. You have until the count of three and then it's one spank for every second you procrastinate."

Indulgent, her ass.

"One. Two. Thr—"

Shoot. She threw her hands back and pulled apart the cheeks of her ass, putting herself fully on display. This was way, way too embarrassing.

"Just in time," he said in a low voice.

She heard him move towards her. There was a squirting noise. Lube. Well, that made sense. She could guess what was coming next. A dab of lube went on her puckered entrance then his finger prodded at her back hole.

"Relax, sweet girl. It's just my finger to start."

To start? Awesome.

He slid his finger deep inside her asshole and she gasped. In. Out. Oh Lord, her arousal started to grow. Spiralling higher and higher as he rubbed lube around. She didn't know why, but having her ass played with made her so hot.

Then he pulled his finger free and something rubbery and firm replaced the digit.

"This is a bigger one than you've taken before but you can do it, Abby-girl. Just relax and breathe out. That's it." He slid the plug deep. It burned slightly and she could definitely feel the difference in size, but as her body adjusted to the feel, her clit started to throb and her nipples ached.

"Right, you can stand up." He held her waist to ensure she was steady as she stood. Then he went around to the side of the bed to pull back the covers. "In you go."

"But...aren't you going to..." she waved her hand at herself unable to say it.

He raised an eyebrow. "What?"

Grr. "I can't sleep with a plug in my ass."

"I'm sure you'll get used to it."

"But what about..."

He just waited. Shit. He was going to make her say it.

"I'm aroused."

"Are you?" he asked silkily, coming towards her. "Spread your legs."

Lordy. Lordy. She spread her legs.

"Wider," he commanded.

She pushed them apart as far as she could without losing her balance. He cupped her mound then slid a finger through her folds. "My, my, someone liked having their bottom played with." He leaned in and kissed her lightly as he withdrew his fingers. "But someone has also been naughty and naughty girls don't get to come. Into bed you go."

He prodded her along with a sharp smack to her ass. She climbed into bed grumpily.

"And just so you know, I would consider you playing with yourself very naughty behavior. And it would result in you being banned from orgasms for a week. And if you think I wouldn't know, you are very mistaken."

How was he always one step ahead of her? He handed her Boss Hog which she hugged to her chest as she curled up on her side, the plug seated deep in her ass. Then he tucked her in, turned off the lights and kissed her forehead.

"Night, night, baby girl. Sleep tight."

"I'M GOING WITH YOU," Abby insisted.

"You certainly are not. It's too dangerous. You'll stay here with Clint and Charlie. And you will mind my brother." Kent narrowed his gaze at her.

"I will not. I'm not staying here while you go talk to Mr. Markovich on your own. I'm coming and that's that." She stomped her foot and glared up at him.

He pointed towards the corner of the living room. "Naughty corner. Now."

He'd woken her up from her nap with his mouth on her pussy. She'd take a nap without arguing every day if she got woken up that way each time. Then he'd taken her from behind and as she'd lain there, curled in his arms, in a haze of satisfaction, she'd remembered to ask him if there was anything going on she needed to know about.

That's when he told her about the meeting tonight.

"Kent!"

His gaze narrowed at her. "Corner. Now. And you just got ten for not obeying immediately."

Grr. Sometimes he made her so mad! Part of her was telling her to give in to him. That she didn't want to ever make him regret their relationship. She wasn't a person who usually enjoyed fighting. She preferred to make people happy not mad.

But this was too important.

"Fifteen," he said warningly.

She couldn't believe how unreasonable he was being. But she found herself stomping over to the corner. Last thing she wanted was for it to turn to twenty. She pressed her nose to the corner.

"Stick that bottom out."

She pushed her ass out, feeling herself growing red as she realized the sight she must make. She was naked. She still had the plug in from earlier. She hadn't cleaned up from their lovemaking. She stood there in the corner and fumed, her mind racing for a way to make him see reason.

She had to go with him. This was her mess. No way was she letting him go fight her battles for her. It was tempting to let him do that. She was way out of her comfort zone. But Mr. Markovich wanted her there. What if he got angry with Kent if she wasn't with him? She didn't know what she would do if something happened to him.

"Abby, come here."

Okay, his voice was as cold as she'd ever heard it and she shivered slightly. Turning, she watched him with trepidation.

"Are you mad at me, Daddy?" she asked in a small voice.

He was sitting on the bed, watching her. Suddenly he sighed. "I'm not mad, baby girl. Come here."

The look on his face was now softer. And she practically raced over, banging into him and sending him flying backwards onto the mattress with her sprawled on top of his chest.

"Sorry," she breathed out.

He chuckled and ran a hand through her hair. "I can always count on you to make me smile."

"You should have told me about the meeting before now, Kent," she said seriously.

He sat up, settled her on his lap. "You're right," he replied surprising her. "I was trying to protect you."

"I know you were. You always protect me. But there are some things I need to do or know about. You can't shelter me from everything."

"I can try," he muttered.

"Kent," she said cajoling. "I love being your Little and your sub, but that doesn't mean I want to be completely shut off from the rest of the world. It doesn't mean I need you to solve all of my problems."

"You're out of your depth with this one."

"I know I am. Which is why I'm lucky to have you. I still want to go. I'll do exactly what you say. I just, I'd be a mess worrying about you."

He huffed a breath. "Who knew you could be so stubborn?" He didn't sound happy but she got the feeling she was winning.

"All right, you can come. But before you get excited, you won't be leaving the truck. You'll have a bodyguard the entire time. You will do exactly as they say, because they're going to have my permission to do whatever it takes to keep you safe, understand?"

She understood it was as good as she was going to get. "All right."

SHE GLANCED around at the group gathered in what they called the command room. It basically looked like a meeting room in any generic building. There were about a dozen desks and chairs, as well as a projector mounted to the ceiling.

Or it would have seemed like any other meeting room, if not for the group of badasses filling it. She stared at them, totally floored. It was like they sucked all the air from the room with their manliness. There were only four of them plus Kent, but it felt like there were way more.

She recognized Zeke but she hadn't met the other three men. One had very dark hair with hints of silver, a body that was thick with muscle and had an intense focus about him that made you wonder what would happen if he ever aimed that focus on you.

She shivered at the thought.

Yikes.

But if she'd thought that guy was big, the next one had him beat and then some. He towered over the others, his biceps had to be thicker than her thighs and that was saying something. His hair was closely shaved.

The last guy was the only one who had glanced her way when she'd walked in with Kent. He had a surfer vibe about him. Blond hair, blue eyes, deep tan. Not as muscular as the other guys, she had a feeling that didn't make him less dangerous.

The door opened and she turned to see Clint walk in. Beside him, surprisingly, was Charlie. She was carrying a small paper bag in one hand. She stilled like Abby had done when she'd first entered and gazed around with her mouth slightly open.

"Whoa, it's testosterone city in here." She waved her hand in front of her face while Clint gave her a firm look.

"Don't worry, cowboy, they have nothing on you." Charlie patted his arm.

"You guys ready?" Clint asked. "Thought Abby could come back to our place."

"Shit," Kent swore. "Forgot to call you. Abby is coming now."

Every male pair of eyes turned to her. She gulped and felt her legs weaken at the disapproving glares she was getting.

"Girl, how are you still standing?" Charlie whispered. "That's a whole lot of manly disapproval right there."

She nodded. It was.

Clint's scowl was the worst in her opinion. "She's what?"

"She's coming," Kent said grimly.

"You lost your mind?"

They were all staring at Kent as though they thought the same but didn't want to ask.

"No," Kent said shortly, staring at Clint. "She's coming."

Clint rolled his eyes heavenward. "What's the world fucking coming to."

"She'll stay in the truck the whole time. Macca and Jed are in position. Zeke and Donovan will have my back at the meet and Bain is gonna be watching Abby."

The big guy turned to glare at her now. Uh-oh. Kent was leaving this guy to watch her? Was he mad? He looked like he broke legs for a living. The scowl he was giving her was a mix of disapproval and dismissal.

Okay, then. Cool. Yikes.

Why couldn't she have the surfer dude?

"Corbin is staying here to act as contact for everyone." The surfer nodded. "Everyone good?"

"I got permission to do what I need to in order to protect her?" Bain asked in a low rumble.

Shit. Shit. Shit.

"Yep," Kent replied. "You have free rein. She gives you any trouble, you take care of it then tell me later."

Bain gave a short nod. What the hell did that mean? Take care of it?

She was in trouble.

Charlie leaned into her, taking her hand. "You can still change your mind. I was going to bake cupcakes. We can decorate them, make a mess, get on a sugar high and make Clint stomp around like a growly bear."

"It's tempting. Very tempting." But she took a deep breath. "But I have to go."

"If you say so. Word of advice?"

She turned to the other woman. "Please."

"I'd do exactly whatever that big guy says. To the letter. You do not want to end up over his knee. With arms like that..." Charlie shuddered.

Abby's breaths came in shallow pants. "He wouldn't

spank me."

"What do you think Kent meant when he gave him permission to do whatever was necessary? You give him any problems and your ass is toast. Double toast because I'm sure Kent will roast it again when you get home. I mean, I used to think he was the easy-going brother, but I've since learned otherwise."

Oh hell.

Charlie gave her hand a final squeeze before walking over to Kent and giving him the small bag. She watched curiously as Kent kissed Charlie's forehead. What was in the bag? She wanted to ask, but then everyone started moving out. She waved goodbye to Charlie before following everyone to Kent's truck. The men all carried weapons which made her even more nervous. She couldn't keep up with their long legs without running, which she wasn't going to do. She was horribly unfit, as well as clumsy as hell. Kent turned; saw she was behind and stopped to wait for her.

He held out his hand and she slipped hers into his.

"Did you really give Bain permission to spank me?" she asked quietly.

"Baby, we're going into an unknown situation. You can't defend yourself. You've never done anything like this. And you're the most precious thing in the world to me. I still can't believe that I agreed to this. But I did, so I'm going to make sure you're as safe as I can. So, I can concentrate on what I'm doing and won't get distracted worrying about you."

"Oh. God, Kent, I didn't even think of that."

"Just do whatever Bain says, all right? If there's any trouble he'll get you out of there and keep you safe. Truthfully, I'm not expecting any real trouble. Markovich knows me and my reputation. If I thought there was any true danger then I'd have Clint tie you up and watch you."

Right. Of course, he would.

"But that doesn't mean there isn't an element of the unknown. So Bain has permission to do whatever he has to, we clear?"

"Yes."

"Good."

When they reached his truck, the others were standing around.

"I don't want Markovich seeing you if we can help it. Zeke, you and Donovan take the other truck. Bain will ride with me to stay with Abby."

Kent lifted her into the backseat of his truck and did up her seatbelt. The drive was in silence. It was late afternoon by the time they reached the clearing in a wooded area off the highway. It was one of the places that had a couple of picnic tables and a toilet, but was rarely used after a newer picnic area had been put in further up the road.

Two dark cars were already parked right at the back of the parking area. Kent parked up facing them. Zeke pulled in next to him.

Kent turned around to stare at her as he undid his seatbelt. "Keep her safe."

"Got it," Bain replied.

Bain exited the truck when Kent did and moved around to the driver's seat. She peered around the seat as she watched Kent approach Mr. Markovich, who had gotten out of one of the cars. Two goons were behind him, one of whom was Gray.

Zeke and Donovan hung back a bit.

"Keep back," Bain said sharply as she leaned further out. "I want you out of their line of sight."

She noticed Bain didn't take his eyes off his surroundings.

"I wish we could hear what they're saying."

"Kent's telling Markovich that he's not happy about the incident the other night in the parking lot of Suck 'n Blow. He's especially angry over him making you pay your brother's debt."

"What? How do you know that?"

"Everyone is wearing a mic." He was silent. "Yep, roger that."

"What?" she asked again, confused.

He sighed. "I'm answering Macca."

"Oh, he's out there? Where is he?"

"None of your business."

"Well, that's rude. What are they saying now?" she asked.

"You always talk this much?" he muttered.

"Nobody has ever complained that I talk too much."

"You do."

She glared at his back. Then poked her tongue out.

"I saw that," he said in a low, rumbly voice.

She sat back in her seat with a thump. She chewed at her thumbnail nervously, ruining Kent's good work from the other night.

"What's taking so long?" She shifted around on her seat.

"You need the toilet?" Bain asked.

She froze. "No." Well, kind of. "I'm just nervous."

"Settle in. He'll be done soon. Your man is tough and smart."

"Were you in the SEALs too?"

"None of your business."

She sighed. "Are you always like this?"

"Like what?"

"Um, grumpy, untalkative."

"Been talking more than I usually do. Shit."

"What? What is it?" She reached for her seatbelt. Why, she didn't know. Wasn't like she could get out there and help.

"Stay where you are," Bain snapped. "Markovich wants to see you."

"Oh. Shall I get out?"

"No."

No. Right. He didn't want to expand on that?

"Got it," he said.

"Got what?" she asked, confused.

This time he turned to her. "Kent is going to let Markovich talk to you, but you stick right by me. You move more than three inches away from me and I'm gonna haul you back. You disobey me and first chance I get, I'm gonna blister your ass. Don't care if you're the boss's girl or not, got me?"

"I-I got you."

"My only focus is you. You are the body I am guarding. Everything goes to shit and I will get you out of there, my focus is not on anyone else and neither is yours. I am your world right now. Got me?"

"But Kent—"

"Can take care of himself. He's got Zeke and Don there. It's you and me, got it?"

"Got it."

"You don't talk to anyone without an okay from me or Kent, got it?"

"Yes."

"And you stick to my left side. Not in front, not behind unless I tell you. Okay?"

"You're making me really nervous."

"Good. Nervous will mean you do as I say. Nervous is good. I'm going to get out and come around for you. Number one rule?"

"I do what you say."

"And?"

"I stick close to you."

"Right. Wait there." He climbed out and moved cautiously around to her door. He opened it and leaned across her to undo her seatbelt which she had forgotten to do.

"Climb down," he told her.

She slid down, nearly tripping over her big feet and landing in a heap at his feet. He didn't say anything, didn't even seem to notice, which she was grateful for. He moved and she did her best to move with him. She didn't focus on anything except getting to Kent. When they grew close, Bain stopped her with a hand on her shoulder.

She wasn't sure what to do. No one was talking. So, she waved at Gray. He gave her an incredulous look and she felt slightly embarrassed.

What to do now? Bain said not to talk. But that was damn hard when she was so nervous. She fidgeted, shifting her weight from foot to foot.

Finally, Kent spoke. "As you can see, she's here. Now, I want your agreement that she's off-limits. Don't care what beef you have with her brother; she doesn't come into it."

"I'm keeping the money I already have."

"Fine," Kent growled.

"I want to speak to her for a moment."

She opened her mouth to reply, she was right here after all, but Bain made a low, warning noise. Right, she was supposed to stay quiet unless given permission. Sheesh. This all seemed silly to her. How many times had she met safely with Mr. Markovich and Gray?

"Fine," Kent said. He then half-turned to her. But his expression didn't change from badass. She had to admit, it was a turn-on.

"Abigail, how are you?"

"Fine, Mr. Markovich, and you? Hey, Gray."

Gray sighed.

"Don't mind Gray, he's on bodyguard duty," Mr. Markovich said. "Guards aren't supposed to speak."

"Oh right."

"Abby, are you well?"

"Me?" She looked at him, startled. "Why wouldn't I be fine?"

Mr. Markovich was an attractive man. Older, probably in his late forties, he always dressed well and smelled nice. But he wasn't a good guy. She knew that. However, he'd always treated her fairly.

"You're with this man of your own free will?" he asked.

"Kent? Yes, of course, I am."

"You're certain?"

"Yes. Why do you keep asking? I want to be with Kent. I love him."

Oh shit. Oh fuck. Had she just blurted that out? There was a moment of silence.

"Enough," Kent barked. "You've talked to her. We have a deal?"

"Yes, we do." Mr. Markovich stared at her strangely. "Goodbye, Abby."

"Bye. Bye, Gray."

She wasn't offended when he didn't say goodbye in return.

"Bain, get her in the truck." Bain walked her back and helped her in the back, doing up her seat belt for her. Kent said something to him as he approached and Bain climbed in the other truck. Kent climbed in and started his truck, pulling out. She turned to see Mr. Markovich watching them as they pulled away. He'd seemed different tonight. Slightly sad.

Okay, now she felt silly sitting in the back seat while he was in the front.

"Can I move over to the front?" she asked.

"No," Kent said.

There was some tension that she didn't know the source of. "Are you mad at me for getting out of the truck?"

"Of course not, I'm the one who told Bain to bring you out."

So it wasn't that.

"You're still mad at me for coming with you?"

"Did you mean what you said back there?" he asked, pulling to the side of the road. He put the truck into park and then turned to stare at her intently. "That you love me?"

She bit her lip. "Did that make you angry?"

"Did you mean it?"

"Yes," she said in a quiet voice.

"Good," he said before putting the truck back into drive and heading down the road.

Good? That was it, good?

Okay, now she was starting to get a bit mad. She crossed her arms over her chest.

"Did you know he wants you?" Kent asked suddenly.

"Who?"

"Markovich. He wants you."

"No, he doesn't." Wants her? What did he mean?

"He did. It's why he wanted to see you. Any sign you weren't happy and I think he would have tried to take you from me."

"He didn't want me. He was taking money from me each week for a debt that wasn't even mine! He's a bad guy."

"It was a good way to see you each week. I wouldn't be surprised if he was going to make a move soon. He was surprisingly easy to convince to give up extorting money from you."

Oh. She shook her head. She couldn't believe it.

"He wasn't...he didn't want me."

He just sighed. When he pulled up outside his house, he was still acting kind of weird. He came around and opened her door as usual, helping her down. But instead of putting her on her feet, he swung her up into his arms and carried her inside.

"Kent! What are you doing?"

"You love me." He got them inside then shut and locked the door without budging her at all.

"Yes. I love you."

"You love me," he repeated as though he couldn't believe it.

"Yes. How do you feel about me?" How did he feel about her?

He reached the staircase then paused to glance down at her. "Baby, I think I fucking fell in love with you that night in the back room of that fucking awful bar that you'll never visit again."

"You did not." She blushed as he set her down next to the bed.

He cupped her face between his hands. "I did."

"It's not possible to fall in love like that."

"Baby, I did," he growled. "Are you seriously arguing about when I fell in love with you?"

"I guess that is a bit silly, isn't it?"

"It is," he growled. "Now get naked. I'm in the mood to tie you up and fuck you. I cannot believe I fucking took you into that situation tonight."

"I was safe."

"You may not have been."

"But I was," she soothed, knowing that was his greatest fear.

"You have five seconds to get naked," he commanded.

"Five seconds, I can't get naked in five seconds!"

"One."

"Okay, okay, I'm going!" She'd never gotten naked so quickly, she threw her clothes onto the floor, something she'd never usually do. But she still had her bra half on by the time he got to five.

He shook his head. "That's gonna cost you." He strode over to his magic bag of tricks and pulled out a silken scarf as well as a spreader bar. He wrapped one end of the scarf around the headboard. "Up here on your hands and knees with your arms out in front of you. Place your chest flat on the mattress."

She shot him a worried look but got into position. He wrapped the scarf gently around her wrists. The bruises were mostly gone but he was still so gentle with her.

"Spread those legs," he commanded.

She widened her legs and felt him place the cuffs around her ankles. Then he ran his hand down her ass before lightly slapping it. Again and again, he smacked her ass. Building up a heat in her bottom. The spanks became harder and faster until she was gasping and groaning, the heat in her ass becoming a deep burn that she knew she was going to feel for a long while.

"Fuck, that's a beautiful sight. Nothing more gorgeous than a bound sub with a red ass, is there? Bet you're wishing you moved quicker, aren't you?"

"Yes, Sir." Sort of. Part of her knew he needed this and she wanted to give it to him. Part of her also liked the burning in her ass. Especially as she knew what was coming next.

"I need your ass tonight, baby girl. We're moving up to one of the bigger plugs. You ready for this?"

"As ready as I'll ever be, Sir."

Rustling noises, that telltale sound of lube being expelled from the bottle. Then his finger ran between her ass cheeks, pushing it deep inside her, spreading lube around. She moaned softly. She couldn't help it. She loved this feeling of being penetrated.

"That's my girl, relax for Daddy."

Two fingers. Oh hell. Felt so good. And so full. He withdrew his fingers and slowly started to insert the plug. Her insides were stretched. The burn now just wasn't on the outside of her ass. She took a deep breath out, forcing herself to relax.

KENT STARED down at the plug disappearing into her ass. His cock throbbed with the need to take its place. He wanted to drive himself deep. Hear her whimpering as she struggled to take his dick.

Okay, calm down.

Slow down. Take your time. You have to prepare her. Make it good for her.

He twisted the plug when it was halfway inside her. He'd hated having her anywhere near Markovich. He'd wanted to attack the bastard for even thinking he got to breathe his precious girl's air. But common sense had prevailed.

Just.

But now, he needed this. To be in complete command. To demand her submission. As Sir and Daddy. He finally seated the plug deep and just took a moment to stare at her. Then he started to strip.

"I need a taste of that pussy, sweet girl." He lay on his back between her legs and grabbing hold of her hips, pulled her pussy down to his mouth. He started by lapping at her. Just soft, slow licks of his tongue that he knew had to be driving her insane. Her body shook over him. Her breath coming in soft pants.

"Sir!" she cried out.

"Yes?"

"More? Please?"

"More what?" he asked.

A beat of silence. He went back to his gentle exploration. Fuck, the taste of her was amazing. Freaking addictive.

"Please touch my clit. Make me come. I need you. I need to come. Please, Sir. Please, Daddy."

"Poor baby. So wet. So hot. Let me see what I can do." This time, he concentrated on her clit, flicking at it in hard drives of his tongue. Faster. Faster. He felt trembles rock her body, then she stiffened, her cries growing more frantic and as he felt the first wave of her orgasm hit her, he moved his tongue to her entrance and drove it home. She convulsed around him and he drank her down, reveling in her cries.

He lapped at her as she came back down from her high, her thighs trembling. His cock ached; his balls so tight he was in pain. Coming out from under her he moved to lay next to her, rolling onto his side to face her as he ran his hand up and down her back.

"How you doing, baby? Okay?"

She turned her head. The look on her face could only be described as pure bliss. "Yeah, you could say that."

Leaning in, he kissed her lightly then deeper. Need drove him. Fiery. Hard. All-consuming.

"I need you, baby. So fucking much."

"Take me. I'm ready for you."

He grinned at her fiercely. "That's my girl."

Without waiting another second, because he wanted inside her now, he moved around behind her on his knees and grasping hold of the bottle of lube, he squirted some on his hand to rub up and down his thick shaft.

He had to clench his jaw together in order to maintain his control. Fuck, he was too close to the edge. He took a moment just to breathe and calm down before playing with her, driving the plug in and out, twisting it, listening and loving the way her moans filled the room.

Finally, he drew the plug fully out then threw it away and grabbed hold of his shaft.

"Here we go, baby girl. Stay nice and relaxed for me." Fuck him, if that wasn't one of the best sensations in the world. There were better, of course. Fucking her pussy. Watching her smile at him in happiness. Her calling him Daddy.

But this was definitely up there. He pushed past the tight ring of muscle. Her pants grew harder.

"All right, baby?" he asked, pausing for a moment.

"Don't stop. Don't stop."

"No fucking chance." Unless she asked him to. Hell, he was so wrapped around her little finger, he thought he'd do just about anything for his sweet girl.

He pressed forward until he was fully seated inside her. Both of their skin was slick with sweat. His heart raced, his breath coming in fast pants. He felt like he'd already run a marathon.

Pulling back, driving forward. Over and over. He reached around her hip to find her clit and rubbed it lightly as he fucked her ass with thrust after thrust. Her cries told him she was close again already.

"Sir! Daddy!"

"Yeah, you're going to come for me again. I want to feel you pulsing around me, sucking me inside you. Taking me. That's it. Take me, baby girl."

He felt the orgasm rush through him, building in his lower back then rushing out. Abby screamed and she clenched down around him. And that was it.

He was gone. Diving into bliss. The world fading around him as he fell into his girl.

~

TWENTY MINUTES LATER, Abby was yawning as she felt Kent move.

"Where are you going?" she asked. She was exhausted and snuggly. He'd already cleaned them both up, wasn't it time for sleep?

"Got something for you. Left it in my truck." He brushed his lips over her forehead. "Stay here and I'll go get it."

Now she was wide awake. She sat up, waiting for him, her curiosity fully piqued as she saw him return with the mysterious paper bag that Charlie handed him earlier. He sat on the mattress next to her, facing her, his thigh brushing hers.

He cleared his throat, looking nervous.

"Kent?"

"Sorry. Just hoping I did the right thing. I know how much Bun-bun meant to you and that it was painful when he was destroyed."

She bit her lower lip. She felt like a bit of a wimp to be so upset over a stuffed toy, but she'd had him a long time.

"Well, he wasn't repairable, you know that."

She nodded.

"But I did grab a piece of his ear for you. Then I had Charlie sew it up." He pulled Bun-bun's ear from the bag. It didn't have any stuffing and had been sewn neatly up the back where it had been ripped. "I thought you might like a piece of Bun-bun to keep. But if it's too weird or not right then don't feel you have to—oomph." He grabbed hold of her as she threw herself at him.

"Baby, you're shaking. It was the wrong thing to do?"

She reached for the piece of ear and held it to her nose, rubbing it back and forth. "No, Kent, it's perfect. You are perfect." She sniffled, rubbing away her tears. "I just can't believe how perfect for me you are."

He kissed her softly. "Only as perfect as you are for me, sweet girl."

24

Abby sat in the fort she'd built with Charlie and Ellie. Charlie and Clint had a huge dining table and it had taken four blankets to cover it, as well as a lot of cushions. They'd snuck in some bags of sweets and chocolate and were gorging themselves. She had Boss Hog and her Bun-bun ear. Charlie had her favorite toy, Inky. Ellie had her teddy.

"Oh man, we're almost out of the snacks. Dare you to sneak into the kitchen and get some chips," Charlie said to her.

"Oh no, Clint nearly caught me last time," she replied. "Your turn. It's your house. He's your daddy."

"And he's standing just a few feet away from you," Clint said dryly, making all three girls cry out in surprise.

He pulled up the edge of a blanket and sunlight shone through. Clint sighed. "Just how much junk have the three of you had? Christ, Bear is gonna kill me."

It still amazed Abby how at ease Charlie and Ellie were with their Little sides, but they both told her that it had taken a while and they weren't always comfortable around other people. But then Clint wasn't just another person.

"It's a mess in here," he grumbled.

"Daddy is a grumbly bear today," Charlie told them in a not-so-quiet whisper, making Abby and Ellie laugh.

It was hard to believe she'd only been here a month. She now couldn't imagine living anywhere else, as though this was the place she was meant to be. With people who accepted her for who she was. Little and sub. She'd put her house up for sale. There was no point in keeping it and surprisingly she wasn't as sad as she thought she would be to say goodbye to it.

Kent had left three days ago for a business trip. She hated not having him around. The only saving grace was that he'd arranged for her to come stay with Clint and Charlie.

For years, she'd lived alone and it seemed she now couldn't even do three nights without Kent. She'd felt slightly silly having to come stay with Clint and Charlie, but they'd totally opened their house to her. Charlie had kept her occupied with games and movies and baking while Clint made sure she went to bed on time and didn't get too sad.

Kent was due back in the morning, though and she couldn't wait to see him. She'd just enrolled in an online course in creative writing which started in a few weeks. Kent still didn't want her leaving Sanctuary without someone with her. They hadn't heard a thing from Bartolli or her brother, but he wasn't letting down his guard.

She heard some deep voices coming from the down the hall. Her heart raced. She knew that voice. She stood without thinking and banged her head on the table.

"Owie! Ouch, owie!"

"Oh, Abby, are you okay?" Ellie asked. "Do you want me to kiss it better?"

Tears flooded her eyes and her head throbbed. Partially from the pain, but mostly because she wanted to rush to see if that really was Kent.

"I'm okay, thanks." She crawled out from under the table just as he entered the dining room. Happiness filled her. He entered the kitchen and everything was right in her world.

"Abby! What's wrong?" he rushed forward, concern on his face.

She felt silly as tears dripped down her face. Ellie ran to Bear who had walked in behind Kent.

"Ellie," he said in a low voice. "You were supposed to be home half an hour ago."

"Sorry, Daddy. We were having so much fun. Abby banged her head, though. She needs a magic kiss."

"Oh, sweet girl, where did you hurt your head?" Kent asked her.

"It's okay," she whispered even as she pointed out her boo-boo.

He kissed her head gently. "There, all better with Daddy's magic kisses."

She nodded. Then she threw herself into his arms. "I'm so happy you're home."

"Oh, baby. I'm happy too." he rocked her gently. "I missed you. I didn't like being away from my girl."

"I didn't like it either." Then she felt like she was being selfish. "But I'm okay. Clint and Charlie took care of me." She sat back to give him a smile.

Kent raised his eyebrow. "Did they? Just how much sugar have you been eating?" He glared at his brother, who shrugged.

"It kept them happy."

"You are the biggest softie," Kent told him. He glanced behind to where Charlie was standing by the fort they'd made. "You built a fort? Are you all right?"

"What do you mean is she all right?" Clint asked.

"She usually builds forts when she's stressed and wants to hide," Kent explained.

Clint frowned. "Abby?"

"I'm all right. We just wanted a fort to play in."

Both men stared down at her.

"And maybe I was getting a bit stressed about things. I was missing you and worrying about Max," she told Kent. She hadn't heard from Max again. She was worried about him. But she'd also heard nothing from Bartolli's goon. She knew Kent had put the word out that she was under his protection. Warmth filled her at the thought of the way he took care of her.

He pulled her close and kissed the top of her head. "I missed you so much that I think I'm going to have to take you with me next time."

"You think that's wise?" Clint asked. "We still don't know where her brother is or what Bartolli is going to do."

"If I take her with me, then I'll also bring someone to watch over her when I'm not around."

"Not Bain," she said hastily.

He grinned. "You don't want Bain as your babysitter?"

"He makes a terrible manny," she commented.

"I dare you to call him that to his face," Kent told her.

Her eyes widened. "I value my life." She sighed. "I just wish I knew when all this would end."

"I know. Me too," Kent told her. "In the meantime, I'll keep you safe."

"And you are always welcome to stay with us when Kent's away as well," Clint told her.

"We might have to have a talk about sugar consumption," Kent grumbled.

"Jesus, all I get around here is complaints," Clint moaned.

Kent placed her on her feet. "Come on, baby. Let's go home."

She sighed. Home. With Kent.

That sounded absolutely perfect.

EPILOGUE

"**D**addy!" Abby rushed towards the door as Kent came through into the hotel room. She jumped and he caught her as she wrapped her legs and arms around him.

"Somebody is pleased to see me," Kent said warmly.

"Probably just happy I'm no longer in charge," Bain said dryly as he stood and stretched, putting down the book he'd been reading.

Kent raised an eyebrow as he set her down? "Problems?"

She wrinkled her nose and glared at Bain. "The manny is being an old grump as usual."

Bain made a low, rumbly noise.

"Now, baby, you know the manny doesn't like being called grumpy."

"I hate you both," Bain told them. "She's mad at me because she opened the hotel door without my permission and I sent her to her room for half an hour."

"You did what?" Kent growled down at her.

"It was room service. I ordered it." She bit her thumbnail. "Sorry."

"More of an apology than I got," Bain said.

Kent rested his hands on her shoulders. "You know these rules aren't because Bain or I want to be mean. They're to keep you safe."

"I know, I just forgot. I'm sorry."

"Not just me you owe an apology to, is it?" Kent said sternly.

She turned to the large, grumpy man. "Sorry, Bain."

The big man nodded.

"Bain, can you give us a while?" Kent asked.

She got a shiver of trepidation at his tone. The big man just walked into his room without another word. They had a suite with a living room and two bedrooms with attached bathrooms. Kent led her over to a sofa.

"Sit down, baby." He sounded worried. Concerned.

She sat with an inelegant plop. "What is it? Is something wrong? Is it Max?"

He crouched in front of her. "Corbin found him. I'm so sorry, baby. There's no easy way to say this..."

"He's dead, isn't he?"

Kent nodded. "Yes, sweet girl. He's in a morgue in Seattle. They must have found him somehow. I'm so sorry."

"Oh God. Oh God." Numbness filled her. "How long has he been dead? What happened to him?"

"His body was found out by Beaver Lake. It had been dumped there."

She placed her hand over her mouth. "I feel ill."

He hastily stood and picked her up and raced her to the bathroom where she lost the burger she'd ordered from room service earlier. Kent held her gently, kept her hair back for her and when she was finished, he wiped her face gently with a wet cloth and handed her a toothbrush.

She leaned weakly against him. "How did he die?"

"I'm not telling you that, sweetheart," he told her as he picked her up. This time, he carried her into the bedroom and laid her on her side of the bed. Then he lay next to her, curling his body around her back and holding her.

"Please. I need to know. Please, Kent."

He sighed. "Gunshot wounds. Several of them."

She sobbed in a breath. Then another one. Then her body started to shake. "I k-know he was a-awful. But he was s-still my brother."

"I know he was."

"He d-didn't deserve t-that."

"No, baby. He didn't. It's all right. Cry it out."

Tears rushed down her cheeks. "He w-was the s-sweetest kid. I don't know w-where things went wrong."

"You know it wasn't your fault, right? None of this was your fault."

"But m-maybe I should h-have given him m-money when he called."

"Oh, baby. You can't think like that. You can't predict the future. Max brought this all on himself. It wasn't your fault. Please, don't think that. We offered to help him and he threatened me, remember?"

"I know. You're right."

"You just let it all out, baby. I've got you. I'm here. I'm here. I'm never letting you go."

She cried until it felt like she was empty. Her tears dried up and her sobs faded. Kent rolled her so she was facing him. He reached back to grab a tissue from the box on the bedside table.

"Blow." He held the tissue up for her.

She blew her nose and he wiped her face. Then he kissed her lightly on the lips.

"So does he just get away with it? Bartolli?" she asked.

Kent sighed. "I'm gonna keep in touch with the detectives in charge of the case, but Bartolli is smart. He wouldn't leave any evidence. I'll do my best to make him pay, no matter what the cops find."

"No, don't," she said hastily.

He stiffened. "What?"

"I don't want you going up against him, risking yourself. Max is gone. He's never coming back, no matter what. I think we should just leave it alone. Please, Kent."

"Okay, baby."

"What now?" she croaked. She felt so drained. She couldn't think. Couldn't move. Max was dead.

"You let me take care of that. I'll arrange to have his body released. Do you want a funeral back home?"

"I-I don't know. I guess."

"It will be okay, baby." He held her tight. "I'm here."

"Don't ever let me go," she whispered. "Losing Max is hard. But losing you, it would devastate me."

"Never," he swore fiercely. "You will never lose me. I know I can be overbearing and overprotective and demanding but I will always be here for you. I love you, sweet girl. Now and always."

"Now and always."

EXCERPT FROM MASTERED BY MALONE

Mia took a step and stood on the hem of her pants. She immediately dropped the linen, trying to grab for the railing to keep herself from falling, but her fingertips slid off the wooden banister as she flung forward. She tensed, letting out a cry of alarm as she waited for her body to hit the stairs. But instead of slamming against wood, she came up against a hard chest. The person who caught her, let out an oomph as they braced themselves against the banister to keep them both from flying.

She took in a shaky breath. Then another one. She didn't want to look up. She knew it wasn't West or Jaret or Tanner who'd caught her.

She knew it was *him* and she did not want to look up.

He just held her against his chest for a long moment. Her feet weren't even touching the ground, they just dangled in the air. She had the crazy thought that she could just snuggle in against him as though they were cuddling.

Then he set her down. Disappointment hit her hard.

Stupid.

She took a step back. "Sorry about that. Thanks for catching me." She tried to move around him, but he grabbed hold of her shoulders, holding her there. "Umm, Malone? You okay?"

Why wasn't he saying anything? She risked a look up into his face, saw how tense his jaw was. He was glaring down at her. Was he mad?

"Uh, is there something wrong?"

"Something wrong?" he repeated.

"Yes, is there something wrong?"

Silence.

"You're...um...acting odd. Did I hurt you?"

"Hurt me?"

Why was he repeating everything she said? "Did I hurt you? When I fell against you."

"Did you hurt me? Hurt *me*? Fuck." He stared down at her. Then he moved one hand to cup the side of her face, wrapped his arm around her back and pulled her in to kiss her.

And, oh, boy, what a kiss it was. Her body sizzled from the tip of her toes all the way up to her hair. He didn't just kiss her, he possessed her. He took complete control and all she could do was hang on for the ride.

When he drew back, she couldn't help but make a small sound of protest. She wanted more. Needed it. But instead of kissing her again, he swung her into his arms, one under her legs, the other around her back, and he turned, carrying her downstairs.

"What are you doing?" she asked. She wrapped her arms around his neck, terrified he was going to drop her. But he didn't even show a hint of strain as he carried her straight into his office and then set her down on the leather sofa that lay in front of the fireplace. He started to pace back and forth, and she just sat there for a moment, watching him, taking him in.

Her lips still tingled, and her clit throbbed. Damn, if that's what it felt like to kiss him, what would it be like to take things further? To have him touch her, taste her, take her?

She cleared her throat. She got that he was angry. She just wasn't sure why. She inched her way forward on the sofa, ready to stand. He must've seen her movements because he turned around and pointed a finger at her.

"Stay."

She ground her teeth together. She wasn't a damn dog. Her heart was still racing from her near miss. And that kiss. What the heck did that kiss mean? She had no idea. All she knew was that right now, the last thing she wanted or needed was an Alec Malone lecture.

"Thanks for catching me," she said. "But I need to go tidy up the mess I made. I've got to get the sheets in the wash. And I'm gonna be late getting dinner started if I don't get a move on."

He moved closer, his hands on his hips as he loomed over her. "You fell down the stairs."

"Yes, well, I just tripped. I'm sure I would have been all right. Sure, I might have had a couple of bruises—"

"You tripped halfway down the stairs," he interrupted her. "You could have broken a leg or an arm or hit your head or anything. This has to end."

"What has to end?" she asked.

"This habit you have of getting yourself into trouble," he snapped back at her. "Why the hell were you trying to carry your weight in linen down the stairs? You couldn't see anything. You didn't even see me coming up the stairs."

"I thought I could get it all down in one go. And I tripped because my pants keep slipping down. And I don't make it a habit of getting into trouble, you know. Do you think I wanted to fall? Do you think I want all these things happen to me?"

How could he go from kissing her to scolding her like a naughty teenager caught out after curfew?

He blew out a deep breath. "You need to take more care. No more carrying heavy things down the stairs. Got it?"

"This a new rule, is it?"

His jaw was tense as he glared down at her. "Yes. Another rule. And why are you even doing the washing? Your job is to cook. It's not to clean my grandmother's lamp. It's not to hang out the washing. It's not to wash all the linen. It's to cook. And it's to do as I tell you. I am in charge of your safety and I will get you to that damn trial in one piece, even if no one told me the biggest risk to you would be you."

She looked up at him for a moment. All right, so obviously that kiss hadn't meant much to him. Certainly it didn't mean he cared about her.

She stood. Not her home. Not her family. She needed to remember that. "Fine. Sorry for overstepping my bounds. I'll get out of your way."

She got to the door when he called out to her.

"Yes?" She turned back to look at him. Maybe he was going to apologize for being a jerk. Miracles did happen, right?

"Your pants are slipping because you've lost weight. You need to eat more. You need clothes that fit better."

"Is that it? Nothing else you want to add that you find lacking about me? Maybe my hair? Or my makeup?"

"You don't wear any makeup."

Awesome. She guessed he liked curvy girls who dressed with style and were made-up from the minute they got up until they went to bed. Not walking disasters who tripped over their own pants.

He moved over and sat at his desk. "If that's all, I have work to do."

Damn, he was an ass.

Printed in Great Britain
by Amazon

25411480R00158